"Shultz's Seas⟨...⟩ ⟨...⟩rom Darren being a⟨...⟩ ⟨...⟩ wife's poisoning murder. Whoever did this is truly evil." Jack's image dimmed. "I'd rather believe it was the building. I'm going to keep researching."

Charlene settled back. "I can ask Kass and Kevin what they know about the place. Have them return to the Spellbound with paranormal investigation on their minds instead of movie night with friends. Considering how that turned out, they'd probably be on board."

"There has to be a way to clear the bad mojo," Jack said. "I fear for Darren's safety until that happens. Unless he embraces it? Makes the haunting public?"

Charlene wanted to protect Darren and give him the time and space to mourn his wife without the pandemonium of paranormal investigators.

"Let's try to stay focused," Charlene said. Jack was practically an encyclopedia with all that he'd learned. "Someone—"

"Or something," he countered.

"Poisoned Elise. Darren is a suspect, but I don't think he did it. I believe that despite their arguments, he would've given her whatever she wanted. More money, more designer clothes, more houses. Sad as that is, he might have used his money to make up for his lies."

Jack nodded. "I can see that."

"Which means we need to find the real killer before Darren winds up in jail."

"Or," Jack said, "before the theater kills him . . ."

**Books by Traci Wilton**

MRS. MORRIS AND THE GHOST

MRS. MORRIS AND THE WITCH

MRS. MORRIS AND THE GHOST OF
CHRISTMAS PAST

MRS. MORRIS AND THE SORCERESS

MRS. MORRIS AND THE VAMPIRE

MRS. MORRIS AND THE POT OF GOLD

MRS. MORRIS AND THE WOLFMAN


**And writing as Traci Hall**

MURDER IN A SCOTTISH SHIRE

MURDER IN A SCOTTISH GARDEN

MURDER AT A SCOTTISH SOCIAL

MURDER AT A SCOTTISH WEDDING



**Published by Kensington Publishing Corp.**

# Mrs. Morris
## and the
# Wolfman

## TRACI WILTON

Kensington Publishing Corp.
www.kensingtonbooks.com

KENSINGTON BOOKS are published by

Kensington Publishing Corp.
119 West 40th Street
New York, NY 10018

Copyright © 2023 by Traci Hall

All Kensington titles, imprints, and distributed lines are available at special quantity discounts for bulk purchases for sales promotion, premiums, fund-raising, educational, or institutional use.

Special book excerpts or customized printings can also be created to fit specific needs. For details, write or phone the office of the Kensington Sales Manager: Attn.: Sales Department. Kensington Publishing Corp., 119 West 40th Street, New York, NY 10018. Phone: 1-800-221-2647.

The K and Teapot logo is a trademark of Kensington Publishing Corp.

First Printing: September 2023
ISBN: 978-1-4967-4137-0

ISBN: 978-1-4967-4138-7 (ebook)

10 9 8 7 6 5 4 3 2 1

Printed in the United States of America

This story is dedicated to my family for their wonderful support of this crazy writing dream! It is also dedicated to the readers who make this journey possible. Thank you!

# Acknowledgments

I'd like to thank John Scognamiglio and the team at Kensington. It takes a village to bring a book to life and I'm so appreciative. And of course, Evan Marshall, agent extraordinaire. Thank you for making the magic happen behind the scenes.

# CHAPTER 1

Charlene Morris arrived at the refurbished Spellbound Movie Theater at half-past six with Avery Shriver riding shotgun. When they'd first met, Avery had been sixteen with orange hair and a nose stud. Now eighteen, Avery planned a low-key summer before starting college in August—she'd worked her booty off and earned full tuition at Boston Academy.

Charlene had no children of her own and considered Avery family. Charlene and her resident ghost at the bed-and-breakfast, Dr. Jack Strathmore, joked that they'd become late-in-life parents to a teenager, and they couldn't be happier.

"There's Seth's car. I texted him that we were running late." Avery pointed across the crowded lot to a silver Camry that belonged to Avery's new boyfriend. Charlene chose a spot next to it.

For Avery's graduation, Charlene's mom and dad had given Avery a light blue Civic, gently used. The only reason Avery hadn't driven herself was because she and Seth were headed to the beach with their friends for a Saturday night bonfire after the double feature of *The Wolf Man* and *Frankenstein Meets the Wolf Man*.

"It's already packed," Charlene said, spying her friend Kevin Hughes's truck. The ladies exited the SUV. She hated to be late but hadn't counted on how many times a teen girl had to change clothes to get just the right casual vibe.

The historic three-story brick building had a flat rooftop sporting castle-like crenellation. It had been many things since first built in the 1800s. During the last few years, the brickwork had fallen into disrepair as the building had been empty and derelict.

Darren and Elise Shultz had moved from Saint Mary's, Pennsylvania, to Salem six months prior and saved it from the wrecking ball. Opening a theater was a dream come true for Darren, who'd made over a million dollars creating specialty seasoned salts. They'd picked Salem because Elise was from here, and her sister, Patty Wagner, owned a bakery that would supply the soft-baked pretzels at the theater, making it a family affair.

Charlene, new business liaison for Salem, had welcomed Darren and Elise with open arms. Her bed-and-breakfast thrived, and Brandy Flint, president of the City of Salem business board, had talked her into accepting the position to share her expertise as part of the community.

"Someday I want a car like Darren's," Avery said as they walked past the sleek black Tesla. It screamed understated success.

"I'm working on a passenger van." Charlene

kept her tone droll. "The Pilot will have to suffice for a while longer."

"I think you should forget the van and order the gazebo and hot tub." Avery peered at Charlene from over the rim of pink sunglasses. The teen was adorable in short cutoff jeans, sneakers without socks, and a T-shirt advertising *Spellbound Movie Theater.* Her soft light-brown hair bounced at the tops of her slender shoulders.

"You've been talking to Minnie," Charlene said.

"Maybe." Avery laughed, guilty as charged.

Charlene could attribute the B-and-B's success directly to her housekeeper's magic in the kitchen, and it had earned Charlene's amazing reviews online. Gaining positive reviews was part of her marketing strategy, and she'd shared that tidbit with Darren and Elise for the movie theater.

She was impressed by the updated building, as well as the miracles time and money could buy. What had leaned sadly to the left was now rebricked and straight. Outside aesthetic, check. Movie specials to bring in the crowds, check. This was just the sort of venue to draw people into Salem. There was no city better at making lemonade from lemons.

"Hey! Can you get the door?" a female voice called from behind them.

Charlene turned as Avery said, "Sure!"

A stylish brunette woman in a leather miniskirt with suit jacket and three-inch black heels held a bouquet of purple-blue flowers. "I can hardly see," she said, shifting them to one side of her face. Long lashes with cat-eye liner showed off mirthful brown eyes.

Avery opened the door, and the scent of fresh

popcorn with butter and salt escaped. Charlene had been clueless about designer seasoning salts until meeting Darren. They weren't his passion, though; that had been the movie theater, so he didn't mind pouring money into the venture to get it off the ground. Elise backed his project all the way.

"I'm Klara Maxwell," the woman behind the flowers said. "Darren's salt sales rep from Pittsburgh. You see that new car out there? Well, I aim to ensure he can afford ten of them by this time next year. We're going global!"

Charlene laughed at the young woman's enthusiasm. It reminded her of when she and Jared, her beloved soul mate, had worked at the ad agency in Chicago. There was a lot of energy in creation, and vibrant salespeople made a world of difference in a product launch. This was the first time she'd met the rep, and Darren spoke of Klara highly.

"I'm Charlene, and this is Avery." She was glad they weren't the only late attendees. "Nice to meet you."

The door shut behind them.

"And you," Klara said, long lashes blinking as she took it all in. "Wow."

The interior of the movie theater rivaled the bright lights of a casino. Yellows, blues, reds. Plush carpet beneath their feet, a popcorn machine, pretzels, soda. She even smelled roasted peanuts.

"This is so cool!" Avery removed her sunglasses and scanned the deceptively dim lobby. There were no other moviegoers down here, but laughter was audible from upstairs. Her gaze was drawn to the teen boy across the lobby by the popcorn machine.

Movie posters of *The Wolf Man, Frankenstein Meets the Wolf Man, House of Frankenstein, Dracula, The Mummy, Frankenstein,* and *Frankenstein's Bride* were in mega color on the walls. It was like going back in time. Charlene could appreciate the art of the old posters if not the movies themselves. She was willing to keep an open mind.

Darren's vision all along had been to bring the movie theaters from his childhood to life. He'd grown up in Germany and escaped what he referred to as his personal hell in the cavern-ish sanctuary of darkness. *The Wolf Man* franchise starring Lon Chaney Jr. was his favorite series, and he and Franco knew all the lines.

Franco Lordes was the film expert at the theater. Things were digital now, but Franco's expertise was in the old-fashioned reels. He could repair them and had a reverence for them shared by Darren.

You just never knew who might get you in this world. Charlene didn't care for Hollywood, old or new, but she was all about the buttery, salty popcorn that Darren somehow elevated to new heights with his unique flavors. According to Elise, he had a palate on par with the top chefs of the world.

"Welcome!" Darren called as he and Elise strode toward them. He was dark-haired, and Elise was a blonde. Darren was just a smidge taller than Charlene at five-eight compared to Elise's five-foot even. He had a muscled chest with a broad forehead, and she was petite to her toes.

"Klara!" Darren roared her name, laughing as he carefully accepted the bright purple-blue flowers and took the vase from her hands. "Only you would dare bring wolfsbane to my opening night."

Elise blinked prettily. Diamonds winked from her earlobes as well as her fingers, and she wore an ivory sundress. "Wolfsbane? Isn't that poison and supposed to ward off werewolves?"

"All in good fun," Klara said, her nose lifted slightly at Elise.

Tension simmered between the ladies. Competition for Darren's attention?

"Also known as monkshood, because of the shape of the blossom." Darren pointed to the flower but didn't touch it. "Among other names that I won't get into. I should put this in the office so nobody accidentally gets poisoned. Thanks for adding drama, Klara!"

"You brought dangerous flowers to the theater?" Elise stated, clearly appalled.

"It's a joke. We're watching *The Wolf Man*," Klara explained as if Elise was ignorant of the werewolf lore. "Wolfsbane will keep us all safe just in case of a werewolf attack." The sales rep bared pearly white teeth.

"I know that, Klara." Elise's lower lip pouted. "I've seen the movie a hundred times."

Franco, tall and thin, with great big green eyes and a dark goatee, his dark hair an inch all around his scalp, set his tray of popcorn back on the counter in exchange for the flowers. It was plain to all that Elise was not enjoying the jest. "*Even a man who is pure at heart . . .*" he said.

Darren continued with an eye twinkle, "*. . . and says his prayers at night. May become a wolf when the wolfsbane blooms.*"

"*And the autumn moon is bright.*" Franco and Darren each howled. "The wolf's next victim will have a mark of the pentagram on their palm," Franco said theatrically. "Hands out, everyone!"

Charlene, Avery, Klara, and Darren all showed their palms. Elise folded her hands together and said, "That's silly."

They all lowered their hands. Charlene discreetly studied the ladies.

"It was meant to be lighthearted," Klara said, dismissive of Elise. Interesting dynamic between two important women in his life. "Darren, this place is spectacular. I skipped dinner so I could gorge on popcorn."

"And the soft-baked pretzel rods. Patty helped Seth set them out. Have you met my sister yet?" Elise asked Klara, Charlene, and Avery.

Charlene and Avery shook their heads.

Franco took the flowers toward a door marked *OFFICE* behind the concession stand.

The prelaunch party for friends and family was twofold. One, to make sure tomorrow's opening day would go smoothly. Second was as a thank-you for everyone's help. The strategy to bring in customers with free weekend matinées if they bought a season pass for the summer lineup of movies had been Charlene's idea.

Elise and Darren had designed a logo of an old-fashioned film reel in black and white with a noir vibe. They would give out novelty red-and-white-striped popcorn holders, with free refills, and an all-you-can-drink soda container that read *Spellbound Movie Theater*, tomorrow only. They'd advertised in print, radio, and social media and expected to sell all three hundred seats.

"I'll introduce you." Elise led the way across the plush maroon carpet in the foyer to the tiled lobby closest to the concession stand, where things were bound to get sticky from spilled drinks and food. Tile was easier to clean.

"Have you seen *The Wolf Man* before?" Klara asked Charlene. Her heels clicked against the tile as they neared the counter full of snacks. Bright boxes of candy beckoned from behind the glass.

"Once as a kid," Charlene said. If she admitted she hadn't been a huge fan, she'd be kicked to the curb. "Avery hasn't seen any of the films, so this is her first foray into cheesy horror."

Darren turned around from where he'd stopped at the counter and bestowed a smile on them all. "It's my obsession," he admitted. "Elise prefers romantic comedies."

"You don't like horror movies?" Avery asked Darren's wife. The two times Elise had been at the bed-and-breakfast for business planning meetings, Avery had been at school.

Elise crinkled her nose. "Not really. The plan is to have Noir Night on Fridays in the small theater, romantic comedies on Saturdays, then Sunday will be older movies for a discounted price. The main theater will have top headliners, of course. We did the cost evaluation, and it makes more sense to only be open on the weekends unless someone books for a private party."

"Tonight, we will be in the largest theater with stadium seating." Darren grinned like he was a kid again. "We're offering a tasting selection of seasoned salts and a tray so you can dip your popcorn or pretzel and try them all."

"My favorite is the white truffle." Klara's eyes glittered with anticipation as she glanced at the counter and the trays. Popcorn popped merrily in a boxy clear-glass machine. A cute teenager in a *Spellbound Movie Theater* baseball cap kept smiling at Avery.

Could this be Seth?

"I like the roasted garlic and the dark chocolate. Not together," Elise said with a self-deprecating chuckle. "Separate."

"We could try it, *schatzi*. The sweetness of caramelized garlic combined with the bitterness of a dark cocoa?" Darren licked his lips as if imagining the taste. "If it's good, we will name it after you, Elise."

Elise brightened. "I'd love that!"

"I can't get enough of the herb and chili flake." Darren rubbed his palms together. "The secret is to start with German sea salt for a base, and there's no limit to what you can create."

"This is your baby." Klara clapped her hand around his forearm. "You've done great, Darren. Your gift for flavors has made your movie theater dream come true."

Elise had mentioned during the business launch meetings that she longed for children and hoped to start a family. Darren had tabled the discussion until after the premiere of the movie theater opening. Charlene knew Elise wished for success in more ways than one.

"Thanks, Klara. I couldn't have done this without you."

Elise lost some of her glow at Darren's comment.

Unaware, Darren faced Charlene and Avery. "Lon Chaney Jr. really makes this movie." Darren pressed his thumb to his fingers and shook them toward the ceiling. "The suffering he conveys with his eyes, the horror when he realizes—"

"Wait!" Avery said, totally into the new experience. "Don't spoil it for me, now."

Franco left the office to join them before the snack counter, the door ajar. "*The way you walked was thorny through no fault of your own,*" he droned, hands before him. "*But as the rain enters the soil . . .*"

"*. . . the river enters into the sea, so tears run to a pre-destined end,*" Darren said, immediately falling into the verse. Charlene assumed it was from the movie.

"*Your suffering is over. Now you will find peace for eternity,*" Franco concluded.

Charlene and Klara laughed while Elise barely hid an eye roll.

"Avery!" Seth greeted the young lady over the hum and *pop, pop, pop,* of the popcorn machine. His good looks were evident despite the cap and movie theater uniform of a crimson polo and tan pants. Brown waves, blue eyes, a lanky physique. "Matthew said since it's a practice night and we're giving everyone the same treat for the movie, I can sit with you until intermission."

"Awesome!" Avery sidled closer to the popcorn machine. Seth filled the second-to-last tray with popcorn, then the final one. Patty added a carton of soft-baked pretzel rods. Charlene noticed they had names on them. Darren's was already mounded with golden popcorn and salt, as was Elise's. Matthew's, Patty's, Seth's, and Charlene's had a sampling tray with a variety of salts. Silver canisters were on a stand that was labeled *Shultz's Seasoned Salts.*

"I'm so sorry we're a few minutes late," Charlene said.

Darren waved her apology away. "We will start in ten minutes, at six forty-five." With a glance at his watch, he and Franco hurried up the stairs.

Matthew Sinchuk, the movie theater manager, turned from where he was stacking the empty novelty popcorn boxes in a special tray with *The Wolf Man* on it. Every month they would have different designs. He was forty, slightly older than Darren, with a small paunch beneath his polo shirt tucked into khakis. Tie. Silver-framed glasses, thick auburn hair. They'd met at one of the launch meetings. "Hi there, Charlene, Klara. Charlene, here is yours. Avery."

They each accepted their sampling tray. "What a nice touch with the names," Charlene said.

"Thank you! I thought it would be fun if our special guests had a little keepsake." Elise rested her elbow on the glass counter. "Hey, Patty, meet Charlene! She owns the bed-and-breakfast. I think you two should talk pastries. Patty makes blueberry muffins that are heaven-sent."

Charlene appreciated the connection Elise was making, but she would give up Minnie's magic in the kitchen over her dead body.

A thick-figured brown-haired woman placed a carton of soft pretzels, still steaming, on the last special tray next to the novelty popcorn. "Hello."

Patty was as cute as Elise with the same upturned nose and bright blue eyes. "Nice to finally meet you! Our dad wouldn't be pleased with the lower profits since his death. I've had to learn by trial and error, unfortunately. I'm willing to accept any advice."

"Anytime," Charlene said. "Join the City of Salem Business Association. You won't regret it!"

"This new venture will only help spread the word that Wagner's Bakery isn't going anywhere," Elise said.

Charlene liked that Elise came to her sister's defense.

"Thanks to you and Darren, I'll have my name on each tray of snacks." Patty rotated the cardboard box to show the back where Wagner's Bakery's address and phone number were displayed.

"My background is marketing, and that's prime real estate," Charlene assured her.

Klara chimed in, reaching for the sampling tray that had her name on it. "Sure is. Should have said *Shultz's Seasoning Salts*, but I wasn't consulted."

Elise ignored the sales rep and smiled at Avery. "You can choose water or a soft drink from the machine over there. Free refills with your bottle."

"Thanks!" Avery happily perused her tray of treats. "There are even little gummy bear candies."

"We hope to entice customers for private parties," Elise said.

The lights dimmed twice.

"Five minutes to showtime!" Matthew tossed a package of Swedish Fish at Seth. "Go on. Get your popcorn so you can sit with your girlfriend. No such breaks tomorrow, though, got it?"

Seth grinned. His freckles added to the teenage girl's dream. "Thanks, boss." He scooted around the counter to shake Charlene's hand. "I'm Seth."

"Charlene," she said, charmed.

Seth joined Avery by the soda machine while Charlene chose water. She had nothing against sweet drinks, but when she had one, she preferred a margarita.

Klara nibbled a piece of popcorn from her tray. "Are you coming, Matthew? Patty?"

The manager nodded. "We'll be right there. Going to lock the doors, grab a root beer, and extra of the chocolate salt." He gestured to the array of labeled canisters. White truffle, chocolate, roasted garlic, herb, white cheddar, chili flake. Coconut.

"Aren't they all so good?" Elise took her box of treats as well as Darren's. They had full trays with their favorite flavor rather than a little of each. "Matthew, let's make time for a chat tomorrow morning, to go over what happened yesterday." Her expression held the remnants of annoyance.

Matthew whipped off his silver-framed glasses, his eyes narrowing as he stared at Elise, not at all subdued regarding the subject. "You bet."

Charlene, ever so curious, wanted to know what was going on. Opening a business was often highly stressful.

"Darren is probably already in our seats." Elise batted moisture from her eyes. "This is such a special night for him."

"You both have worked really hard," Charlene said, recalling how they'd come to her house with a file folder of plans, and now, six months later,

their dream of opening a movie theater was coming true.

Once Elise helped Darren reach his, then he
would discuss starting a family. "It's important,"
Elise said. "I want him to succeed."

Patty grabbed the sampling tray with her name.
"I sure hope the movie lives up to the hype."

They all climbed the carpeted stairs to the second floor. Seth held the door to the theater open
for them. Red velvet curtains and gold ropes were
reminiscent of old-time theaters. The seats were
spacious with tables between them so you didn't
have to put your food and drinks on the floor.

"I love it here!" Avery peered out at the thirty
other folks, all friends, with their dates, from the
Salem Business Association. Just like in the old
days, a cartoon played before the feature film.

Seth took an aisle seat, and then Avery, then
Charlene. Klara chose the next one down. "Mind
if I sit with you? Franco said I could watch the show
in the projector booth on the third floor with him,
but I think these seats are going to be more comfortable. This is very exciting." The sales rep sat
back and crossed long legs made longer by her
miniskirt.

"It is," Charlene said.

Klara leaned forward so she could look at Charlene, Avery, and Seth. "What's your fave so far?"

"Chocolate," Avery said. "For the popcorn. For
the pretzel rods, I prefer the chili flakes."

"Good choices," Klara confirmed.

"I like the herbs for the popcorn and the truffle
for the pretzels," Seth said. "But to be fair, I al-

ready tried them during training for the concession counter. It's such a great idea."

Klara tilted her head as if mentally calculating
marketing figures with the demographic of teens
versus adults. "What about the roasted garlic?"

"It's great," Seth said with a slight blush as he
glanced at Avery, "but not for a date."

"Fair!" Klara chuckled and dipped her popcorn
into the roasted garlic salt. "I am free as a bird
today." She tossed the kernel in her mouth and
chewed with exaggerated delight.

"What's your favorite, Charlene?" Avery asked.

Charlene had just tried two so far. White cheddar and Dijon. "I don't know yet till I try them all,
but these soft pretzels with the Dijon salt might be
my new addiction."

The lights flickered.

"Almost showtime," Seth said. "Cool black-and-
white cartoon."

"Hang on. I'll be right back," Elise said in a terse
tone. "Excuse me." She passed by the row, practically tripping over feet in the dim lighting.

"Are you okay?" Charlene asked.

Elise shook her head. "Our popcorn must have
gotten mixed up. Darren prefers the crushed herb
and chili, and he got mine with the roasted garlic.
As if I'd want to make him unhappy! I bet you Matthew switched the popcorn salt on purpose."

Elise left the theater for the concession area.
The heavy red drapes around the doorway fluttered, and Charlene felt a chill.

Klara pursed her lips. "I wouldn't be at all surprised," the sales rep murmured, "if poor Matthew
is about to get fired."

# CHAPTER 2

After that pronouncement, Klara followed Elise out of the theater, leaving her novelty popcorn tray at the small table by her seat.

"Wow. I guess Elise and Matthew don't get along?" Avery said. They talked in a hush so as not to be heard over the cartoon in the background.

Seth dipped a pretzel into the white truffle salt. "Elise looks sweet, but she's got a temper. Patty is the nice one. Yesterday during training, Elise ripped Matthew's head off for not closing the office door. He said he did, but it was open. Franco joked around about it being opened by a ghost, and Elise lost her mind."

Charlene knew ghosts were real, but it hadn't been an easy adjustment to her Midwestern sensibilities. "She doesn't believe in them?"

Seth raised a brow and sipped from his soda bottle. "Ghosts are an accepted fact in Salem for a lot of people." He peered at Avery, then Charlene. "Matthew has worked as a manager in this building during the last two businesses. He believes he's seen things."

Darren and Matthew had discussed how the third time would be the charm for Matthew managing this property.

Avery sat back. "Like what?"

"I dunno." Seth shrugged. "Shadows. Like out of the corner of your eye? Salem has a lot of paranormal activity."

"Do you believe in ghosts?" Avery asked Seth. Charlene listened carefully.

"Sure do. Our house is haunted by a little girl about five or so." Seth unwrapped a treat-sized package of Swedish Fish. "I've never seen her, but Mom and my brother have. She likes to open the refrigerator."

"How awful! You should talk to our friend Kevin, or Kass," Avery said. "Maybe they can help banish her for you."

Perhaps the little girl could travel into the light that waited beyond this plane of existence, Charlene thought.

"Why?" Seth licked the salt from his thumb. "She doesn't bother anybody."

"It just seems sad, that's all." Avery dabbed the tip of a soft-baked pretzel rod into the chili salt. "Will she be stuck there for eternity?"

"How should I know?" Seth asked. "I'm not an expert. Mom says the little girl doesn't seem to be in pain or afraid. She's just . . . there."

Someday she'd need to write a handbook on this particular paranormal experience. While Charlene and Jack figured out what his "rules" were, she was learning by experience. Charlene had never seen a ghost other than Jack.

The definition of a *ghost* was an apparition of a dead person that manifested itself to the living. Generally harmless, whereas a *spirit* had demonic connotations. Ghosts were thought to be caught in an echo of time, which would explain the phenomenon at Seth's house.

Jack was just . . . Jack. So far, Charlene was the only one who could see him. He couldn't leave the property, the scene of his murder. Maybe it was the same for the little girl—had she been murdered too?

Charlene wanted an invite to the Gambles to see for herself—but tagging along as Avery's . . .what was she to Avery? They loved one another but weren't physically related.

Avery was too old to need a mother. Despite the hardship of growing up at the teen house without parents to care for her, Avery had earned a four-year scholarship and now had a forever home with Charlene.

The teenager had her room at the B-and-B—Charlene had insisted she take the single at the end of the house with a hint of a view of the oak tree. Avery said she didn't mind sharing a third-floor bathroom, and it wasn't always in use by guests. After living at the teen house with ten or more kids, this was plenty private.

Charlene imagined holidays spent together for as long as Avery wanted, and there was a small, selfish part of herself that hoped Avery would settle down in Salem and never leave.

Elise returned with a medium-sized tub of popcorn and the canister of herb and chili salt for Darren. Her eyes were red-rimmed and her cheeks pink. Had she let Matthew have it for the mistake? He was the manager, though Seth and Patty had been adding popcorn and pretzels to the trays.

Klara came back right afterward, gaze thoughtful as she retrieved her snacks. "I've decided to join Franco in the projector room upstairs. I've never watched a movie from where the action happens," she said with a laugh. "I'll see you all later."

Matthew slipped in as the door closed behind Klara, and the manager found an aisle seat.

The cartoon ended, and the movie started. Charlene was transported for the next hour to Wales. *The Wolf Man* stood on its own merit; though it was a little corny, the story itself was solid. The black-and-white movie was the perfect delivery for the tale. The anguish of the man trying to fight his wolf nature, then the father, thinking his son was mentally ill . . . to have the father then kill the son at the end. Or so the viewer was left to believe.

Man versus his inner beast. There was something poignant about it all.

Just before the lights went on, Elise passed down the row again, coughing, but trying not to, with Patty at her heels.

The bright lights showed the interior of the theater and rows of velvet seats as folks got up to stretch or get more snacks. There was Kass Fortune, who owned a tea shop in the pedestrian mall; Kevin Hughes, who managed Brews and Broomsticks, a local bar, as well as running a paranormal tour business, which Kass sometimes helped out with. His girlfriend, Amy Fadar, was an actress and also worked with Kevin on the tours. Archie Higgins with his wife from Vintage Treasures; Sharon Turnberry, and her husband, John. Lucas Evergreen, who owned the bookstore. The Flints had sent their regrets, and Charlene got the not-too-subtle hint that movies weren't their thing.

Charlene wondered if Elise was all right, coughing and holding her stomach. "I'll be right back," she told Avery, then pointed to the empty chair next to her. "Where's Seth?"

"At the concession to refill popcorn with Matthew," Avery said. "He'll be back! Having fun?"

"I am—I'm going to make sure that Elise is okay."

Avery nodded and sipped from her plastic cup.

Charlene went to the restroom, where Patty was offering Elise a drink from a water bottle. The pair were side by side at the farthest sink. Patty whispered, "You don't have to put up with that nonsense. Darren married you, not her."

Charlene wished they would have shut the door all the way, and that she hadn't intruded on the private moment. She brazened it through as if she hadn't heard anything out of the ordinary. Of course, she realized they had to be talking about the sexy Klara. "Are you all right, Elise?"

Elise peered up at Charlene with wide blue eyes. The skin around her neck was red. "I'm fine. A kernel caught in my throat." She rested her hand over her stomach. Her ivory sundress was flattering to her slim figure. "I don't feel well, but it's just because I ate too much popcorn. I'm like a kid and can't stop myself."

Charlene went into a stall since that was what you were supposed to do when you went to the bathroom, closing the door.

"Darren should fire her," Elise murmured. "But he won't. She's made him too much money. If I hear the word 'global' one more time!"

"Oh, honey," Patty said. "I'm sorry. Just give it a little while longer. Once you get pregnant, all his attention will be on you. Do you think you could be preggers right now?"

Elise sobbed. "He doesn't want a baby, Patty! Never."

What? That wasn't the impression that Darren had given regarding a family. He'd told Elise to be patient. What had changed? Other women entered the bathroom, and Charlene flushed, escaping from the stall where she'd been trapped. She went to the sink and washed up, smiling at Kass and Amy.

She sent an empathetic glance toward Elise. Marriage was not an easy road. She'd noticed the antagonistic remarks between Elise and Klara. As if getting his attention was a competition.

Honestly, Darren had shown nothing but love for Elise, so Charlene hoped that what Elise suspected was wrong.

Unfortunately, women liked men with money and didn't always care that someone else was already with that man.

"What did you think of the movie?" Kass asked. Her long hair reached her hips, and it was loose today, Cher-esque with bangs.

"I loved it," Charlene said.

"A little corny," Amy offered. "But not bad for

nineteen forty-one. I'm up for the next one! How many are there?"

"Five," Elise said.

"Four too many." Sharon Turnberry snickered. She'd joined the line for the ladies' room, her bright red hair not any natural shade.

At that, Elise smiled, sensing an ally in her movie tastes. "Enjoy the pretzels and popcorn and be sure to come tomorrow for the free matinée. We'll have horror movies in the smaller theater and the latest features in the large one."

"Action-adventure or romantic comedy are more my speed than *Frankenstein Meets Dracula* or whatever comes next," Sharon admitted ruefully.

"Mine too!" Elise laughed.

Sharon tucked a brilliant red curl behind her ear. "Though this is a lovely theater. I'm so glad you and Darren have brought it back and made it safe. I swear, each time I drove by to the Wharf, I half expected it to be condemned or brick crumbles on the ground!"

Avery entered the line for the restroom. "It's like high school—everyone gathered for gossip in the bathroom." All five sinks were in use.

"Nothing's changed," Kass said. "Hey, kiddo."

"Hi, Kass!" Avery smiled at Charlene. "Wait for me?"

"Sure," Charlene said. Now she had an excuse to linger as the others entered the stalls, with Avery being last. Kass dried her hands after washing up with a paper towel.

Patty peered at her sister with concern in her blue eyes. Her brown hair curled at her collar bone. Elise seemed especially pale in her shadow.

"Maybe you should go home," Patty suggested. "Get some rest."

"No, ma'am." Elise straightened and braced her hands on the counter behind her. "That's the last thing I should do. Fleeing the playing field is a move of surrender, don't you remember?"

Patty eyed the ceiling. "Dad's long gone, sis. Which is a shame because he'd set your husband on the right path for so much as thinking of straying."

"We don't know for sure," Elise said softly. "Let's get back. I would say before Darren starts to worry, but he's so involved with Matthew and Franco that I doubt he's missed me. He thought I put the wrong salt on purpose! I was going to ream Matthew, but he wasn't there when I went to get different popcorn."

The sisters left, and Kass raised a dark brow at Charlene. "Trouble in paradise?"

"I hope not." Charlene peered after Elise and Patty. "I really like the Shultzes."

Avery came out and washed her hands at the sink. "I can see why this movie is a classic. And the black-and-white cartoons? Totally old school! I'm hooked for the next few months of Friday Noir Nights. Seth likes them too."

"It's perfect for Salem," Kass laughed. "We love our monsters, witches to werewolves!"

"Right?" Avery dried her hands and tossed the paper towel into the trash. "Let's go! Bring on Frankenstein. Seth keeps talking about how there's a deeper philosophical meaning to the movies, but I just like the scares."

Charlene nodded. "Because they aren't too scary. Just the right amount."

"So," Kass said, nudging Avery as they walked out of the restroom, "who is the cutie I saw you talking with earlier?"

"Seth Gamble, popcorn maker." Avery glanced at Kass with a sweet smile. "He's going to community college here in Salem. Business management."

"Nice. Well, this is your time to shine, Miss Boston Academy. Criminology degree. I'm blown away every time I think of it, but I know you can do it." Kass smiled encouragingly. "You're going to be great—the tea leaves predict it."

Kass did tea leaf readings in her shop, where, after a person drank a cup of tea, Kass divined messages from the way the leaves were arranged. She'd given a reading to Avery as a graduation gift. Avery would not have the traditional type of life, according to the oolong, but she'd be happy.

Salem was geared toward non-tradition, and happiness trumped everything.

Charlene still hadn't done a reading for herself. Once a person started to believe in the paranormal, well, it was hard to put the cork back in the champagne bottle. She was concerned she'd get in over her head. Jack was plenty for her to accept . . . also, she was learning to trust her intuition more.

They headed toward their seats, and Charlene took a mental snapshot for her resident ghost, who missed things like this. Bright light illuminated movie posters. Red wallpaper, gold trim. Popcorn and salt, roasted peanuts, cushy leather reclining chairs. It was all such a sensual treat.

"It's cool, but spooky," Avery said as they arrived at the door leading inside the theater.

"Why spooky?" Kass's hair swung at her hip. "I love the ambiance. Dark red drapes, rich mahogany accents. We could be in a nineteen-twenties theater, it's so posh."

"I keep thinking there's someone behind the curtains," Avery admitted with a giggle.

"This place is haunted," Kass said. "I can feel it. My psychic shields are working overtime." Their friend walked ahead to her row.

"Seth doesn't believe me." Avery paused at their chairs. Their novelty popcorn trays were on the attached tables. Charlene scanned the walls and curtains around them but noticed nothing out of the ordinary.

Elise coughed, then again. Charlene turned toward the end of the row and Elise and Darren. Elise held a napkin to her mouth.

Darren patted her shoulder, his expression the epitome of a concerned husband. Had he and Klara done the wild thing behind Elise's back?

Charlene just didn't want to think about it. Too sad. She looked for Klara, but the sales rep causing Elise's distress wasn't around. She must still be in the projector room with Franco.

The lights flashed twice—a warning that the second movie was about to start and to get to your seat before it was dark.

"Have a drink, *engel*," Darren said as he handed Elise a water bottle.

She pushed it away. "No! Can't breathe!"

"*Liebling,* please." Darren smoothed a lock of

Elise's blond hair from her cheek. "Don't be dramatic right now."

Was Darren embarrassed by Elise? Had Elise accused Darren of messing around?

"I didn't mean to be upset about the salt mistake," Darren said.

"I didn't do it!" Elise shoved the popcorn tray off the small table, and yellow puffs flew across the floor and aisle. "Matthew," she wheezed, "or maybe Klara."

"Elise!" Darren said, sounding stern.

Charlene hadn't heard him use that tone while they'd been at her house for the business meetings to plan the theater launch.

Suddenly Elise's eyes bulged. Her cheeks darkened in the dim theater. Spittle foamed at her lips. Charlene glanced at Avery and Seth, who were in conversation from their seats and hadn't noticed the scene. She stepped toward Elise.

"Darren!" Elise clawed at the collar of her sundress and her eyes rolled back as she fainted and slid from the seat to the floor.

"Elise!" Darren cried.

The lights went out as the second feature started to play. The crackle of the old film reel was the background to the low music of the overture.

Charlene used her phone as a flashlight, her gaze focused on Elise's pale sundress in the dark. "Avery, call nine-one-one. Seth, go upstairs and have Franco turn off the movie. We need the lights on. Hurry!"

Avery jumped up from her seat, holding her phone. She'd been staring back at the curtain and now faced Charlene. "What's going on?"

"Elise is choking. We need an ambulance," Charlene said as Darren not-so-gently settled Elise's head on his lap, opening her airway. "Now!"

Elise dragged in breaths.

Avery dialed 911.

Charlene thought of calling Sam, Salem's leading detective, as she always did in these awful emergencies she sometimes found herself part of, but this wasn't a crime. A tragedy, yes, unless they got help in time.

"What's wrong?" Seth put his tray down on the table attached to the theater chair.

"Go upstairs!" Charlene said again, with more urgency. "Tell Franco and Klara to stop the movie. Avery?"

"On my way," Seth said. He glanced at the dark shadow of his boss and his boss's wife sprawled on the floor before darting out of the theater to the hall, then up the stairs.

Charlene heard Avery calmly give her name as she told the operator that emergency services were needed at the new Spellbound Movie Theater.

One of the owners was choking.

Charlene's heart beat crazily out of time as Darren patted Elise's cheeks, then tilted her head back. He listened for breaths. It was obvious that Elise was struggling but still breathing on her own.

"Elise?" Darren's tone had changed from annoyed to scared. "*Schnucki?*"

The lights turned on, and the movie paused in mid-rotation. Charlene watched Elise carefully, afraid to look away. Elise had to be all right. She felt helpless, but Darren was doing everything right. He'd stretched out Elise's body and was crooning to her in German. Sounded like a lullaby.

Darren dabbed at the spittle on her lips with a paper napkin. What if Elise had suffered a reaction to the salt? Could someone be allergic to salt—or something in the seasoning? Elise had eaten roasted garlic.

It wasn't long before Matthew arrived and banged open the door from the hall to the seats, leading the medics from the ambulance, and the police, into the theater. Not Sam. She didn't text him, as that would break their friendship policy. Nothing personal through cell phones and all police business would be conducted through the station.

Sam was handsome, smart, capable, and she didn't have time in her life right now for such a wonderful man. Not while she had a ghost at home. Jack had given up heaven for her, and they were such great friends. Romance, if it was to happen, would need to wait.

She'd discovered in the past year that Sam was quite content pursuing his detective career while flirting with her and wasn't in such a rush either.

Unlike Darren and Elise, they had time.

# CHAPTER 3

Charlene was relieved to see Officer Bernard on call. The Haitian policeman was one of her favorites at Salem PD. He nodded at Charlene and smiled at Avery. He'd once taken Avery on a ride-along in the patrol car—rather than scare the teenager, it had whetted her appetite to be a police officer.

"What's going on?" Officer Bernard asked as the EMTs surrounded Elise. The medics urged the rest of the folks to step back as they lifted her onto a stretcher.

"Elise Shultz choked on her popcorn," Charlene said.

Salem wasn't such a small city that everyone knew everyone else, but it was close. A new business in a historic building, specifically a movie theater, had made the news. Officer Bernard sighed. "They just moved here, right?" He stepped forward to peruse Elise, on her back, eyelids fluttering. The medics belted her on the stretcher.

"Will she be okay?" Avery asked.

"I hope so. She needs to get to the hospital." Officer Bernard eyed the gold ceiling and the red drapes along the walls with a shudder. "This building has its secrets."

"What do you mean?" Avery asked, rounding her gaze to be wide and innocent.

Officer Bernard made room for the medics around Elise as they wheeled her out of the row to the aisle. "You'll learn for yourself how to decipher truth from fiction, but Salem has a mystic underbelly beneath the witchy tourist stuff. What's this?"

He stopped the popcorn tray with *Elise* written on the side from being trampled and cordoned off the spilled puffs.

"It was a keepsake for Opening Night," Seth said. "We all received one with our names on them."

"Everyone?" Officer Bernard clarified.

"Yes." Charlene lifted her gaze from the floor and the spilled popcorn. Darren's was empty, and there wasn't much left in Elise's novelty tray. "Darren had some of Elise's flavoring on his popcorn by mistake. She got him a fresh tub."

Matthew tugged at his tie. The small print on the fabric was howling wolves. "I'm not sure how it happened, but yes, Elise wanted just the roasted garlic seasoned salt on hers, and Darren wanted the herbs and chili flakes. There was a problem, and Darren had some of the roasted garlic too."

Officer Bernard located the tray of popcorn that had *Darren* written on it. The wadded-up white napkin with pink spittle made the officer pause. "Hmm. Is this blood? Was there food coloring in any of the flavored salts?"

"No," Seth said. "Darren emphasized they were made from all-natural ingredients during the training session for the salts."

"I'm sure it's just a choking accident," Patty said, her voice trembling. "Elise needs to be at the hospital. She didn't feel well."

Darren, red-faced, shot his arm to the side. "It was just a little of the roasted garlic salt and not a big deal. Elise wanted everything to be perfect for me, and she went to the concession stand for fresh popcorn and my favorite salt."

The silver canister of herb and chili flakes was on the floor underneath Darren's chair.

The medics, with Elise on the stretcher, reached the end of the aisle. Darren followed without a backward glance.

The EMTs turned right in the hall and disappeared. Darren hustled after them and out of sight to the waiting ambulance, no doubt to ride with Elise to the hospital. Could the pink on the napkin be blood from the popcorn lodged in Elise's throat? It was awful to witness someone choking and not be able to help.

Patty bumped into Charlene as she raced by with Elise's designer purse over her shoulder. "My sister will want this. I should go. Should I go?"

"Why don't you wait here, ma'am," Officer Bernard suggested. "Let me ask some questions first."

Patty stopped abruptly, leaning toward the door where her sister had been whisked out as if she wanted to go anyway.

Sam arrived in the doorway, all six-foot-six of muscled detective; his thick mustache and dark brown eyes immediately scanned the scene of spilled popcorn and didn't rest until he saw Charlene and Avery together.

"Sam!" Charlene stepped toward him as if drawn by an invisible string.

"I heard Avery's name on the scanner for an accident at the theater and thought I'd check it out. This is the soft opening?" Sam looked around the refurbished movie theater. "Nice place. Too bad."

Darren and Elise had put a million dollars at least into their passion project to create a profitable business showcasing Shultz's Seasoned Salts.

Officer Bernard had donned thin rubber gloves and now put the canister of seasoned salt into an evidence bag. Darren's tray was also in one, and Elise's in another. Why would he do that? It was obviously a choking accident.

Avery sidled up next to the officer. "Officer Bernard, what are you doing?"

Because she'd declared an interest in police work, the officer explained, "What you first see when you arrive on the scene isn't always the truth." He turned to Sam. "Detective Holden, I'm glad you're here. I'd like you to examine something." He gestured to the tissues with pink on them. "Now, Avery, why don't you wait in the hall with Charlene?"

Avery nodded, crestfallen that she couldn't learn more—but she didn't pout or argue to get her way. "All right."

Officer Bernard raised his voice. "If everyone could wait in the hall?" The people left in the theater moved to the exit, whispers about what could have happened circling among them.

Sam tucked his hand into the pocket of his slacks and joined the officer. "What's going on?"

The two bowed their heads together, Officer Bernard with a hat, Sam bare-headed, and Charlene allowed Avery to nudge her away from the scene.

"I bet he saw something suspicious," Avery murmured.

"Like what?"

"Like, if that's blood on the napkin . . . how did it get there? Was she choking that hard? I didn't hear her, but the music from the movie was starting. What if there was something in the popcorn that shouldn't have been?" Avery sighed. "I can't wait to be a police officer, Charlene. I want to solve crimes and help keep our community safe."

Kass, Kevin, and Amy joined her, Avery, and Seth as they waited along the gold-and-mahogany banister in the hall.

"What's up?" Kevin asked.

"Elise choked on her popcorn," Charlene said.

Avery gave Charlene a tiny head shake, to warn her against saying anything else. The girl was going to be a natural fit for the police department.

"What a date," Seth said, trying to make light of the situation. He removed his cap and tucked it in his back pocket, freeing his wavy hair.

Avery shrugged. "I'm so worried about Elise. I'm not sure I'm up for a bonfire party on the beach."

"Oh," Seth said, masking his disappointment well. "Understandable."

Sam came out of the theater, hands at his sides. Speaking above the murmurs of conversation, he said, "We're sorry to have detained you, but you are all now free to go. We will be in touch with further questions if necessary."

In other words, get lost.

Sam went back into the room. He was methodical; Officer Bernard too. Did he agree there was something suspicious going on? He wouldn't act on a hunch—he required facts. The napkin would need to be tested for blood.

Klara and Franco arrived from the third-floor projector room. Charlene knew from the tour a month ago that on that floor there was also a special room where they stored the films that weren't digital.

"Hey," Matthew said, looking at Franco. His poor tie was a wreck. "Where've you two been?"

"Trying to stay out of the way." Franco smoothed his goatee, his green eyes sharp as he took them all in. "How's Elise?"

A ringing interrupted the conversation. Patty, waiting next to Matthew, answered her phone. She paled, then screamed, dropping the device to the plush carpet in the hall. "No! No. Elise is dead. My beautiful sister is dead!" She crumpled, and Matthew caught her by the waist.

Charlene's eyes welled with tears. It seemed unreal. She reached for Avery, who began to sob as she returned Charlene's hug. She ran her hand in circles over the teenager's shoulder. This was not the night of celebration they'd planned.

Poor Darren. Poor Elise! And Patty. It was a nightmare.

"Dude!" Seth exclaimed, his mouth rounded in

shock. He snapped it closed. "That's awful. I mean, *awful.*"

"Maybe this place should be left to rot," Franco said, in a daze. His body was long and gangly, like Jack Skellington from *The Nightmare Before Christmas.* "I've seen lots of movies where the buildings are malevolent. *Amityville, Poltergeist. House of Evil . . .*"

"Those are all houses, man. I've worked here in one capacity or another over the last fifteen years," Matthew said. "People suck. I also blame the building."

Patty scrubbed her plump cheeks, but the tears kept coming. "I need to get to the hospital to see Elise. They won't move her until I get there, will they?"

"I'll drive you," Matthew offered, backing up a little to create space between them as she clung to his arm.

"Thanks." Patty peered up at Matthew. "I just. I can't. Poor Elise!"

The pair left. Charlene watched them go, wondering how best she could help in this situation.

Seth nudged his elbow against Avery's arm. "I think you're right . . . I don't feel like partying tonight either. You're sure you don't mind skipping the bonfire?"

"Nope. Call me later?" Avery straightened, her body trembling as she took a steadying breath.

"Okay. See you, everyone." Seth walked out as if he had cement in his shoes dragging him down. The brim of his cap peeked from his back pocket.

"I can't believe it," Avery whispered.

Kevin, Amy, and Kass all shared hugs. "Let us

know if you hear anything," Kevin said, his arm in Amy's as they turned for the stairs leading down to the lobby.

"I will," Charlene said.

Kass traipsed after them in her long-legged stride, blowing a kiss to Charlene and Avery over her shoulder.

Franco and Klara kept staring at the closed theater door where the accident had happened, and where Sam and Officer Bernard were collecting evidence. "Evil lurks," Franco said. He wore a snug black T-shirt over black pencil jeans as if wanting to accentuate his thinness. "What are the cops doing in there? What do you think happened to Elise?"

"Don't know. I'm outta here. I've got to find Darren. He'll be falling apart." Klara scooted past them down the stairs, still fashionable in her heels and short skirt. She was a pretty woman. Had she been having an affair with Darren?

Franco pulled a pentagram necklace from under his T-shirt, then showed Charlene and Avery his palms. "No mark of the wolf. I'm safe." He hurried up the stairs and out of sight. She heard the slam of the film-room door.

"That was weird." Avery's brow scrunched as she watched where Franco had vanished. "Let's go home."

Franco's response had been strange—in the end the movies were just movies, meant to entertain. "Want to stop for ice cream?" Charlene wasn't in the mood, but she had no clue how to cheer Avery up after this tragic event.

"No, thanks." Avery put her phone in her shorts

pocket. "After all this junk food, I think I want some comfort food—like soup."

Charlene checked the time. Seven. She had a full house over the next few months as summer in Salem was gorgeous. "The guests will be out on their dinner cruise for a while yet. Would you like lentil or chicken and rice?" Minnie had both in the fridge.

"Chicken and rice." Avery stepped toward the stairs.

With a last look back at the closed door, Charlene followed Avery to the empty lobby. The medics were gone as well as the special guests.

The office door was open, and Charlene decided to close it in case the police left without doing so. She peeked in. The space had also been given a makeover with bright white paint. The walls were bare compared to those covered with movie posters everywhere else in the building. There was a modern desk with a computer monitor, two chairs, and a side table. Where were the purple-blue flowers?

"The wolfsbane bouquet isn't here." Where could it be? Maybe Klara, knowing it was poisonous, had taken the flowers back to avoid questions from the police. Charlene's nape tingled.

She whirled around in alarm, her fingers to her thumping chest.

It was only Avery behind her.

Avery gave a surprised laugh at Charlene's expression from where she waited by the concession counter. The popcorn machine was off, the novelty popcorn trays stacked for the next day. "What are you doing?"

"Closing the door!" There was no reason to make Avery worry even more than she already would, so Charlene didn't elaborate. She jiggled the knob to ensure it was locked and then they left the theater.

Avery turned on the radio when they got into the car, a signal that she didn't want to talk as they drove home. Every time Charlene glanced toward Avery, she was staring out the window, humming along to pop music.

Charlene, never having had kids, didn't know if there was something she should be doing for Avery considering the trauma of the night. What was supposed to have been a victory celebration for a new Salem business had ended with Elise dead. Choked on popcorn. Or worse.

It didn't get easier, death.

As they crested the hill leading to the mansion with seven bedrooms, not including Charlene's suite, Avery straightened. "I love this view. I'm so glad that this is my home now."

"It is beautiful," Charlene agreed, remembering the first time she'd seen it. It had taken her breath away. Will Johnson, Minnie's husband, kept the large green lawn mowed and the flowers abundant. Trees lined the back of the property, and the top of the oak tree was visible over the roof of the house. The widow's walk had a brass telescope for her guests to view the stars or the ocean. "I'm so happy you're here, too."

Parker Murdock, a local handyman, had created an elegant sign that read *Charlene's Bed-and-Breakfast*, which was in the front yard by the long driveway. A separate garage was to the right, and a cellar was on the left. There really was enough room for Parker to build a gazebo on the expansive grass.

Passenger van first.

Charlene had no regrets over taking the plunge and buying this place sight unseen to escape her grief, and her mother.

Now, almost two years later, her grief had lessened, and she actually enjoyed both her parents. Jared would always live in her heart.

The loss of a spouse made her think of Darren. She would reach out to him tomorrow and offer her condolences. She understood his bereavement too well.

Charlene slowed as she turned toward her home. A silvery-gray Persian lounged on the top rail of the white porch, her tail swinging in feline contentment. "Have you noticed the railing is Silva's favorite spot in the evening?"

"That cat is so fat I'm surprised she can get up there," Avery remarked with a chuckle.

"I know it. She's still quite the hunter, despite her size." Charlene parked in the driveway and opened her door to slide out. Jack appeared and tickled the plus-sized cat on her perch where she dozed.

Silva jumped awake and swatted at what must have seemed to Avery thin air.

"Silva is cray-cray." Avery exited the Pilot and walked to the stairs, glancing down at her shirt. "Oh, no! I have a butter stain."

Charlene locked the car doors with her key fob. "We can toss it in the wash. Hi, Silva." She fluttered her fingers at Jack.

Jack was tall—not as tall as Sam, but still well over six feet. He presented himself like the stylish gentleman he'd been before his death. His essence was invisible unless he made the effort. When he'd first manifested for her, he'd been in a dark-blue smoking jacket with an unlit pipe, his dark hair smoothed back. His turquoise eyes popped.

"You're back early," Jack said. "I thought the double feature wouldn't be over until midnight."

Charlene was no longer the gullible woman he could trick into answering him when they had witnesses, though Minnie and Avery both believed she had a terrible habit of talking to herself. Another peccadillo was keeping the TV on in her suite for company. Coverage for her and Jack's conversations.

"I'll start the soup," Charlene said as they entered the foyer. "Do you want to dash upstairs and change?"

"Yeah. Thanks, Charlene." The young lady, all of eighteen, took the stairs two at a time without any effort.

"She's like a gazelle with those legs." Charlene reached the kitchen. Certain they were alone, Charlene said, "Jack. Elise Shultz is dead."

Jack's image shimmered with astonishment. "What happened?"

Charlene set her purse on the kitchen counter. "Choked on popcorn, we think." She pulled the soup from the fridge.

Silva twined between her legs to get attention, treats, and kibble. On the feline wish list, treats would be first.

Jack floated the foil bag of liver-flavored treats to the kitchen table. "You *think*?"

Charlene warmed the chicken and rice soup on the stovetop and heated hard rolls in the toaster oven.

"Officer Bernard collected the novelty popcorn containers. Evidence? There was a napkin that looked like it had blood on it, possibly from Elise choking so hard." She listened for Avery on the stairs but heard nothing. "Elise didn't feel well during the intermission. Officer Bernard and Sam were sequestered in the theater while we waited in the hall, so I fear there might be more to the story."

She also quickly filled him in on Elise's concern that Darren had been having an affair with the salt sales rep, Klara.

"And Klara hurried out of there," Charlene said. "No sign of her or the flowers."

"Very interesting." Jack crossed his arms. "I suppose Sam will drop by?"

"Or Officer Bernard." Charlene stirred the chicken and rice in the pot.

"It'll be Sam," her jealous ghost said. "Just to visit with your beautiful self and eat all of Minnie's croissants."

She laughed as she heard Avery gallop down the stairs to the kitchen, holding the stained tee. She'd switched from the *Spellbound Movie Theater* T-shirt to a *Taylor Swift* one.

Silva waited with a tail-flick by her bowl.

"What's funny?" Avery spread her stained shirt by the sink.

"Silva, pouting for treats." Charlene switched off the heat on the stove.

"I'll get them for her." Avery opened the bag Jack had set on the table and gave Silva two. "I need to sprinkle baking soda on the butter stain, according to Google." She put the treats in the pantry and returned with the baking soda. "I hope this works! This shirt is super soft."

"What would we do without Google?" Charlene checked out the stain the size of a dime, then looked down to see if she'd gotten any butter on her own clothes, but her floral top and capris seemed fine.

"There was the library and newspapers," Jack answered her question from his position by the fridge.

"Beats me. Didn't you have to actually wait for answers?" Avery elbowed Charlene to show she was teasing. "That soup smells great. I guess demolishing junk food for dinner isn't smart anyway."

Charlene got out the bowls. "How much popcorn did you eat?"

"Seth loaded us up with refills during the show. It was so good I didn't mind the extra butter, but now . . ." Avery placed her hand over her tummy.

"She appears all right," Jack said, studying Avery closely.

"Ah. I was so engrossed in the wolf man's plight I didn't notice him leaving for more popcorn." Lon Chaney Jr.'s performance had captivated, just as Darren had promised. Charlene turned off the toaster oven, then poured them each a steaming bowl of soup and set the rolls on side dishes.

"Minnie's feeding us even when she isn't here," Avery noted with a good-natured smirk.

"Thank heaven." Charlene blew on the soup too

hot to eat just yet. "I'm all right for basic cooking stuff, but she's next level. Did you hear Elise trying to set up a meeting between us and Patty, since her sister runs the bakery? Minnie would keel over at an intruder in her kitchen."

Charlene's smile fled.

Elise was gone. Dead. It was wrong to find humor in things.

Avery slurped a spoonful, oblivious to the jumble of thoughts in Charlene's head. "Minnie is amazing. Why should she have to share the cooking with anyone? She told me that she loves it."

Charlene sighed. "Are you okay, Avery? I mean, it's not easy. Someone just died practically in front of you."

Avery stirred the chicken and rice, glancing at Charlene. "It's super sad. I just want to know what happened to her. Could we have helped if we'd acted sooner?"

Jack fluttered between them. "You realize that if Elise was killed by foul play, you both might be at risk?"

Charlene dropped her spoon to the bowl with a clatter. "What . . ." She stopped and glared at Jack. "I want to know what happened too. How do you feel, Avery?" Charlene did a mental inventory of her own physical symptoms. She felt fine.

"Your eyes aren't dilated. You aren't sweating," Jack said. His essence swooshed coolly over her skin as he examined her.

"Better now, thanks to the soup. Also, I'm glad we have air-conditioning so we can justify hot food in the summer." Avery dipped a roll in the creamy broth. "Can we watch *Friends* for a while?"

"You bet." Charlene and Avery both enjoyed re-runs for a familiar laugh.

What if Elise's popcorn had been tampered with?

"Neither of you is exhibiting symptoms of being poisoned," Jack said.

Charlene held her fingers to the pulsing vein at her throat.

Jack crossed his arms, in protector mode. "I'll watch television with you to make sure it stays that way."

*Thank you, Jack.*

# CHAPTER 4

Charlene entered the kitchen at 8 a.m. the next day, a bit bleary-eyed from lack of decent sleep. Her guests, three couples who had started as strangers a week ago and just might end up life-time friends, had come home from the dinner cruise by ten and they'd stayed up playing cha-rades until midnight. She and Avery had jumped in to play as well.

Minnie was in her element, creating a Sunday morning feast with quiche, scrambled eggs, bacon, fresh-squeezed orange juice, melon chunks, and banana-nut muffins.

"Morning," Charlene said, going straight for the Keurig. She added cream to a mug, then the dark roast. "How are you today?"

"I'm fine, but Elise Shultz is all over the news." Minnie wiped her hands on a dish towel and faced Charlene. "She was a hometown girl, you know. The Wagners have had a bakery in town for generations. Collapsed at the movie theater—as you must know, since you and Avery were there."

"We were." Charlene gave her coffee a cautious sip. "It's very sad. Did they say what she died from?"

"I thought choking." Minnie raised her brow. "Is there more to the story?"

Jack appeared in front of the refrigerator, and Minnie glanced at the burst of cold to see if she'd accidentally left it open.

"Hmm." Minnie turned back to Charlene. "What else is there?"

"We're not sure." She'd planned to talk to Jack after charades, but he'd been gone. They didn't always know if he'd be able to show himself. The longest time he'd been away had been four days, and by the end of that stretch, she'd worried that he might not return.

Avery arrived in the kitchen wearing shorts and a light-blue T-shirt, her shoulder-length hair up in a ponytail, revealing the delicate spider tattoo at her nape. "Morning." She helped herself to a glass of orange juice. "Did you see the news, Charlene?"

"Not yet." She glanced at Jack, who watched Avery as if to verify she was still okay and hadn't eaten anything bad. She found his protectiveness very sweet.

"It's all about Elise." Avery sipped. "Darren is a person of interest."

"What?" Charlene shook her head, having witnessed their partnership. "That can't be right. He loved her very much."

But had Darren been cheating? Elise had been upset that Darren had thought she'd put the wrong seasoned salt on his popcorn and had blamed Matthew or Klara.

"I was on the phone with Seth all night. Darren sent out a group text at five this morning that he still wants them to go to the movie theater today for the grand opening. That Elise would want him to continue. Now, that's weird, isn't it? I mean, your wife just dies, and it's work as usual?" Avery took another drink of juice, her tone disapproving.

Bizarre. Why would Darren do that? Unless there was more to their relationship than met the eye. "Seth mentioned yesterday that Elise had a temper."

"Right?" Avery grabbed a napkin and wrapped it around the base of her glass. "Seth heard Darren and Elise going at it to rattle the roof right before everyone else got there yesterday. Had to be around four."

"What about?" Charlene drank her coffee, the morning gift from the gods.

Avery's ponytail slid across her neck when she shrugged. "Seth didn't know, and Darren switched to speaking German. Matthew had to knock on the door to let them know the staff was there and could hear. Terrible, huh?"

It was too bad. People were rarely as they seemed.

"Let's talk more after breakfast and join our guests in the dining room." For once, Charlene wouldn't have to explain what had happened as they'd been far from the scene on a dinner cruise *if* there was a crime. Right now, it was simply a tragedy. "Can I help, Minnie?"

"Here you are," her housekeeper said, handing her an egg-and-bacon quiche on a trivet.

"Thanks." The steam rising from the savory pie smelled heavenly.

"What's the plan?" Minnie picked up serving tools.

"These folks will all be gone by noon, no late checkouts today." Charlene stepped past the kitchen table. Avery brought a tray of toasted bread and Minnie carried scrambled eggs with cheese.

"Awesome!" Avery said. "Plenty of time to strip the beds and begin cleaning."

"We'll still need to hustle. All four suites will be full this afternoon, and a single. Fresh towels, flowers, baskets of wine and snacks for each room. The Seafarer's Festival has us booked." Charlene loved it when business boomed.

They moved as a team to the dining room. Charlene smiled at the happy faces around the table. "Good morning! Please help yourselves."

Charlene and Avery sat with their guests while Minnie ducked back into the kitchen to start on the dishes.

She had just finished her slice of quiche when the doorbell rang. Minnie answered it, then paused at the dining room door, which was open to the foyer.

"Charlene, Detective Holden is here to see you." Minnie blushed.

The crush her housekeeper had on Sam was adorable, and he flirted with her shamelessly—all in good fun, of course.

Avery looked up from her banana-nut muffin,

obviously wanting to be part of the conversation. Sam had to be there because of Darren and Elise. Charlene shook her head for Avery to stay put; she'd fill her in later.

"I'll be right back," Charlene said to her curious guests.

Sam waited for her in the living room in front of the fireplace. It being a warm summer day, there was no need for it to be lit. The window on the side of the house showcased tubs full of bright assorted blooms.

Jack, also wanting to hear what Sam had to say, waited in half-form by the window.

"Sam! I'm so sorry Elise is dead. How did it happen?" The detective sat in the yellow brocade armchair, and she took the one across from him. He wore a short-sleeved gray polo and black slacks.

"Me too. At thirty-two, Elise was way too young to die." Sam smoothed his chestnut-brown mustache, thick and glorious and his one vanity.

"Avery said Darren is a person of interest?"

Sam chuckled. "Can I ask the questions for a while?"

Charlene squirmed on her chair. She tended to take charge—her curiosity often got the better of her. "Sorry. Go ahead."

Jack emitted a low laugh and moved closer to the pair, his image strengthening. "He's got you there."

Silva entered the room and brushed up against Sam's slacks. Sam stroked her back, and she purred before jumping up next to Charlene. The bell on Silva's collar jingled. They'd finally found a brand she couldn't sneak out of and yet still had the safety breakaway feature so she wouldn't get caught on a branch.

Charlene found it hard to believe she'd never been a cat person. She petted behind Silva's ears, and the feline closed her golden eyes with a rumbling purr.

"So." Sam crooked a knee and rested his forearm on it. "I've talked at length to Patty Wagner, Elise's sister. She's broken up, understandably so."

"They seemed close," Charlene said. "I only met her last night at the theater. They were catching up in the ladies' bathroom during intermission."

His brow rose. "What about?"

She hated to repeat the conversation because if it was true, it would cast a bad light on Darren. He'd done everything right last night as he'd tried to save Elise. "How did she die? Did she choke?"

Sam eyed the ceiling and then her. "She didn't *just* choke. What did the sisters talk about?"

Charlene considered what to say, and how to say it, to be fair. "Well." She scratched the fur around Silva's collar. "I don't think Elise liked Klara, the seasoning salt sales rep, very much."

"Klara Maxwell?"

"Yes." Charlene watched Sam's reaction.

Cool as a cucumber, per usual, as he asked, "Why is that?"

"I don't know for sure, but Elise seemed worried that Klara and Darren might have had something going on. I didn't hear any *facts*." Charlene raised her hand. "Elise wanted Darren to fire her but feared he wouldn't because Klara made him so much money."

Sam pulled out his tablet to read his notes.

"Same as what Patty told me. Klara wants to take the salts *global*. They've already started in Germany because that's where he buys the salt. I'll talk to Klara today."

That was a good tangent to follow, more so than Darren, to her mind. "Klara had brought a bouquet of wolfsbane to the opening, which upset Elise so much that Franco hid the flowers in the office."

"Why would that upset Elise?" Sam flipped to a fresh page.

Jack, gone one second, and in full colorful form the next, appeared next to Sam. Silva meowed. "Wolfsbane is also known as monkshood, and *aconitum napellus*. It's poison, Charlene," he said with concern. "You didn't tell me that last night. Just that there were flowers."

Oops. She hadn't meant to keep things from Jack. Of course, he would know this, as a doctor. Charlene petted Silva. "Elise was upset that Klara would bring something potentially dangerous to the movie premiere, even as a joke. According to legend, wolfsbane is supposed to keep away werewolves."

"Huh." Sam jotted that down. "Wolfsbane. I was more of a sci-fi kid growing up instead of into horror, so I'm not up on the lore. Anything else?"

"Franco, Darren, and Matthew knew the movie by heart and were quoting lines. Klara jumped in, which also annoyed Elise."

Sam continued writing. "Sounds like Elise was jealous of more than just Klara. How did the Shultzes seem to get along?"

"They were loving to each other. Maybe Darren

was more demonstrative, but Elise didn't shy away from him. Even with not always agreeing." Charlene thought back to the meetings they'd had. Elise had offered sound opinions and grasped the financial part of the business dealings very quickly. "They were here at the house a few times." She gave Sam a half smile. "You're speaking to the new business liaison for the city of Salem."

"Since when?" A smile peeked from his mustache.

"I was offered the position in February." Charlene crossed her ankles. "Brandy Flint is president of the board, and she thought my marketing skills might be useful."

"I can see that." Sam's brown eyes glinted with humor. "You're very welcoming and friendly—to everyone but me."

"Sam!" The man had the power to make her stomach flutter. "No breaking the rules. You're here for a case, not to fraternize."

"We never have time to socialize," Sam said regretfully. "And if I aim to get promoted, there's more travel in my future. Rover is going to forget all about me."

"Dogs are loyal," Charlene said. Sam had an Irish setter she'd never met that stayed with a friend from the department when he traveled.

"Good riddance." Jack brushed his hands together. "Sam can't solve a case here in Salem without you."

That wasn't true, and Jack knew better, but this was his way of poking at Sam for using her conversation skills to his advantage. She happened to have the gift of gab—which required listening as well as talking.

She didn't want to think about Sam being away more often.

"What did Darren and Elise argue about?" the detective asked.

"Not argue—disagree," Charlene corrected. "Over the last six months, I heard Elise mention several times that she wanted to start a family. Darren asked her to wait until the theater was up and running." She recalled how upset Elise had been in the bathroom about Darren saying he didn't want kids. That had been different from the conversations she'd heard at the launch meetings.

"That's a touchy subject in a marriage." Sam tapped his pen to the page.

It had been something she and Jared had both wanted, but it hadn't happened. "Elise agreed to wait. Darren listened to her suggestions respectfully, but she conceded that it was important to him because this was his baby. He'd been dreaming of a theater like the one from his childhood since he started making money with the specialty seasoning salts."

"And in return, Elise hoped to get her own baby later," Jack said. He'd been at the meetings as well, behind the scenes.

"How did Elise take that?" Sam asked. "Was she mad?"

"No." Charlene rested her arm on the armrest. "But that's what I meant—she calmly agreed to talk about it after the launch. I didn't see any sign of the temper that I've heard from others she had."

Sam's brow furrowed as he digested this information.

Minnie brought in a tray with two coffees—Charlene's with cream, Sam's black, and a banana-nut muffin for the detective.

"I thought you might like some coffee." Minnie placed the tray on a small table between them. "The muffins are fresh from the oven this morning."

"Thank you! At least one of you likes me," Sam joked. "Charlene is stubborn, Minnie. What can I do?"

"Patience," Minnie advised as if Charlene wasn't there. "A world of patience." The housekeeper left while Charlene spluttered.

Jack disappeared in a flurry of jealousy that Minnie might take Sam's side. Minnie didn't know anything about Jack.

"She's right. I get it." Sam broke off a piece of muffin, and the scent of banana tinted the air. "And she can cook. You think Will could ever give her up?"

"Never." Will and Minnie were soul mates and bonded through love and family. "Can we please talk about Elise? How did she die, Sam? I saw the pink on the napkin. Was it blood, like Officer Bernard thought? And what did you mean, 'not just choking'?"

Sam swallowed his bite and followed it with coffee, thinking, stalling.

It made her crazy.

Jack returned, pacing by the window. "I'm too curious about what he's going to say to stay gone."

She raised her mug to Jack and drank. Sam wasn't the only one who needed to be patient.

"Numbness and tingling are the first symptoms of poisoning," Jack continued.

"Officer Bernard thought he saw flecks of foam on her lips," Sam said, picking up his tablet and pen. "Did you?"

Charlene recalled Elise's mouth as Darren had held her head on his lap. "Not foam, but Darren wiped her lips. I thought the pink might be blood from her coughing so hard. She mentioned at intermission that she didn't feel good and blamed it on eating too much popcorn. She also said she had a kernel stuck."

Sam lowered the pen. "Officer Bernard is a trained policeman with a decade in the field. That experience matters. He noticed something outside the obvious and luckily brought it to my attention before the trays and popcorn all got trampled."

"I like him." Charlene sipped her coffee, taking comfort from Silva's warmth at her side. "He put the canister of the herb and chili blend Elise had brought from the concession stand in an evidence bag. Elise's popcorn salt was the roasted garlic. Could she have been allergic to it somehow? She probably ate Darren's too, since she'd gotten him a fresh tub. His was empty."

"Darren said there wasn't very much on his. The roasted garlic may have accidentally been added while Elise shook it on hers." Sam scanned his notes. "He said Elise brought the trays up, so he didn't see her shake it."

"We all entered together, Patty too. Matthew came up later."

"Matthew Sinchuk, the manager?"

"Yes." Charlene sighed and helped Silva to the ground. The cat stretched and stalked toward Jack by the window overlooking the flowers in the side yard. "Seth said Elise really ripped into Matthew, where the employees could hear, in the office."

"Seth? The kid who is hanging around Avery?"

"He's nineteen, and she likes him," Charlene said. "Be nice."

Sam shook his head. "Nope. Seth had access to the popcorn as well."

"True. He runs the machine." She'd seen him scoop popcorn into the trays, with Patty adding the soft-baked pretzels. Charlene cupped her mug of coffee. "He told Avery on the phone last night that Elise and Darren had argued."

"Do you know what about?"

"Seth didn't know."

"Do you have an idea?" Sam asked.

Charlene realized this didn't sound good and hesitated. "In the bathroom, I overheard Elise tell Patty that Darren had decided he didn't want a family. It might have been a reason to argue." And lose control. Not helping Darren's case.

"After asking her to wait for kids until the launch." Sam had a drink of his coffee.

"I suppose so." Charlene could only really attest to what she'd heard.

"So, Elise yelled at Matthew regarding the office door. And Darren—but we don't know about what. Elise had a temper," Sam said.

"Maybe. I never saw that side of her." However, Elise had wanted Darren to fire Klara. Her demeanor in the bathroom with Patty had seemed sad and hurt. Not angry.

"People are complex." Sam checked the time on his watch.

"Another thing Patty was commiserating with Elise over was her starting a family." Charlene thought again of the conversation in the women's bathroom. "Is there a way to see if she was pregnant? Elise was acting sick. Patty had asked her if she was expecting, and that's when Elise said Darren didn't want kids. She never answered the question. What if she'd gotten pregnant already?" Too late. What would Elise do then?

"That could be argument-worthy," Sam said. "Good catch. I'll check with the coroner."

"Thanks." What if Elise had wanted kids so badly that she hadn't waited for Darren's okay after all?

Sam stretched his legs out, deceptively casual. "Can you tell me more about this wolfsbane? Describe it for me?"

"It's a pretty purple-blue flower and doesn't seem at all dangerous." If she'd seen it outside, she might have picked it and put it in a vase herself. "Darren also called it 'monkshood' because of the shape of the blossom."

"But it is dangerous, Charlene," Jack said. "Aconite is a common poison used throughout history against an enemy. It would take a large, or concentrated, amount to be fatal, though. A smaller dose might just cause a stomachache."

Like what Elise had complained about. She focused on Sam and not Jack. "There's a famous line in the movie that Darren and Franco both quoted, something about when the wolfsbane blooms is when the werewolf comes out, but I don't remember it exactly."

"Not a fan?" Sam kept writing without looking at her.

"Oh, no! I liked it—just not enough to memorize it." Charlene placed her coffee on the side table. "It has to do with an 'autumn moon.' I was glad this is the month of June when I heard the verse."

Jack said, "Sam needs to know that aconite's roots and seeds are the most lethal. When consumed, it increases the influx of sodium through the channels causing excitability, which might lead to heart failure. The poison can paralyze the nerves and lower the blood pressure—that's if there's been a big dose. A smaller one causes numbing of the face and mouth. Possibly attributed to why she was choking, and why it wasn't sudden."

How could she tell this to Sam without sounding like an encyclopedia?

"I see you thinking, Charlene," Sam said.

"That obvious?" She half-smiled, wishing Silva was still at her side.

Jack paced behind Sam.

"I heard that even touching the flowers of the wolfsbane can be toxic," she said, circling the point. "Do you think it might have affected her breathing?"

"The coroner will do a full battery of tests, but I'll give him my notes as soon as I finish here." Sam patted the notebook, done with sharing.

Could the flowers have been sprinkled on the popcorn? She didn't see how, as the bouquet had been brought to the office right away and wasn't near the counter with the popcorn trays. Franco had tucked them safely out of sight.

"This might not matter, but as Avery and I were leaving last night, I realized the office door was ajar. Since Darren was with Elise, I decided to shut it for them." Charlene bowed her head. "I peeked inside the room."

"Yeah?" Sam sounded interested all of a sudden.

"I know Franco had stashed the flowers there." Charlene raised her head. "They were gone. There wasn't so much as a petal lying on the floor."

Sam tugged his mustache. "Elise was *poisoned*, Charlene. I'll let the coroner know about the wolfsbane right away. Now, be honest with me. Was Darren Shultz anywhere near the popcorn trays before the movie started?"

# CHAPTER 5

Jack manifested behind Sam, and Charlene wished for telepathy to ask her ghost if they'd been wrong about Darren's character. Could he have killed his wife, Elise? It didn't make sense. She dropped her gaze to Sam, trying to keep her expression neutral. It was difficult because she wanted to shout that Darren had to be innocent.

"Darren, yes," Charlene conceded, "but there was a group of us milling about."

"Who?" Sam poised his pen over his tablet. "The movie was to start at six forty-five, according to Franco. He said you were late?"

Charlene swallowed a smart remark. "Avery and I arrived at the same time as Klara, with the flowers. The bouquet was so big we had to open the door for her."

"I'd sure love to find them." Sam tapped the paper. "Who all was around the counter?"

"Darren. Patty, Seth, Matthew, Klara, Franco,

me, Avery. Elise." Charlene gave a little shrug. "I'm sure you've talked to Darren. What does he say?"

"That he's innocent. But they all say that." Sam finished his coffee. "I had him in for questioning last night and released him this morning with a warning not to leave town."

"I guess he'll be at the theater," Charlene said, trying to make sense of it all. "Seth told Avery they're still holding the grand opening today. Free matinée of *Dracula* in the small theater and *Jungle Escapade*, the latest action-adventure with Chris Rocket, in the large theater."

Sam's jaw gaped, and he closed it, rubbing his chin. "Unbelievable. Charlene, I find Darren's reaction to his wife's death odd."

Charlene recalled how Darren had sung a quiet song to Elise as he'd stroked her hair. "Sam, Darren was singing to Elise last night while he cared for her. He did everything textbook for how to handle a choking victim until the ambulance arrived. He wasn't cold toward her at all." She'd taken part in a safety course the city offered and had learned CPR.

"I don't believe it," Jack said. "That's not the man we saw here, Charlene."

"The only reason I didn't put him behind bars already is that every man is innocent until proven guilty. I am searching for that proof. The man's a genius at creating salts. A chemist." Sam's eyes had a predatorial gleam. "The good news is that the poisoning would be personal to Elise. I'll talk to Klara and ask about an affair. And I'll check on the possible pregnancy. Thanks for that, Charlene."

"Why is that good news?" There was nothing good about this at all. She felt terrible. And she feared Sam was investigating in the wrong direction.

"I don't think Darren will be a danger to any other employees at the theater. I bet this Klara woman will be a gold mine of information." Sam pocketed his tablet and stood. "I hope I don't regret letting him go."

Charlene also rose, her hands before her.

"Will you tell Avery to stay away from the theater, and Seth the popcorn boy, too, until this is over?" Sam brushed cat hair from his slacks. "He's on my list to interview as well."

"I'll ask . . . but I can't *tell* her to do anything. Was the poison in the seasoned salt? Which flavor?" They'd tried them all. Charlene's stomach tightened.

"I'm not sure yet. It will take time." Sam strode toward the foyer, and Charlene followed. "Thanks for the coffee." Silva meowed from behind the foyer table with the beautiful shell planter.

"You're welcome." Waiting made Charlene feel helpless. "What now?"

Sam opened the door. "You excel at pampering your guests, so, do that. I'll do my job—which is to find who murdered Elise and toss them in jail. Think this case is gonna be easy." He wagged a finger. "Stay away from Darren and the theater, too, all right?"

Charlene didn't answer, but Sam had already turned to skip down the steps. Rose-scented summer air filtered into the house. Jack appeared on

the front porch and gave Sam's behind a kick of
his leather loafer.

Sam didn't notice, instead getting into his SUV
and honking good-bye. Charlene burst out laughing once they were inside the foyer and quickly
shut the door.

Avery joined her with big eyes. "Is Sam gone?"

"He is." Her laughter dried like an oasis in the
desert. "Honey, Elise was poisoned, and the detective kindly asked that you stay away from the theater." She was torn about his request for adding
Seth to the mix. If she was Avery and was told not
to see someone, well, it would just add appeal.

"Poisoned?" Avery paled beneath her summer
tan. "Like, they think Darren killed her?"

Charlene clasped Avery's forearm. "It seems
that way. Of course, Sam will do due diligence."

"Does Sam know about the seasoning salt mix-
up?" Avery asked.

"He does. But Officer Bernard only gathered
the herb and chili flake salt! They'll need to get
the other canisters."

Jack stood in the kitchen hallway. "What if the
poisoned salt is on both of their popcorn trays?
That might clear Darren."

"You're right," Charlene said.

Avery shook her head. "I didn't say anything."

Jack chuckled and disappeared, his ghostly
voice saying, "Gotcha!"

"Sorry." Charlene tapped her temple and frowned
at the spot where Jack had been over Avery's shoulder. "Inner dialogue."

Avery rubbed the nape of her neck, a habit she

had to touch the spider tattoo when nervous. "What were you right about?"

Mm. "Well, I wasn't sure it was a good idea to tell Sam what I heard in the bathroom between Patty and Elise. The possible affair with Klara. Darren changing his mind about wanting a family. But now I think it was the right thing to do."

"Totally was! Hey, should I call the station about collecting the roasted garlic canister?" Avery pulled her cell phone from her back shorts pocket.

"Yes, please." Charlene turned her back on the front door. "I've had my fill of a certain detective today."

Avery crinkled her nose, and her diamond glistened. "It's cute! He likes you."

She stepped toward the dining room, not wanting to touch that subject with a dozen ten-foot poles. "While you do that, I'll say good-bye to the guests." It was a reprieve Charlene didn't mind at all.

Why did Sam always get her so flustered?


At the happy hour that afternoon, Charlene had a very full house. The Welch family of four from Portland, Oregon—Bob and Joanie, and their twelve-year-old twin sons, Sheridon and Braydon, on summer vacation for a week from their carpentry business.

The Cohens from Minnesota—Spencer and Natalie; their seven-year-old daughter, Lara; and three-year-old son, Christopher. The parents were teachers.

The Lopezes—Maria and Georgio from San

Diego, California, were visiting Salem for the first time.

In the last suite, the Millers, Dustin and Cora, from San Francisco, were scientists on holiday. They'd been referred by friends who'd spoken highly of Charlene's. Dustin was an astronomer who was very interested in the full moon coming up, and her telescope on the widow's walk.

Sheila Flynn, a medical student about to begin a residency at Harvard, was in a single for a few nights, and that only left her one available room. Charlene surveyed the guests in the living room and poured some pinot grigio into her wineglass.

Minnie had just gone home after a long day. She couldn't manage without her housekeeper who didn't mind doing the extra work occasionally, and Charlene always paid her well for the effort. They worked in tandem here at Charlene's. "Ready?" she asked Avery, who waited by the sideboard.

"Yep!" Avery removed the silver tops of the warming dishes, and garlic permeated the room.

"Hello," Charlene said to her guests. Everyone had something age-appropriate to drink, including her. She raised her wineglass.

The people turned her way with smiling faces.

"We are so glad to welcome you here before you take off for your evening excursions or dinner plans! Just a little bite or two to tempt you before you go. Mini crab cakes, pita chips, spinach dip, and last, cold cheese-tortellini salad." Charlene gestured toward the side table heaped with food. "Help yourselves!"

"This is a feast," the twin in the red shirt said;

the other wore blue. They were identical, so Charlene had no idea which was which.

Their dad, Bob, had a full, bushy dark beard, and their mom, Joanie, was pretty with round cheeks. Bob drank an artisan beer, and Joanie was enjoying a chardonnay from Flint's Vineyard. Avery handed the boys each a plate so they could start on the appetizers. They answered with enthusiastic thank-yous.

Lara Cohen, a seven-year-old brunette cutie, attached herself to Avery. The precocious young girl wanted to know everything about witches.

Natalie and Spencer's toddler son, Christopher, was balanced on his mother's hip. She smoothed his auburn curls. "I'm interested in the witches as well!"

Spencer gave an apologetic shrug. "I teach middle-school English literature. I want to see the House of the Seven Gables. Nathaniel Hawthorne!" Lara's hair was more brown than auburn and wavy without the corkscrews that Christopher had. Spencer had brown hair, and Natalie's was auburn, straight and shiny. "The Peabody Essex Museum."

Lara tugged Avery's T-shirt. "Can you come with us?"

Avery glanced at Charlene with a question in her gaze. How far did being a good hostess go?

Charlene hurried to Avery's rescue. "Lara, when I was a little girl, I used to visit museums with my dad too. We had so much fun, and then afterward, we'd get ice cream." It had been her dad's way to remove her from her mother's line of fire.

In the meantime, it fed her curiosity about history and art.

"Ice cream?" Christopher asked, his thumb to his lower lip.

"Ice cream!" Lara clapped. Undeterred, she yanked on Avery's hand. "Can you come?"

"I'm sorry, sweetie." Avery patted Lara's shoulder. "I work here."

Lara frowned.

Avery kneeled down, eye to eye. "What if you tell me all about the museum later? I'll push you on the swing out back."

"Yes!" Lara hopped up and down with excitement, knocking Avery back, but the teen was agile and righted herself before falling into the side table.

"Swing!" Christopher called, kicking his heel to Natalie's thigh.

"Not now, hon." Natalie leaned toward Charlene. "I thought he'd want a nap after the day of travel, but he is raring to go."

"It's such a beautiful evening. If you go to the Commons on Washington Square, there's a park, and a bandstand that's a Salem landmark," Charlene said. "Food options are anything from pizza to lobster."

"I want a lobster roll while we're here. Maybe two." Natalie patted her stomach. "It's vacation."

Charlene laughed and moved on to visit with the Lopezes, Maria and Georgio. "Hello! You mentioned when you arrived that this is your first time in Salem. What part of California are you from?"

"San Diego." Maria was an attractive Hispanic woman with a bright smile and flashing dark eyes.

"Have you been?" Georgio asked. His once-brown hair was now heavily threaded through with silver and gray and quite striking.

"Not yet, but it sounds amazing," Charlene said. "I've heard so much about the food scene from other travelers that it's made my bucket list!"

"San Diego is known as America's Finest City, because of the gorgeous coastline." Georgio cracked the top off a bottle of sweet tea. "I'm interested in comparing it to Salem's."

"When you arrive, look us up and we can suggest some sights for you that you shouldn't miss, like Balboa Park. Or the San Diego Zoo, which is *fantastico*." Maria drank a local amber beer. The couple was probably in their sixties.

"I will! Thank you." How sweet of them. "So, what do you do when you aren't traveling to new places?"

"Retired navy. And Georgio from the marines. We have a second career in a little corner convenience market, but it was time for a vacation." Maria held Georgio's arm. "We aren't getting any younger."

"My brother died last year," Georgio said, grief in his tone. "Only sixty! Too young. So, we decided not to wait to travel anymore."

"That's so smart." Charlene sipped her wine, enjoying the fruity notes. "I bought this place after my husband died. I'll be in Salem two years in September." The time had flown by, and her fears of failure were banished. "Life is short. You should travel and do what makes you happy."

"Didn't I tell you I had a good feeling about this place?" Georgio said. "We also love seafood, and I want to take part in the Seafarer's Festival."

"What do you mean?" Charlene hadn't attended the festival yet but knew it was a celebration of Salem's coastal history, and there were booths and kiosks everywhere to cater to the tourists.

"I'm going to enter the fishing competition. Cash prizes." Georgio rubbed his fingers and thumb together.

"I didn't know about a competition. Well, good luck." Charlene clinked her glass to his bottle. "Let us know how you do!"

Charlene next joined Dustin and Cora Miller, forty-year-old scientists on holiday from Berkeley, in San Francisco. Dustin, bald, was an astronomer, and Cora, in stylish cat-eye black frames, did research for the college. They were talking animatedly with Sheila Flynn. The Millers were from Cali, and Sheila from Rockport, Maine, but it turned out that Cora was a Flynn before she'd married Dustin, and they were deep in conversation about possible family connections.

All the self-affirming gurus touted being in the flow and then success would follow. Charlene, filled with joy, was clearly meant to be a hostess.

"What are you going to medical school for?" Charlene asked Sheila. The young woman was in her mid-twenties, with red hair and freckles. Big green eyes.

"I want to be a pediatrician." Sheila sat on the ottoman by the sofa, her wineglass dangled between two fingers.

Jack appeared over her shoulder, his energy exuding approval. "A true calling." He missed being a doctor.

"That's wonderful," Charlene said.

"We don't have kids." Cora smiled at Dustin and squeezed his hand. "Don't want them and never did. You're a saint, Sheila."

"No." Sheila grinned and shook her head. "I'm one of five children is all."

"That's a lot of mouths to feed." Dustin mock-shivered.

"Catholic parents," Sheila said with a shrug. "What can you do?"

"Be a doctor," Cora laughed good-naturedly.

Charlene went to the bar that she'd had Parker Murdock design for her. The man was a recluse for the most part, but he knew how to make a piece of wood come to life. He'd created the wine cellar downstairs as well, that only she and Jack used. It was the one place she was guaranteed privacy to speak with her ghost.

Bob Welch admired the sturdy piece with reverence. There were slots for wine stems, cupboards for tumblers, and plenty of space for spirits. "Where'd you get this beauty?"

"Custom-ordered." Charlene stood back to show him the ice machine built underneath.

Bob tugged his thick beard. "By a master. Does he have a shop or something?"

"No," Charlene said. "Parker works by word of mouth only."

"Too bad." Bob patted the cabinet.

"If you want, I can pass your name along." Charlene wondered if this was a sign from the universe that she should talk with Parker about the gazebo. "Did you have something in mind?"

"Not really. Just one artisan to another. Wood-work is a specialty." Bob smoothed his palm over the curve of the maple countertop. "This man listens to the wood and follows the grain."

"I like this guy," Jack said.

Charlene smiled. She did too.

At a quarter past five, the guests were all ready to hit the town. Salem had so much to offer for any age group, and the festival just added more fun options. The new guests had kept her mind off of the theater, Darren, and poor Elise.

She and Avery cleaned up the kitchen, with Silva meowing pathetically for scraps. Which, of course, both she and Avery gave to her.

It was no wonder Silva had put on a few pounds. They'd blame the fur. What was that saying . . . I'm fluffy, not fat?

"That Lara sure likes you," Charlene said as she started the dishwasher.

"She's adorable, and smart." Avery sprayed cleaner on the kitchen table and swiped it down. "I think it's great that they're going to the museum. I never realized you and your dad used to do that. I mean, maybe you told me, but I don't remember. That's cool."

"It was a treat for the two of us." Charlene wiped water drops off the counter and stepped back. "Want anything to drink? I'm going to refill my wineglass."

"Iced tea sounds good—I can get it." Avery poured it from the pitcher in the fridge, adding extra ice so the liquid almost sloshed over the top.

"There's hardly any tea there with all that ice." Charlene admired a heavy pour.

Avery shrugged. "I like to crunch it up."

"That's bad for your teeth!" Charlene clamped her hand over her mouth. "Forget that. I sounded like my mother."

Avery showed her teeth—strong, straight, and white. "So far, so good."

They sat at the kitchen table just to chat. It was nice, and Charlene took in a deep breath. "How are you feeling?"

Avery sipped carefully, not spilling a drop. "All right, I guess. Seth texted to see if he could come over after work?"

"Oh." Charlene thought about this. It hadn't really been something she'd included in the reality of Avery, a young adult woman, wanting to spend time with a young adult man. She tapped her fingers on the table. "This is your house too."

Avery laughed and swirled the ice in her tea with a spoon. "You should have seen your face just now. It's not about sex."

"Avery!" Charlene bit the inside of her cheek to keep from overreacting. There was a reason you started with little kids—to get used to the big ones.

"Well, I just don't want you to think that." Avery scooped an ice chip into her spoon and put it in her mouth.

"Okay." Charlene sipped her wine, wishing she'd brought over the bottle. And where was Jack when she could use a refill?

"Seth just wants to talk," Avery said. "Darren is sending them all home. The theater was a nightmare because Elise's death was on the news. The reporters hounded Darren. The line for the free matinée was around the block before they even arrived for work at two. He decided not to let any of the movie guests in, which caused even more trouble."

"Oh, no." Charlene easily imagined the chaos. Darren had been crazy thinking he should adhere to his launch schedule. Was he that out of his mind with grief?

"It was pretty bad." Avery chased a chip of ice with her spoon. "Darren locked himself in the office and didn't answer for hours, even though Matthew and Franco both tried to talk to him. Seth was worried they'd have to call the fire department to knock the door down, but Darren finally came out."

"Seth is welcome here," Charlene said. "I mean it—this is your home too. Invite your friends."

Avery grinned. "He'll be here in fifteen minutes. I figured we could get the dirt from him since Sam hasn't told us anything else." She kept her phone on the table, no doubt waiting for Seth to text.

"I can't tell you the amount of time I've spent in my life waiting for Sam to call," Charlene confessed with a rueful smile.

"He probably can't tell you much. It'll be hard when I'm a police officer. I'll want to tell you everything." Avery stirred her tea.

"I'll want to hear it," Charlene admitted.

"I guess there was a police officer outside the theater all afternoon too, to keep an eye on Darren," Avery said.

Charlene sipped her wine. "You were so calm yesterday. Calling for help. Asking questions. I think you have the temperament to be a really good officer, Avery. If that's what you want."

"You do?" Avery smiled wide.

Their conversation was interrupted by a knock on the door. Avery hopped up to answer it. "Seth! Come on into the kitchen."

"This is your house?" Seth looked around with big eyes. He was still in his *Spellbound Movie Theater* uniform and smelled faintly of popcorn.

"I live here," Avery said, with a hint of pride.

"She does," Charlene said.

"Can I get you something to drink?" Avery offered when Seth sat down at the rectangular table.

"No, thanks. I'm full of soda. Popcorn." Seth ruffled his longish hair.

"I'm sorry you had to go to work today," Charlene said. "It must have been tough."

"It was a zoo. People screamed 'murderer' at Darren and pounded on the doors to get in when he decided not to sell any tickets." Seth plopped his forearm on the table. "Darren wasn't in good shape, folks. Bloodshot eyes, scruff all over his face. That man must have to shave twice a day. I've heard of bros like that. I don't envy them."

Darren's hair was coarse and thick, deep brown like his eyes. Seth had zero facial hair and probably didn't have the shaving problem.

"I feel awful for him," Charlene said. "The police were there?"

"Officer Lennox patrolled the lobby. She's gotta be at least thirty." Seth made Charlene feel the weight of her forty-three—almost forty-four—years. "She confiscated all the seasoning salts that were at the theater."

Avery looked at Charlene. "I left that message

with Officer Bernard about the roasted garlic canister. They'd only taken the herb and chili. Guess he got it."

"The policewoman watched Darren like an osprey about to catch a fish," Seth said. "It's totally obvious she thinks Darren did it. I don't blame him for hiding out in his office."

"What do you think?" Charlene went to drink her wine, but the glass was empty.

"I can't imagine it." Seth drummed his fingers to the table. "Scratch that. Before today, I couldn't imagine it. This afternoon, Darren was acting like one of those wild beasts in the movies. Said the cops were out to nail him."

"What did Officer Lennox do?" Charlene got up and poured herself a glass of water.

"She split around four when she realized Darren wasn't leaving his office, with the box of salts. The rowdies in the parking lot were gone, so she had no other reason to stick around. Darren even freaked out his buddy Franco." Seth twisted his fingers together. "Those two are tight, knowing all the movie lines."

"Why was Franco so bothered?" Avery asked.

"Matthew kept going on about the building being haunted. Elise's spirit was just one more ghost to add to the crew." Seth raked his hair back and let it fall.

Charlene noticed Avery noticing Seth's long locks and hid a smile. "Did Matthew say that to Darren? I don't think he'd find it comforting."

"Not that I know," Seth said. "But me and Franco got to hear his opinion on repeat. Day two and I already want to quit my job."

"You might not have one for long." Avery clicked on her phone and scrolled through her pictures.

"Darren is sure to realize that Spellbound needs to be put on hold awhile," Charlene said. She returned to her chair.

"Hope so. What do you think this is?" Avery passed the phone to Seth.

"The curtains at the theater?" Seth gave the phone back.

Avery passed it to Charlene. "Well?"

Charlene slowly studied the grainy image of what seemed to be the curtains behind them at the movie theater, as Seth had guessed.

"Am I missing something?" Charlene squinted to bring the hem of the drapes into focus.

Avery grabbed the phone back and used her fingers to zoom on where Charlene had been looking.

"There," Avery said with a hint of frustration.

Charlene took it again.

Studied it.

The temperature in the kitchen dropped significantly and Charlene bit her lip as Jack manifested behind Seth, giving him the stink eye.

Well, Avery was a teenager and was probably going to have lots of boyfriends. Jack needed to relax.

"There," Avery said, tapping the phone in Charlene's palm. "I told you I felt someone watching me. Since when do ghosts wear Crocs?"

# CHAPTER 6

Charlene thought it was a stretch, but possible, that the dark-blue blobs beneath the drapes could be shoes.

"I don't know, Avery." Charlene passed the phone back to her. The truth was that Jack wore clothes specifically for Charlene. A ghost could have shoes. Would they show up on film? Was the image anything but a blur captured by an imaginative teen?

"I think we should show it to Officer Bernard. I like him." Avery set her phone to the side. "He won't make me feel silly if I'm wrong. But I'm not. You'll see."

"Why would someone hide behind a curtain during a movie?" Seth asked.

"I don't know," Avery replied with an edge. "Why would someone kill Elise?"

"You're right." Seth propped his forearms on the table and leaned toward Avery. "It's a mess. Want me to drive you to the station? We can get a burger afterward or something downtown at the Seafarer's Festival."

"He's too smooth, this guy," Jack said with icy disapproval.

Seth looked around the kitchen and rubbed the back of his neck.

"Yeah. That sounds great," Avery said. "We were just hanging around at home anyway. Is that okay with you, Charlene? I hate to ditch you."

"Don't worry about me, hon." Charlene smiled at them both. "I've always got a million things to do."

The teens left. Charlene refilled her wine, picked up Silva, and went to her suite, where she and Jack could talk freely.

"What do we know about that kid? I think Sam's right. He's trouble," Jack said.

"Seth Gamble is fine." Charlene closed and locked the suite door. "He's cute, and cool, and into Avery."

"Better not be," Jack growled.

"Hey!" Charlene put Silva on Jack's favorite armchair, quickly changing the subject before things went too far down a figurative rabbit hole. "What have you been doing?"

"Researching wolfsbane. Aconitine is an alkaloid chemical that contributes to the toxicity of *aconitum napellus*. It's been used in ancient times as a medicine but also a poison. Plants that can heal, can kill if not used properly." Jack grazed a palm over his smooth chin. "Like the dual nature of the wolfman himself, come to think of it."

Charlene set her wineglass on the coffee table. "I don't trust the herbal remedies. I'd rather go to the doctor and get a prescription in a nice orange bottle."

"I felt that way too," Jack said with a wink. "Now, like so many things, I find it fascinating. My memory is even better than it used to be when I was alive."

"Lucky!" He deserved a perk or two. "I'm curious as to *how* the poison was applied to the popcorn. We just know it was poison, but not what kind."

"You're right. Seeing how interested Sam was in the wolfsbane bouquet makes me wonder if it was aconitine." Jack tilted his head. "When dried, the properties would be easy to mix with sea salt. Darren's hands-on with his salt creations."

During one of the movie theater launch meetings here at the B-and-B, Charlene and the Shultzes had been discussing salt. How Darren came up with unique flavors in their home kitchen then rented an industrial kitchen when he made large batches. He bought his sea salt in bulk from Germany, but the process was as simple as boiling salt water from the ocean and letting it evaporate.

"That makes a plus for Sam's case, that Darren killed Elise by adding poison to her roasted garlic salt. He was upset and didn't eat it. Elise brought him a fresh tub of popcorn and the canister of herb and chili." Charlene blew out a breath. "But it couldn't have been that particular bouquet."

"Exactly. The fresh petals aren't as potent. From the questions that Sam asked you, I think they're gravitating toward something added to the salt. But *why*." Jack stood in front of the TV, where he'd been watching the news. His image wasn't strong, and she could make out the commercial break about a company selling car insurance.

"That's never easy." She perched on the arm of the love seat. "There are so many variables. And once you start asking questions, more questions pop up . . . I'm exhausted just thinking about it."

Jack floated her pen and a notebook to her. "You should probably jot some things down as you like to do."

Charlene laughed and accepted Jack's offering. Doodling allowed her brain to pull things in from her subconscious. "Perfect. We need to start with the victim." She scrawled an *E*, but added a *D*.

"Was the target Elise? Was Darren supposed to eat the roasted garlic too? I assume, because Elise was killed and Darren is fine, that the poison must be in the roasted garlic canister. Her favorite. Did you taste it?" Jack asked.

Charlene's stomach tightened. She had tried it and found it delicious. "The sampling tray had thimble-sized salts in them of assorted flavors. My favorite was the Dijon."

Jack's energy chilled with anger before he calmed himself. "Probably not enough to harm you. If it was added to all the roasted garlic, which is an assumption. The poison could have been sprinkled over Elise's popcorn alone."

Her cell phone rang, and Avery's picture showed on the screen. "Hey!" Charlene put the device on speakerphone so Jack could hear.

"Hello," Avery said, her tone triumphant. "Just wanted to let you know that Officer Bernard

seemed very interested in the possible shoe connection. Thanked me for the reminder about the
canisters of seasoned salts, too."

"That's really great, Avery!" Charlene and Jack
shared a smile.

"He's the kind of officer I want to be. Well, like
him, and Sam, and Officer Senta. She's awesome."

Charlene sent a little prayer heavenward that
Avery would be okay. "You've done your civic duty
now, so try to have some fun. Don't dwell on the
bad stuff. This is your summer to relax."

"I know how to compartmentalize very well,"
Avery said. "Bye, Charlene!" The call ended.

"She would, too," Jack said. "Poor kid." He leaned
back against her office desk, arms slung low across
his stomach. His turquoise shirt matched his eyes.

"Now she has us, even if she can't see you,"
Charlene said. "You still look out for her."

"I do." Jack blinked and cleared his throat, a
perfect affectation of how he must have been
when he was alive. This man! This ghost. How he'd
taken up residence in her heart.

She swallowed her emotions to focus on the list
she was making. "Jack. You saw Darren and Elise
interact here at the house. I just don't think he
would have killed her."

"I agree." Jack watched her as she doodled. "Especially not at the theater, which was his dream
come true."

"He loved Elise. Elise supported his dreams in
hopes to have her own family."

"Things are often not what they seem." Jack fluttered the edge of her notebook.

They'd learned that the hard way. One couldn't accept things at face value. Not in life, and certainly not in death.

Her doodles were a pentagram in a circle, the sign of the werewolf, mingled with the Spellbound Movie Theater logo and the nostalgic film reel.

Wolfsbane blossoms with their pretty shapes. Pretty, but deadly. Like Klara?

Her attention was drawn to the television as Darren was handcuffed and brought into the brick jailhouse, struggling the entire way. A female officer propelled him forward.

"Jack!"

Jack shifted his attention from her drawings to the television, his mouth lowered in surprise. "Oh, no."

And though they were riveted to the TV for the rest of the night, there were no further updates on Darren Shultz's incarceration.

Monday morning, Charlene and Avery breakfasted with their guests before the families went out for the day. As soon as they were gone, Darren's arrest was all Minnie, Avery, and Charlene could talk about.

"I found his arrest report online," Avery said, showing Charlene and Minnie the picture on her cell phone. "Assault. Resisting arrest by Officer Lennox when she was at his house to question him."

Darren's mug shot was terrible, and he was caught in a half-shave. Her heart went out to him. He'd wanted respect and success in this new business venture. "*Through no fault of his own,*" Charlene said. "We should go see him."

"Quoting Maleva the gypsy now?" Avery snickered. "Why?"

"Maybe we can help. Find a lawyer. I don't know." Charlene shrugged, feeling helpless. "What if Klara went back to Pittsburgh, and he's alone?"

Minnie scooted them both from the kitchen. "Darren could use a friend, and that's reason enough. Say hello to that Sam if you see him."

Charlene grabbed her purse, as did Avery, and drove to the police station. She scored a spot on the street and parked.

"Hey!" Avery gestured toward a sleek new car edging out of a nearby parking space. "That's Darren's Tesla. Why is Klara driving? Where is she going? She hasn't been around *at all* since it happened. Why is that? Guilt for sleeping with Darren behind Elise's back?"

Red-faced with emotion, Avery jumped from the SUV and in front of the Tesla as Klara inched the vehicle forward, just starting to move. Klara slammed on the brakes. Avery splayed her palms on the hood and braced her feet. Charlene swallowed her stomach, as it had lodged in her throat.

Thank God the child had worn sneakers! What if she'd been in flip-flops? What if Klara hadn't stopped?

Charlene hustled out of the Pilot. "Avery!" she demanded. "What on earth are you doing?"

"We need to find out what happened with Darren!" Avery tossed her ponytail as if it was no big deal to block a car with her body. "Why does she have Darren's Tesla?"

Klara, spewing curses, put the Tesla in PARK and got out, slamming the door. The sales rep's summer hat slipped back over her dark-brown hair. It matched the blue of her sleeveless sheath and navy-blue heels. Pointing at Avery with a long blue fingernail, shaking, Klara yelled, "You could have died just now! I don't need someone blaming me for that too. What is your problem?"

"Where is Darren?" Charlene kept her hand on Avery's back in a show of support just in case Klara . . . she didn't know what Klara might do—the woman was furious, and justifiably so.

"He's home on bail after resisting, they say *assaulting,* a police officer who accused him of sleeping with me. *Me.*" Klara patted her curved chest with indignation. "I have a gorgeous girlfriend of my own—I don't need to poach. And she's a lawyer."

"Oh." Avery stepped away from the car and brushed her palms together as if that solved the matter for her. "Why do you have his car, then?"

Klara raised her chin, her expression troubled. "I was driving it home for him since he literally jogged back to his place this morning—he can't stand being confined. It makes him physically sick."

"Sick?" Charlene asked. "Are you sure he wasn't poisoned, like Elise?"

Wincing, Klara said, "I'll drag him to the hospital, just in case, though it's been more than twenty-four hours if it was in his system. I'd heard Salem was wicked, but this is over the top."

"You'll take him?" Charlene exhaled. "Thanks. Let us know, all right?"

Klara caught her hat as it moved in a breeze. "I'm staying at Darren's—in the guest room. He didn't kill Elise. He loved her."

"Is there anything we can do?" Charlene was drawn in by the pain on Klara's face.

"Darren's not in his right mind at the moment." Klara returned to the sleek Tesla. "Ask Patty what she knows. She'll be at the bakery. If not, she has the big house on the lot next to it. Her parents owned it. Elise was sure mad when Patty inherited, and she didn't get squat. Maybe instead of accusing me, you should bother her."

With that, Klara slid in, slammed the door, and started the engine with a rev that could barely be heard, but you still felt the power.

Charlene gave Avery a side hug, then a shake of the shoulders. "Do not ever jump in front of a moving vehicle again. Got it?"

Avery nodded, her eyes bright with adrenaline. "I was just so jazzed up, thinking she and Darren, and then . . . that was obviously wrong." Her body slumped.

"It happens to me too," Charlene commiserated. "Leaping to conclusions that aren't right. I've learned to think first—for the most part."

Charlene was far from perfect. Now that she'd seen Avery vault in front of a car without thinking twice, she had more sympathy for Sam and his frustration with her.

"Now what should we do?" Avery asked. "I could go for a muffin or a Wagner's soft-baked pretzel . . ."

With pursed lips, Charlene gestured to the SUV. Sam would consider this butting into his investigation. She liked to think of it as being neighborly. "We should go straight home."

"But . . . Klara said that asking Patty would be helping Darren."

They both got inside the Pilot.

"Why don't you look up the address?" Charlene immediately remembered the name of the bakery on the side of the popcorn tray. Now, that was incredible marketing. "Wagner's Bakery."

Avery put it in her phone and hit directions. "On Boone and Hemlock."

"Great," Charlene said drolly. "Hope that's not a sign of things to come."

Avery sighed. "Just take a right, and down two blocks. I hope she's open, but how could she be? Her sister is dead. I'd love a croissant."

"How can you be hungry?" They'd had breakfast less than an hour ago.

"Didn't you see my workout just there?" Avery patted her chest. "A girl needs fuel."

Charlene stopped at Hemlock, then turned right. It was an inviting street with trees and businesses. Some were converted houses. Chocolate. Dentist. Doctor. Bakery. "Here we are."

Wagner's Bakery had a light blue door. The roof was decorated in a gingerbread style.

"Like Hansel and Gretel," Avery said. "Should we leave a trail of breadcrumbs?"

"We'll be fine." Charlene parked along the street, and she and Avery got out. Avery tried to open the door. A woman in a lightweight hijab shook her head and pointed to the *CLOSED* sign.

Charlene saw the mammoth house behind the

bakery that Klara had told them Patty had inherited from her parents.

If Elise was mad about it, she hadn't seemed like it in the bathroom while Patty was soothing her. Could be Klara was the one with the gripe and trying to keep the attention off herself.

"Let's see if Patty's home," Charlene suggested. "If not, we can go to Darren's. Offer our condolences in person."

"It might be a little early for that, especially if he spent the night in jail," Avery said.

"We can bring donuts from a different shop," Charlene suggested. "Since there isn't anything here."

They went down the old stone walkway to the home, shaded by thick trees. It was painted a cocoa color with a deep-brown porch, wooden railings, and rocking chairs. She could imagine the Wagners all sitting outside on a summer day drinking lemonade and watching the traffic go by.

"This is pretty," Avery said, nodding with appreciation.

"Idyllic." Charlene glanced at her phone for the time. Ten.

They climbed the steps, and Charlene knocked on the door.

Patty's teary gaze peered out. "Yes?"

"Patty. I'm so sorry for your loss," Charlene said, layering compassion in her tone. "Is there anything we can do for you? Your sister's death is a lot to handle right now."

Patty widened the door, showing slippers and unicorn shorty pajamas. "You're a godsend, Charlene. Avery."

Not the response she usually got to a cold knock on the door. "Oh?"

Patty stepped out to the porch and wrapped her arms around her middle. "I can't bear to open the bakery today, but I have standing orders for clients that I must deliver by noon. A Wagner order is better than a guarantee," she said. Her cheeks were raw from her tears. "Yesterday I stayed on my knees in prayer all day. Sunday, so no orders. But today! You are an answer to my prayers."

"I don't bake," Charlene said. "We saw a woman in your shop?"

"That's Mila. She's a wonder in the kitchen and is filling the orders for me. She's a sweet girl, but shy as all get-out and doesn't drive. In this day and age, can you believe it? I was going to hire a cab or something."

"Do you need us to deliver them?" Avery asked, seeing a solution at once.

"Yes!" Patty sank against the wall of the house. "I've got coffee cakes for the Bank Building, and cupcakes to the Sweet Treats shop by the wharf, and I just can't. Can't. Six total. Elise is dead, and Darren is useless. I've tried calling him to see what he wants to do with her body, but he's not making any sense."

Charlene and Avery exchanged a nod. They could do those deliveries.

"We'd be happy to help," Charlene said.

"I saw on TV that he was in jail. Dumb, dumb man. I know he didn't kill my sister. He loved her." Patty cried into her unicorn pajama top.

After a moment, Charlene said, "We bumped into Klara this morning. Darren is out on bail."

"Good. Darren's loaded, so he can afford it. It's why Elise went for him, in Pennsylvania." Patty brought her thumb to her lower lip.

"Huh?" Avery asked in surprise.

Charlene was surprised too. Not so much about Elise going for a man with money, but that Patty would talk badly about her dead sister. Her newly deceased sister.

"I knew all her secrets." Patty focused watery blue eyes on Charlene. "Even the ones she didn't want me to know. I loved her anyway."

"Family." Charlene took a half step back, wanting to protect Avery from any potentially harmful dirt.

"Yep," Patty said, matching Charlene's paces. "She met this German man online in Saint Mary's, but when she got there, he was after her money, total catfish, so she changed plans. It was about a month later, she'd set her sights on Darren and his seasoned salts. She'd planned all along to incorporate my pretzels."

"How did she meet him?" Avery asked.

"It was no problem for my sister to capture Darren's attention." Patty smirked. "Elise could captivate anyone once she decided to do so."

To Charlene, Patty seemed jealous, and it wasn't nice.

Patty sighed and lowered her arms. "I can't believe she's gone. I'm all alone here now," she cried, gesturing to the house. "The last Wagner."

"I'm really sorry," Charlene said, putting her personal feelings aside to pitch in. "Is there anything else we can help with? Food, phone calls . . ."

"Nobody's left." Patty plopped down to a rocking chair as if her legs were numb. "My folks left me the house even before Elise married Darren. She's been a sly one from birth. Always landing on her feet. Beautiful, smart. Not like me at all. My dad didn't think I'd ever get married."

"If you want to, you could! You have such pretty blue eyes," Avery said.

"And you're an amazing baker." What kind of dad would tell a child they might not get married?

Patty stood shakily. "It doesn't matter. I'm a little odd, I suppose, in that I don't care enough about relationships to work on one. I'd rather bake and read and dream."

"There's nothing wrong with that," Charlene said.

Patty met her eyes. "There is one more thing you could do for me?"

"Sure!" Charlene patted Patty's wrist.

"Get an outfit from Darren for me to bring to the funeral home. I know he's going through a rough time, but I am too." Patty blinked quickly and wiped her eyes. "I'll be better tomorrow. Maybe the next day."

Charlene hugged Patty. She smelled like vanilla. "Yes, of course. Again, I'm so sorry."

"It's all right. Let me call Mila to let her know that you'll make the deliveries. I can't thank you enough." Patty went inside.

While she was gone, Charlene and Avery waited on the porch without talking, and a few minutes later, Patty returned. "Go on down and wait at the shop while Mila boxes the items up for you. She's not a big talker, so don't expect conversation. I don't mind it, but my dad would never have put up with someone he considered on the slow side."

Charlene hid her shock at that remark by glancing toward the chair on the porch. What kind of childhood had this fairy-tale home provided?

Patty scrubbed her cheeks and murmured, "Bastard."

"Is that everything?" Charlene asked. Her tone was too bright for the situation. "If you need something else, just give us a call."

Avery stuck her hands in her pockets. "Bye, Patty." She skipped down the stairs with youthful energy.

Charlene met up with Avery on the path to the bakery. They exchanged a look but didn't discuss Patty's extremely odd behavior.

The door was propped open, and they could hear a woman whistling in the back. The long counter had limited tasty treats as the pastries would be a few days old. To the right of the counter was a cash register. Two chairs and a small oval table were the only seats, but it was obvious this bakery was more of a delivery operation than a sit-down establishment. Scents of vanilla, almond, cinnamon, and yeast filled the interior.

Patty had said the Wagner Bakery had been in the family for generations, as evidenced by the photos on the wall. Black-and-white to full-color snapshots of the Wagners and their customers.

"There's Elise, and Patty," Charlene said, pointing out the cute, plump girls with big eyes holding cupcakes. A thin man with angular features stood behind them, a hand on each shoulder. Could that be their father? Blue eyes, like theirs. While they were happy, he didn't smile.

"So adorable!" Avery moved from the wall of pictures to the array of cookies in the glass case, and of course, the famous soft-baked pretzels. "Do you think these are for sale? I love oatmeal bars. And chocolate-chip cookies. And macadamia-nut anything."

Charlene joined the teenager with a laugh. "We can ask, but if not, I'll buy you lunch after we do the deliveries." Minnie made amazing pastries, and Charlene felt a little like she was cheating as she perused the options.

"That sounds great." Avery tapped her lower lip in serious contemplation. "The white chocolate macadamia nut! Are you sure you don't want something, too?"

"I suppose that chocolate chip might have my name on it."

Mila came out of the back carrying several blue pastry boxes with *Wagner's* printed on the side. "Hallo," she murmured, her soft voice muffled by the fabric. Brown eyes crinkled in welcome, though her face was wrapped in a soft beige hijab. Her body was covered from head to toe. After several trips from the back to the table, each delivery marked with a yellow slip with the address and product, Mila then tilted her head toward the case.

"We'd like a chocolate-chip cookie, and a macadamia-nut one," Avery said.

"No charge," Mila said in a low voice after handing them the cookies in individual paper bags.

"Are you sure?" Charlene asked.

Mila nodded.

"Well, thank you very much." Charlene dropped five dollars into the tip jar by the register.

Mila walked them out, held the door for them, then waved before closing and locking the door behind them.

"We can deliver these on the way to Darren's," Charlene said. "We need to show him support." There were six stops in all.

"And," Avery seconded, "see if he's recovered his mind enough to give you an outfit of Elise's for Patty to take to the funeral home. I don't blame him for checking out a little."

Charlene smiled across the console at Avery. "Not one bit."

# CHAPTER 7

Charlene and Avery dropped off the baked goods that Patty needed delivered as if it wasn't their first rodeo. They'd worked together not only at the bed-and-breakfast, but Charlene had helped Avery learn to drive and study for her tests to get into college.

After delivery number six, they were ready for their snacks from Wagner's Bakery and stopped at a drive-through for iced coffees to wash them down. Charlene parked at a space overlooking the harbor and kept the air-conditioning on. "Productive morning, huh?"

Avery sipped her mocha. "Yep. Fueled by chocolate."

Charlene removed her chocolate-chip cookie from the bag and bit into the chocolate, surprised by the addition of almonds. Her iced Americano was the perfect foil.

"So. What do you think about Patty?" Avery asked. "That was kinda bizarro with how she'd brought up her dad."

"A beautiful home doesn't equal happiness. Unlike ours, which is beautiful and filled with happy people," Charlene remarked.

"People are on vacation and want to have fun, so they come with smiles," Avery said. "And you never disappoint them, Charlene."

"Oh!" She sipped her Americano. "You and Minnie are part of the machine." Silva, and Jack, too.

Around them, tourists walked and laughed, excitement in the air from the Seafarer's Festival with booths of crafts, or food. Artisan items that could only be found in Salem, like a witch's ball. Kass Fortune's specialty teas.

"Did you ever imagine in your wildest dreams that you'd be here, in Salem, owning a bed-and-breakfast?" Avery broke off a chunk of her white-chocolate macadamia-nut cookie and took a bite.

"No. I thought I'd be in Chicago till I croaked." But then, Jared had died, and Charlene had leaped from all she'd known to the unknown. "When I first moved here, I wanted to create an elegant bed-and-breakfast to stand out from the crowd of witches and ghosts. I didn't want anything"—Charlene blushed—"tacky. Quality items that would last through time."

"Like the mirror over the mantel." Avery had heard the story often.

"Exactly. Since I was on a budget, Archie Higgins at Vintage Treasures was my source for local finds. Being on the City of Salem's new business board makes me appreciate how much operating a town is like running a business."

"You could be mayor," Avery teased.

"No, thank you. But I think Brandy was considering putting her hat in for office. I prefer behind the scenes."

"I like her a lot," Avery said. "But I'm like you. I don't need the limelight."

The ladies nodded in perfect accord.

"I love Salem." Charlene wiped cookie crumbs from her fingers with a paper napkin. "It's given me a place to put down roots of my choosing."

"Do you believe in fate?" Avery used her straw to slurp the last mocha goodness from her cup.

"I didn't used to," Charlene admitted. "But I'm more open now to the idea. How about you?"

"I totally do. Like"—Avery darted a glance at Charlene, then looked out to the water—"you had to move here, to meet me."

"We were fated to be friends?" Charlene smiled.

"Fated to be family, duh." Avery offered Charlene the last bite of her cookie.

Charlene shook her head. "That is all you. I feel like we're family, too, Avery."

The clock on the dash blinked half-past twelve.

Clearing her throat, Charlene said, "As nice of a break as this has been, we should head over to Darren's."

"Should we call Patty about the deliveries?" Avery asked.

"I think we can talk to her in person when we bring Elise's outfit."

"'Kay." Avery shifted on the passenger seat and buckled up again. "Sounds fine to me."

Charlene drove to Abbott Street, where Darren lived toward the end of the long block. She'd been to the historic mansion once for coffee with the Shultzes. At some point in the last hundred years, the owners had gutted all the beautiful wood and made it modern white and steel.

Darren hadn't liked the interior, though Elise didn't mind it, she'd said. Growing up in Salem where everything was old, new was different.

What would Darren do with the place now? They'd only been in Salem six months.

The white exterior was four stories with a red door and a slate-paved driveway. Unlike many older homes that had been split into shared housing, this one was still a single-family residence. Elise had remarked that she'd like to fill the place with children, and colorful toys would certainly take away from the stark interior.

"Wow," Avery said when Charlene pulled in behind the Tesla. "This is immense. Awesome."

They got out and knocked on the front door. "I don't know. It's only four bedrooms," Charlene joked. "Ours has eight, including mine."

Klara opened the door, her light-blue hat askew on her dark curls. It was obvious she'd had a stressful morning. Music blasted from behind her.

"Hey." Klara gripped the door handle. "What are you doing here? I thought I said to go bug Patty!"

Heavy metal banged with an emphasis on the drums.

"We did. Patty asked us to come here and get clothes for the funeral home for Elise," Charlene said. "She tried talking to Darren, but he's not . . . well, responding."

Klara's eye twitched. "Understood." She stepped back and widened the door. "You might as well come in. Enter at your own risk."

Charlene perused the white and steel foyer. To the left was the living area with white leather couches and glass-and-steel accent furniture. A white wooden staircase with a navy-blue carpet runner led to the upstairs kitchen. To the right was a small library. Behind the staircase was the master suite and the location of the blaring music.

A kitchen and a formal dining room took up the second floor, and on the third were three guest bedrooms and what Elise had hoped would be her children's rooms.

There was both a basement and an attic for storage, which held all of Darren's movie memorabilia. He'd been collecting for a while, and though Elise hadn't exactly turned up her nose, she'd been vocal about filling the movie theater with the boxes of stuff to get it out of the house.

"I can knock, if you want," Klara offered. She kept her arms around her waist. "Don't know if he'll answer. He might not hear me. Pretty sure he's ignoring me."

"I appreciate you trying," Charlene said. Retrieving funeral clothes was unfortunately not something that could be put off for too long.

Klara dragged her navy heels but went around the staircase. "Darren. Darren!" A loud knock. "Darren—Charlene and Avery are here to pick up a dress for Elise."

"Not now!" Darren shouted.

"You can't ignore this, Darren." Klara tipped her forehead to the door, obviously hurting for her friend. "Tell you what—I'll make coffee, and we can discuss this in the kitchen like adults. All right?"

The music cranked even louder.

Klara turned to Charlene with frustration clear to read on her expressive face. "Come on up. You hungry at all?" The sales rep led the way to the second-floor kitchen. Charlene and Avery followed.

"No," Charlene said, full after eating her chocolate-chip cookie.

Avery shook her head. The pastry had been gone in minutes. "We had a treat from the bakery," she admitted.

"The Wagners can bake. Coffee? Tea?" Klara emitted a soft snort. "I'd offer tequila, but Darren drank it all."

That would explain the ultra-loud music and belligerent attitude. After Jared had died, she'd spent a month in bed not sure what to do with her life without her soul mate in it.

Charlene's heart went out to Darren. Time was the only thing that would ease the pain, but it never went away.

The kitchen was all white with stainless-steel appliances. Top-quality, but cold to her eye. A bouquet of sunflowers was on the kitchenette. Fresh flowers, like the wolfsbane. Had Klara brought those too? A formal dining room was across the hall and had room for twelve. The furniture was also white with nautical and steel accents.

Klara gestured to the kitchen table, round, with four chairs.

Avery sat in the one closest to the window, which looked out over the driveway. Charlene could see the Pilot. Shrubs and hedges marked the space between this house and the neighbors.

"What would you like? This kitchen is stocked

with everything. Elise had to have the best." Klara opened a cupboard to reveal tins of tea, coffee, and hot cocoa. "I can brew something or just put on the electric kettle."

She flipped on the switch of a clear glass pot next to a Keurig.

"Tea sounds wonderful," Charlene said. Nothing caffeinated, as she was still buzzing from her iced Americano. "Anything herbal?"

Klara selected a square tin with individual tea bags and brought it to the kitchen table. "Here you are. I was talking to your friend Kass about her tea shop for a hot minute Saturday night at the theater before things went off the rails. I'd love to help her spread her brand."

"Kass is very gifted," Charlene said, choosing an orange zest and passing the box to Avery.

Avery nodded as she picked a red packet. "Score! Hibiscus and lemon."

Klara set two mugs on the table for them and returned the tin to the cupboard. She chose a packet of instant French roast and dumped it in a mug she'd been using already, according to the berry lipstick smooch on the rim.

"You've been here before?" Klara asked.

"I have, not Avery." Charlene tucked her phone into the side pocket of her purse and placed that over the arm of the chair. "For coffee, when Darren and Elise first moved here."

Klara stirred the French roast with a silver spoon. "Sugar? Honey?"

Charlene and Avery shook their heads as Klara then poured hot water over their tea bags. Orange and hibiscus scented the kitchen like potpourri.

Had Klara known of Elise's suspicions that she was sleeping with Darren? There was one way to find out—chitchat over a cup. "Were you in town for the theater launch?" Charlene kept her tone casual.

"Yeah. The idea was to camp out in the spare room upstairs for a week or two and celebrate the opening of the movie theater, then work on a marketing plan for the seasoned salts. He buys from Germany, so we've already started there." Klara sank her hip against the counter at her back, holding her coffee mug to her chest, her brown eyes welling with emotion. "I had no clue Elise thought Darren would *cheat.*"

Charlene detected the hurt in the words. "You don't think he was?" Avery was quiet and almost invisible as she listened to the conversation.

"He wouldn't." Klara impatiently blew back a wayward curl. "First of all, he loved Elise madly. And second, he didn't have time! Between the move from Pennsylvania, to buy a house *she* wanted, putting the dream of the theater into reality, and creating new flavors with his gifted palate, no. Just. No."

"Where did you meet?" Charlene dunked her tea bag.

Klara got down a saucer from a dish cupboard and set it between her and Avery. "When you're done steeping. We met in Saint Mary's. I was already on his sales force when he ran into that conniving little fortune hunter."

Charlene bowed her head to hide her reaction. Klara didn't like Elise any more than Elise had liked Klara.

"I knew what she wanted, his money, but Darren

didn't care. He fell in love with her face and didn't get past it to realize she had no heart."

"Oh!" Charlene had seen them hold hands and act like a loving couple. "I didn't notice that part of their relationship."

"Elise grew to care for him, I think." Klara snorted. "What's not to love about a millionaire who will give you everything you want? Including moving to this backwater for his dream movie theater so they can use her sister's bakery, right down to the address on the promotion trays."

Avery's grip on her mug tightened.

"No offense," Klara said, realizing how she sounded. "The trays should also say Shultz's Seasoning Salts, don't you think, Charlene? This was for Darren, not just Patty."

"It's hard to know," she said, noncommittally.

"They've been married just over a year." Klara added a touch more water to her mug. "What a damn mess. I can't wait to get back to Pittsburgh. Go, Penguins!"

Charlene shrugged.

"Not a hockey fan? Oh, well," Klara said. "I was born and raised in the city. It's up and coming in the tech scene right now—all the big players have offices there. Amazon. Google."

Charlene placed her tea bag on the saucer. "So, how did you and Darren end up meeting?"

"Well, he moved from Munich, Germany, to Saint Mary's, Pennsylvania, which has a large Bavarian population that he felt comfortable with, you know, to learn English as he started his business," Klara said. "It's only a hundred miles from Pittsburgh."

"That's not too far." Avery dunked her tea bag.

"Like Salem to Portland. We tell the guests about it for day trips."

Charlene nodded. Just another reason she loved Salem. So many things were nearby.

"My girlfriend, DiDi, adores those kinds of excursions close to home. We ended up in Saint Mary's during a fair where Darren was selling his salts as a vendor. I knew right away he had something incredible." Klara sipped her watered-down coffee. "We exchanged business cards, and within the month I'd signed him. It took five years, but he's made his first million-plus. I hope to get his brand all over the world—starting with Germany, where he's from, and where he buys his salts. My ancestry is also German. Grandparents on my mother's side. I joked that we could be siblings."

"That's such a great story," Avery said.

"I didn't know all that." Charlene heard the admiration Klara had for Darren. It was clear she cared, and it was unfortunate Elise had mistaken that for a different kind of love.

Klara's brow hiked. "Why would you? According to Elise, *she* was the reason he'd gone over that millionaire mark."

Elise had referred to herself in front of Charlene as Darren's *engel.* Good luck angel. She'd also told Patty that Darren would never fire Klara, but she'd wanted him to. Did Klara know that was on Elise's mind? It would be a reason to feel defensive about her job. Klara probably made a percentage of salt sales or some sort of commission.

A threat to one's livelihood was a big deal, and some might consider that worth defending.

"How did you and Elise get along while you were here?" Charlene asked.

Klara placed her mug by the sink. "Polite. I flew into Boston on Thursday to talk with some other reps I know for business placement. Salt isn't going anywhere, you know? Used to be a form of currency a long time ago, and it will probably still be used a millennium from now."

"It was? Cool!" Avery said. "I can't live without it on my fries."

Charlene and Klara laughed.

"Salt changed the world," a male voice said right before Darren entered the kitchen. "It allowed food preservation long before our refrigerators." He loped toward the counter as if still feeling the effects of the tequila and grief. He wore slippers, and a robe hung loosely over crimson pajamas that were probably silk.

Klara gave him a relieved smile and pushed toward him from the counter. "Darren! Coffee? Tea? I can make you breakfast. Lunch! Brunch?"

Darren was clean-shaven, his brows trimmed, and his hair smoothed back away from his broad forehead—the man she was used to seeing, unlike his wild mug shot.

"Coffee, please." Darren rounded the island counter to the sink and poured a glass of water from the tap into a tall glass.

"Sure," Klara said, opening a cupboard for a mug. "The water's still hot. French roast all right?"

Darren drained the glass in thirsty gulps, head tipped back. "*Danke.*"

"I'll get it." Klara patted his shoulder. Yes, it was

familiar, but it was also platonic. There was no spark.

Perhaps Elise had been jealous of the friendship itself? Time spent with Klara would be time away from Elise.

Friends were a big deal. Klara had been on the scene five years before Elise, and they had an undeniable connection.

Klara might have been a threat to Elise in more ways than one.

"I apologize for my loud music," Darren said. He averted his gaze, embarrassed.

"No need for that!" Charlene smiled softly at him. "We intruded on your home at a sad time."

Avery murmured in agreement. She was present without making it about her. If that was a useful skill on the force, then Avery would be promoted fast.

Darren drank his coffee, still not quite making eye contact. "You saw the news? I'm so humiliated!" At last, he raised his gaze. "That officer was goading me for a reaction, and, well. I lost my temper. I know better. I haven't behaved so out of control since I was a teenager overcome by hormones."

"Officer Lennox," Charlene said. "I have my own personal albatross at the Salem Police Department. I wonder if she knows Officer Jimenez?"

Avery sipped her tea to avoid a smile. Charlene was not bad-talking—Avery had witnessed the officer's dislike for Charlene firsthand.

Darren chuckled. "Two bullies. We should take them on one day, Charlene. Fight the good fight."

"When it comes to her, I find avoidance works best," she shared, sensing that Darren wholeheartedly believed in right and wrong. Standing up for oneself. It was nice when things worked that way in theory, but in day-to-day life, it was more complicated.

Maybe it shouldn't be.

"Why are you here?" Darren asked, his voice ragged.

"Patty sent us over to ask for a dress for Elise. To bring to the funeral parlor." Charlene and Avery shared a sorrowful glance.

"No." Darren gritted his teeth.

"No?" Charlene straightened. Here she'd hoped they would get the dress and move on with their day with no further drama.

"Elise wouldn't want a dress." Darren blew on his coffee and took a small drink. "There was a favorite pants and suit jacket she liked that made her feel pretty. She was beautiful, Elise, but needed constant reassurance of it." He exhaled as if it was too much to bear. "We all have our scars. I never found her wound, to heal it."

What a deep observation, if dark.

"She knew she was attractive," Klara said, not willing to let that comment slide.

"That's not what I mean." Darren gave his hot coffee another go, his eyes squinting at the heat. "I drank too much tequila."

"Any tequila is too much," Klara joked, her tone light.

"Please, sit, have breakfast. We *are* intruding." However, Charlene couldn't delay picking up the clothes as Patty required them for Elise at the funeral home.

"Elise was poisoned," he said, his shoulders bow-ing in grief. "With my seasoning salts. Mine. I would never hurt her, and that was the vehicle chosen by a maniac. Why?"

"How do you feel? Maybe you should go to the hospital and get checked out?" Charlene suggested.

"That's what Klara said, too, but no. If I die, I die." Darren waved his hand dismissively. "I will be with my love."

Avery kicked Charlene's foot beneath the table to show her reaction. Was he talking about suicide? That wasn't good.

"Your health matters." Charlene regarded Darren with compassion. "I'll drive you to the hospital for a quick checkup. I feel your pain. I know what it's like to lose a spouse."

Darren's face flushed as red as his pajamas. "I don't know what I'm feeling yet. It's too much, and nothing fits! If my *schatzi* was poisoned because of me, then I want to join her for eternity. We are married."

Klara smacked her mug to the counter. "Aren't you religious? Like, Catholic or something?"

"I was raised in a Catholic orphanage," Darren said, pinching the bridge of his broad nose. "My faith is evolving but a bedrock of my life, *ja.*"

"Well, snap out of this *you will let yourself die* funk because suicide is a sin, brother. You can kiss eternity with Elise good-bye." Klara maneuvered so she stood directly in front of Darren. "Now, are you going to the hospital or not?"

# CHAPTER 8

Charlene sat back in her chair in the Shultzes' kitchen surprised by Klara's abrupt declaration. The woman had spunk in spades.

"*Nein*," Darren said, drawing himself up and tying the belt on his robe. "I am not going to the hospital. Other than overwhelming sorrow, there is nothing the matter with me. I'm sure the tests will come back that only my love's popcorn was poisoned, with the roasted garlic salt. I am very in tune with my body."

Klara refilled her hot water and added another packet of instant coffee, stirring vigorously. "Fine. But don't expect me to pick up the pieces." She slurped, upset. "Have you even thought about what would happen if you died? What happens with this seasoned salt legacy you've been going on about for the last five years?"

Darren raised a palm to her. "I can't think about this right now. My wife just died."

"Fair. But you can't give up." Klara lifted his

chin, so he'd look her in the eye. With her heels, they were of a similar height. Both dark-haired. Was that their shared German ancestry? "Promise?"

Jerking free, Darren said, "I won't give up." He almost fell back against the sink. "But I'm lost, friends, and have no idea what to live for. Elise was my *engel.* My life."

"The orphanages in Munich and the entire state of Pennsylvania?" Klara snapped. "You've donated twenty percent of all profit since we first started. Those kids need you."

"My money." Darren scowled.

"Yeah," Klara said, not holding back. "Definitely your money. So what? Without that income, they'd go hungry or without beds. *You* give that to them."

Wow. Charlene had no idea Darren had been so generous with his profits. And it made her contemplate Klara in a different light as well.

Klara was hard as nails but talented, and she cared about Darren as a dear friend.

"That's very kind of you," Avery said. "I grew up in an orphanage here in Salem. Started at Felicity House when I was nine. It was private funding. Just left the teen house for Charlene's. What you're doing does matter, Darren."

Darren examined Avery with interest that pierced his self-pity. "I'm sorry."

Avery smiled. "It was better than living with my mom. She's an addict. It gave me a safer place to grow up."

Charlene patted Avery's shoulder.

"Charlene gives to Felicity House, where the little ones are," Avery said.

Klara and Darren focused on her. Charlene shifted on the chair, not wanting the spotlight on her. She'd been raised by her parents to give back to the community.

"I didn't know that was a cause dear to your heart." Darren put a palm to his. "I will donate too."

"Thank you!" All the better for the kids. "I met Avery at a fundraiser when she was filling in as a waitress."

"Not successfully." Avery laughed.

"It's okay! I convinced her to work for me at the B and B, and I think we've both been happy with the arrangement."

"Beyond." Avery tapped her mug. "Anyway, I think it's wonderful for you to take care of those kids. Why Germany?"

"That's where I grew up, with my sister. We were abandoned in our village as toddlers and if it weren't for the Catholic orphanage and the priests and nuns there, well, we would have died. I couldn't support us as a five-year-old."

"Five!" Klara exclaimed. "I've never heard this story before."

"Because I don't like to talk about it." Darren's slight German accent deepened. "It's in the past," he said sadly. "And it should stay there."

"I never knew you had a sister," Klara said. "Where is she now? Munich?"

"She died." Darren's throat worked, and at last, he said, "I couldn't save her, just like I failed Elise."

"What? How did you fail Elise?" Klara flung her arm to the side. "She was poisoned—not by you, which means not your fault." She faced Charlene. "The Salem PD needs to step up to the plate."

"They will," Charlene said. "You can trust them to get the job done." She'd learned that over time.

"I failed Elise," Darren said again. "She wanted a life of luxury. Success for herself and her sister, Patty. They didn't have an easy childhood."

Charlene thought of the storybook house behind the bakery. The big family porch with four rocking chairs. From the outside, it seemed pretty sweet.

She'd gotten the impression from Patty this morning that their father had been a tough-love kind of parent. In the picture, he hadn't smiled. "Did she say how?"

"Elise was very close-lipped about it—unless she'd had wine." Darren's chuckle held no joy. "Then, *ja,* I'd get bits and pieces. We got married at the courthouse to avoid any religious ceremonies. She was raised Protestant."

"Have you asked Patty?" Charlene figured that he'd go to the only remaining source. She knew from her history lessons that Protestants and Catholics didn't always get along.

"Elise didn't want me to talk to Patty about their past," Darren shared. "She said Patty stole her inheritance."

"What?" Avery asked, leaning forward.

They'd just learned this morning from Patty that she'd inherited the house. She didn't say she'd stolen it.

Klara nodded. "I heard her too. Elise was upset about the house—but only after a bottle of merlot. She was wound up tight."

Darren arched his brow at Klara in warning to be nice.

"Elise wanted a family." Charlene peered toward Darren, wondering why he had told Elise that he didn't anymore. "I assumed to re-create her childhood, but maybe not."

"My head is killing me." Darren rubbed his forehead.

"What is it?" Klara asked. "Hangover? Let me at least make you some toast with aspirin."

"Not just yet," Darren said, putting his mug of coffee down.

Klara blew out an exasperated breath. The sales rep was a tornado of emotions. "I want to help!"

"Why don't you show Avery the house while Charlene and I select Elise's outfit?" Darren's voice shook, and he gulped down tears that had to be drowning him.

"All right," Klara said, jumping on the directive. Like Charlene, she was eager to act on something. Anything.

Charlene looked to Avery, who gave a nod.

"We'll meet back here, then," Charlene said.

Charlene followed Darren down the white staircase to the master suite at the rear of the house. She remembered the way from a few months ago, when she'd been shown the tour. All white and bright and clinically clean.

"I hate this house." Darren opened the door to the suite. Inside, they'd added color in varying shades of blue and green that were restful and calming. "It reminds me of a hospital."

"Your suite is peaceful, Darren. Beautiful."

"It should be for what it cost, but Elise was so

afraid of making a mistake. Not sure who she thought was going to judge her. I should ask Patty." Darren smoothed his hair back. "*Nein.* It doesn't matter anymore."

Darren sank to the edge of the bed, the mattress dipping at his bulk. The robe strained at his muscular arms. A television on the wall was set up for surround sound, and even though the noise was off now, she noticed that he'd been playing Metallica. It was one remote punch away from blasting again.

"I'm so sorry," Charlene said.

He sobbed, and she patted his back as he buried his head in his hands.

It wasn't an adequate comforting, but there wouldn't be one after such a loss. Charlene stayed and offered companionship so he wouldn't be alone in his torment.

After a few moments, Darren breathed in deeply and raised his head. Charlene went to the connected bathroom and wet a washcloth for him, bringing it back to him.

"*Danke.*" He applied it to his face for at least a minute if not more. At last, he stood. "You are very kind, Charlene."

"It's nothing," Charlene said. "I truly understand. Trust me, each day will get easier with time, but there is no skipping ahead in the healing process. Give yourself the space you need to grieve."

"I can't do that." Darren walked to the bathroom and tossed the cloth in the sink, the robe billowing behind him like a cape.

"Why?" She'd learned that one's priorities crystallized in the face of tragedy. How she'd known after Jared's death that she couldn't leave their home, not even for the prayer service at her parents' church, not for work. She'd had nothing to give.

"I have to make Spellbound Movie Theater a success." Darren reposed against the interior door frame of the bathroom. "We put all our joined energy into the theater. Into this house."

"Your baby. So she could have her baby," Charlene said. They'd had the conversation in her living room at a business meeting. Elise had been calm and willing to wait her turn. "What changed, Darren?"

"What do you mean?"

"She told Patty you didn't want a family anymore."

Enraged, Darren pulled his hair with fists above both ears. "Elise wouldn't let it go! She wasn't going to be happy. I let her down in many ways."

Charlene wasn't sure if it was guilt or grief she was hearing. Perhaps both. "How so?"

Darren flung open the closet that had been remodeled to be a walk-in with an overhead light and mirrors. "Check this out."

Gorgeous clothes lined both sides, with shoes neatly organized. For a tiny human moment, Charlene had shoe envy. "This is amazing."

"As if there was ever an occasion to wear such items," Darren said, exuding acceptance of his wife and her foibles. "But it made her happy."

He pulled out a pantsuit, a chic pink Dior with the tags still on it. The jacket was fitted and had a little peplum ruffle; the slacks narrow-legged. It would be stunning on her.

Charlene blinked away tears.

It was like dressing a doll, after the fact.

"Elise stole things from department stores," Darren said, dropping a bomb. "I told her she could afford to buy whatever she wanted. There was no need to steal. After a time, she shopped and would leave the receipts on the table. I never blinked at the cost."

Charlene's envy dissipated. Everyone had wounds that marked them in some way. Darren had known his wife well. "Why do you think she did that?"

"She wanted to be a big deal in Salem and have a fancy house, own a successful movie theater." Darren shook the outfit.

"She wanted a family too," Charlene said, her heart full of empathy for the young woman who had her scars, as Darren had said. "Why was she so angry? What were you fighting about the afternoon of the premiere, before you opened the doors to the public?"

Darren's skin flushed. "I couldn't give her what she wanted most. If it was money, I could make it. If it was clothes, she could buy them. If it was a business with her sister? Done." He brushed his hands together.

"But?" Charlene brought her hand to her earlobes to touch the last gift Jared had ever given her—gold, heart-shaped earrings—and felt hoops instead. It was a testament to her healing over time that they were in her jewelry box and not in her ears.

"No family. I couldn't give her children." Darren held Charlene's gaze, his tortured. "I had a vasectomy long before I met Elise."

The air escaped from Charlene's lungs in a *whoosh*. "Oh. Oh, and you didn't tell her before the wedding?"

"No." Darren yanked his tufted hair back. "I never would have told her. She wouldn't have married me, no matter how much money I had. I told her then in the office. I was just so mad. She kept pushing, saying how she'd helped me, and now it was her turn. Like a kid denied a toy!"

Charlene understood how much Elise had wanted children and empathized with the young woman.

"I let her down!" Darren cried.

The argument explained Elise being slightly off that night. She must have hoped Darren would change his mind, because she hadn't told Patty the whole truth. Partial truths. Was she protecting her husband, or herself? "I'm sorry."

"It's my fault. All of it." Darren stayed at the threshold of the closet with Elise's bounty behind him. The clothes were color-coded on velvet hangers. "I wouldn't change my mind, either. She wanted me to get the procedure reversed."

She knew nothing about vasectomies other than what they were—male contraception. "Can you do that?"

"Sure. But I won't." Darren growled low. "Will not. No child deserves to grow up as I did."

Charlene scrutinized Darren closely. The pulse at his throat and temple throbbed out of sync. "What do you mean?"

"We have a genetic defect in our family that nobody can overlook." Darren shrugged, his German accent thicker now. "It was so bad that our mother was embarrassed by us. The villagers shunned us after our mother died, but the nun visiting saved us and brought us to the orphanage. I hid in the movie theaters in Munich to escape bullies. It was dark. Safe. Children are mean, but adults are too. They punch harder."

Charlene blinked rapidly. Darren appeared just fine to her. She couldn't imagine grown adults beating children. Her heart ached for his pain.

"We were called abominations." Darren stuffed his hands into the pockets of his robe. "People wished us dead. Good Christians, mind you, still thought we should have been locked away or worse."

"Surely not," she said, but she could hear and see the truth from him.

"If my beautiful Elise knew about that, she wouldn't have married me. She wouldn't want children with me. I selfishly kept the news to myself." Darren whirled, giving his quivering back to Charlene. "I hoped I could give her enough that she would be happy."

Charlene was at a complete loss on how to soothe him. He'd been so wrong and yet . . . At last, she placed a tentative hand on his shoulder. "Please remember, despite your pain, all the good you do. You've made amazing choices on supporting orphanages because of those childhood circumstances."

Darren turned toward Charlene and side-stepped away from the closet to pace around the bed. His eyes were manic. "I lied to a beautiful woman and strung her along. Now she's dead! I connect with the wolf man, Charlene. I feel his dual nature." He beat his fist to his chest. "It's why it's my favorite movie."

"We are human," Charlene said. "We all make mistakes."

"You are being too kind. You don't understand at all." Darren calmed enough to return to the closet and went inside.

She did understand, though. Not exactly—nobody's journey was the same—but she understood enough not to judge. "I saw Elise's love for you. Maybe she would have come around to forgiving you."

"We will never know. Someone killed my bride, my *schatzi*, my love." Darren folded the Dior suit into a cloth shopping bag. He added shoes. Earrings. Bracelets, crying with each choice he put in the bag. "For her final journey, she will be dressed like a queen." He handed the bag to Charlene.

"I'll take this to Patty right now," she said softly.

Darren dragged in a ragged breath.

"Please," Charlene continued, "let us know when the funeral will be. I will support you in any way I can."

"Thank you. *Danke*." Darren eyed the ceiling and pushed away from the closet.

"You should rest," Charlene said, gesturing to the bed. The comforter had been mussed as if he'd kicked it around.

"No. No, after you go, I'm going to shower, then head to the theater." Darren's tears dried. His tone held the same determination as when they'd planned the original Spellbound Movie Theater launch.

"Don't work, Darren." She gripped the handle of the heavy bag. "Rest!"

"I have to," Darren said, ignoring her advice. "I need to make Elise proud. She put so much of herself into my dream. It is all I have left of her."

Charlene was so confused about the relationship they'd shared. Would Elise have divorced Darren for lying to her? Her skin prickled.

Could Elise have forgiven the vasectomy if she'd understood why? Or was Darren right that Elise wanted children, more than anything else . . . When Charlene imagined her and Jared in that situation, she didn't know.

They left the bedroom.

Charlene held the handle of the bag of clothes tightly, and the pair went up the stairs to the kitchen. She wasn't sure she could have forgiven a lie like that.

Avery and Klara were demolishing toaster waffles with syrup. Charlene set the bag on the top step, completely supportive of Darren's choices for Elise's funeral outfit. This was one final thing he could do for his wife.

"Breakfast of champions," Klara said. "I've made you two, Darren. Come on, eat for me. I'll feel better about it since you won't go to the hospital."

Darren sank into the vacant chair, a scowl on his face. "You're nagging."

"Out of love. Want some, Charlene?" Klara asked.

"No, thanks." Charlene wished they could go but didn't know how to make a polite exit that didn't seem like fleeing. Darren's grief brought her own feelings of sadness and loss to the forefront, where they hadn't been for a while.

"Klara, I will eat just to keep you quiet." Darren cut off a corner of the waffle. "Do we know what Elise was poisoned with?"

Charlene shook her head. "Not yet." She looked at Klara. "Wolfsbane is poison, and you brought the fresh flowers."

"It was a joke." Klara arched her brow at Charlene. "Do you really think we were in danger of getting turned into werewolves?" She made a circle motion with her finger in the air. Crazy.

"Of course not." Charlene hesitated.

"But?" Klara dropped her fork to her plate with a *clang*.

"Franco put the bouquet in the office," Darren said, as if they were all forgetful. "Nowhere near the popcorn, or the counter, or the salt."

Charlene leaned toward them, meeting their gazes. "Right. When we left yesterday, the office door was open. Darren, you had gone in the ambulance with Elise."

"It was?" Darren swallowed a piece of waffle. "I know I closed it after grabbing my wallet. Should've been locked. It's got to be broken somehow. It's not the first time."

Or Matthew was right, and the building was haunted. It was something she and Jack could investigate later.

"Get to the point, Charlene!" Klara said. "Flowers? I didn't poison Elise, if that is what you're trying to get at here. Sheesh. We didn't get along, but that doesn't mean I wanted her dead."

Darren paled at her blunt statement.

"It wasn't what I was getting at." Charlene sighed. "I'd hoped you'd have the flowers here."

Klara tapped her long fingers with annoyance to the table. "Sometime this century would be great, Charlene."

"They were in the office," Darren repeated sternly. "Franco put them on the desk."

"When we left, I peeked inside before I shut the door." Charlene blew out a careful breath, not wanting to upset him further. "Darren, the entire bouquet of wolfsbane was gone."

Darren finished a waffle, a frown weighting his brow. "You're right. The flowers weren't in my office yesterday, but I was more concerned about the police collecting my salts and their absence didn't register." He made an impatient noise. "Doesn't matter. While the fresh blossoms can be slightly toxic, we would have noticed petals on the popcorn even after the lights went out. The roots and seeds are what can be most deadly."

Klara smacked Darren's arm, her voice high. "I didn't do it."

"I know—ouch." Darren started on his second waffle. "Thanks for making this for me. It's helping me feel more human already."

"What happened to the flowers, then?" Charlene mused.

She should let it go since it wasn't a factor with the popcorn. It would be nice if Sam found out for sure . . . oh, and then, *if* he'd tell her.

"Ask Franco. He was acting weird that evening," Klara said. "All he talked about while we were in the projector room was how he was worried that he and Matthew were both going to be fired. He showed me his pentagram pendant. Like, he's into the whole witch thing."

"Everybody in Salem is," Darren replied in a very dry tone. "Not a big deal."

"He said no pentagram could stop what was coming," Klara countered. "What do you think he meant?"

Charlene and Avery exchanged glances. Franco had shown them his palm and remarked that there was no pentagram before racing up the stairs.

"Who was going to fire him?" Darren asked, irate.

Klara rose and pushed back from the table, staring at him as if he was not quite with it. "Who do you think? Elise."

# CHAPTER 9

"Can you please leave my wife alone, Klara?" Darren tossed his fork to the table.

On that note, Charlene stood and motioned for Avery to rise. "We should get going. Again, I'm sorry for your loss, Darren."

Darren walked them down the stairs from the kitchen to the door, nodding at the bag of clothes and jewelry. "Thanks for taking this to Patty. I'll contact the funeral home later today, but I'm not sure what they can do while her death is under investigation."

Charlene nodded.

"I'll do that after I go to the theater. I want to open the Spellbound this weekend. I don't want whoever killed Elise to take our dream away. I will fight for it." Darren waited at the threshold until they were in the car.

Charlene backed out of the driveway as Avery buckled in, quiet until they reached the road. Once she was certain they were far from Darren's house, Charlene started talking at the same time as Avery.

"You first," Charlene said.

"OMG. Klara is great. But terrifying. She grew up playing football on the boys' team. She thinks it's hysterical, but tragic, that Elise thought Darren was messing around. She swears Darren isn't the kind to do that. He's 'one of the good ones,' whatever that means. You go!" Avery said.

"I agree with that assessment of Darren's character." Charlene headed toward Wagner's Bakery and Patty's gingerbread house. "I don't think he would cheat either. He's got all this guilt, though, for not giving Elise what she really wanted. A family. He lied to her about wanting kids." She didn't mention the vasectomy. It seemed personal.

"She had a gorgeous home, a rich husband, and a business with her sis," Avery said. "She should have been happy, yeah?"

"Happiness is tricky." Charlene and Jared had wanted children and couldn't have them, so her sympathies were with Elise.

"You're happy," Avery said.

"I am," Charlene agreed. "I work on it, though. Trust me, there are times when I want to walk around with my tail between my legs, but it won't help anything. Wallowing just mires you in negativity. Not that you shouldn't feel what you feel! That's important too."

"I know, thanks to years of state-funded therapy." Avery glanced at Charlene. "Growing up how I did has made me more mature than a lot of other teens my age."

"I think you're right." Was Avery thinking of someone in particular?

Avery put on her sunglasses—this pair of light blue. "Jenna gets on my nerves when she's being selfish about stuff. Like the apartment and not going to college."

They'd been thick as thieves during high school. "How is she doing?"

"Good, I guess." Avery scanned her cell phone. "Since she's living with her boyfriend, we don't talk, really."

"I'm sorry about that." Charlene had been like that with Jared—just the two of them were all that mattered. She'd made an effort to make many friends while here in Salem, so she wasn't alone.

"It's okay." Avery shrugged. "We kinda grew apart. Janet said that's normal and to not take it personally."

Thank heaven for Janet, the wise caretaker at the teen house for the older wards of the state.

"It's pretty amazing that Darren grew up in an orphanage," Charlene said. "Moved to a new country and now he's a millionaire." And a widower.

"No limits!" Avery raised her fist in the air and accidentally hit the top of the SUV. "Ouch."

Charlene's heart remained heavy. Loss wasn't easy. "Let's drop these clothes off at Patty's, all right? Then head back to the bed-and-breakfast. *Friends?*" The lighthearted reruns were just what she needed.

"Sounds great to me." Avery's ponytail bobbed over the spider tattoo on her neck as she looked out the window.

Thanks to the congested tourist traffic, the ten-minute drive took fifteen, but at last Charlene parked before the bakery at a little after one. It was closed for business, the interior dark.

They each got out, and Charlene grabbed the cloth shopping bag with the Dior clothes and accessories from the hatch. They walked down the path to the porch, but it was easy to tell that nobody was around. It had a vacant feel.

Charlene knocked, but there was no answer. "I guess I could leave it here on the porch?"

"I think so," Avery said. "It's not like the house is close to the street. Nobody is just going to see it right off."

"True." Charlene placed the bag behind the rocking chair next to the door, her nape tingling. She whirled around, but there was nobody there. Old trees shaded the house and walkway so there were plenty of spaces to hide. "Strange."

"Seeing things again?" Avery teased.

"Or not seeing them, is the problem," Charlene answered with a straight face.

"Such as the shoes in the picture." Avery flowed down the steps with grace. "I told Seth I thought someone was watching us. The photo would make it a higher probability."

"Nice phrase . . . it sounds like something Sam might say." Charlene followed Avery to the car.

Avery hopped into the passenger side, but Charlene still had an itchy feeling, so she checked the back of the SUV and the street before climbing behind the wheel to drive them home. She triple-checked the mirrors, then pulled into the road. "My imagination is working overtime."

"Seth thinks there could be ghosts at the theater, like Matthew goes on and on about." Avery scrolled her phone, probably for messages or videos. It amazed her the amount of content available in ten-second flashes. She feared for the future generation's attention span.

Marketing had changed so much already since she'd left the business behind in Chicago. She used those skills all the time but had Avery to keep her current with social media, like TikTok.

"Matthew has mentioned several times that the building is haunted," Charlene said. "Kass has the same mentality, though, that Salem is loaded with ghosts. What do you think?"

"It's not that I don't believe in them, but would they wear modern Crocs?" Avery sounded doubtful. "Or care about clothes?"

Jack did. Charlene let Avery go on without offering that insight. "You could ask Kass or Kevin."

"That's a good idea." Avery cleared her throat and said in a casual tone, "Seth's invited me for dinner tonight to meet his ghost at the house. His mom's making tacos. Should I go?"

The casual tone meant that it was very important. "Sure! Tacos sound fun. I'm curious about the ghost myself, honestly."

Tagging along to satisfy her curiosity would *not* be okay, she told herself firmly.

"I'll keep you posted," Avery promised. "His mom sounds cool."

"Is Seth an only child?" Charlene slowed to a stop at a red light. The sun was bright in a blue sky. It was tempting to roll the windows down but too hot.

"Nope. He's got a brother, Stephen, who's fifteen. They aren't close—he's a sports jock, and Seth is into video games. I guess their dad left when they were little, and his mom was like, totally fine with raising them on her own."

Probably not a lot of options to do otherwise, Charlene thought. "What does she do?"

"She cleans houses, her own business, and does pretty good." Avery lowered her phone. "They never went without, Seth said."

"That's terrific, Avery." Charlene could tell that Avery was nervous about meeting his family. "Do you want to bake some cookies to take over for dessert?"

"Yeah!" Avery shot off a text as fast as the next thought. "I asked him what his favorite cookie was."

Charlene continued toward home as the light turned green. "Smart."

"Peanut butter," Avery read the answering text aloud. "Do we have the ingredients for that?"

"Minnie has our pantry stocked for Armageddon." Charlene chuckled. "I bet you she does—and if not, you can run to the grocery."

"Right." Avery tucked a piece of hair behind her ear. "In my own car. I keep forgetting! He's thinking about a different job for the summer, you know, in case things fall through at the theater. Even though Darren wants to keep it open, the customers were awful to him. Maybe until Elise's killer is caught, he should wait."

"I agree with you. And I really like Seth."

Avery nodded, a sweet, dreamy smile on her face.

They reached the bed-and-breakfast to find Sam's SUV in the driveway, next to Avery's car. Neither Jack nor Silva was on the porch.

"Sam must have news!" Charlene said, quickly checking her image for dirt smudges or an out-of-place strand of hair in the rearview mirror.

"You look great," Avery said with a knowing smirk.

Busted. "Thanks."

Charlene led the way inside the house and paused to listen for Sam or Minnie in the foyer. Her guests were all out on tours or excursions on this gorgeous day.

Silva meowed from the living room, and Charlene shifted that direction. Sam petted the cat in large-handed strokes that would make any female purr. He'd been seated in an armchair and now stood with Silva in the crook of his arm, her fluffy tail flowing like a luxury scarf.

Minnie turned from where she'd placed a tray of treats. "Charlene! The detective is here to see you. I've brought iced tea and scones. Would you like some?" She wore a floral pink apron over a sundress, her gray curls pinned into submission.

"No, thank you." Charlene entered the living room and smiled at them both.

Sam's hair, dark and thick, was combed. He wore a short-sleeved navy-blue polo with *SPD* on the collar, tucked into tan slacks. They were nice, but she preferred his jeans.

And boots.

He wore leather slip-ons today, and she supposed this was his summer attire. Also attractive—but how could Sam be anything else?

"Hi, Sam," Avery said.

"Howdy, ladies." Sam continued to pet Silva. "You've been out early today."

"It's summer and too nice to stay inside," Charlene said. She wouldn't voluntarily mention that she and Avery had been shooting the breeze with Sam's top suspect.

Why rock the boat when he was in such a relaxed mood? Silva had that effect on her, too, sometimes. He might get angry about it.

Scratch that. Sam would definitely be angry they'd been at Darren's, even though it was to assist with the funeral clothes.

Avery touched Minnie's arm. "Hey, Minnie, can you help me make peanut butter cookies? I'm going to take them over to Seth's house tonight for dessert. His mom is fixing us tacos." Avery patted her tummy as if she hadn't had five breakfasts already today.

"Of course!" Minnie rubbed her hands together, a magician in the kitchen. "I have the best recipe for those if you'd like me to share it with you?"

"Oh, yeah." Avery's eyes sparkled. "He'll think I'm the best cook ever."

"They are pretty good," Minnie said with a wink. "Sure to impress his mother."

The two left Sam and Charlene in the living room, Avery taller than Minnie by a good four inches.

Sam placed Silva on the floor and tilted his head at Charlene. "Seth, as in movie theater Seth? I thought I said for her to stay away from him."

Charlene bristled. "You can't just forbid a

teenager to do something, Sam, or else it's the first thing they'll do. I realize it was a long time ago, but surely you remember?"

"It wasn't that long!" He smoothed his mustache and allowed a smile. "Fine. It's been several decades since I was a teenager."

"Me too," she said.

"I think you're lovely," Sam said.

Her cheeks heated. "Are you here about the case, or to tell me that I'm lovely?"

"I want to take back that rule. I like flirting with you, Charlene, and this makes it impossible," Sam complained.

She hid a smile, while on the inside she jumped for joy. She liked it when Sam flirted too. Only when Jack wasn't around, though, like now.

Where was her ghost, anyway?

"All right. We can reconsider it. Now, why are you here, Sam?" Charlene sat down on the small sofa opposite the armchair Sam had been in and gestured for him to also sit.

The tray with the iced tea and scones was to his right, toward the fireplace. Silva paced between their feet with her tail high.

"The coroner told me Elise Shultz was not pregnant." Sam settled back in his chair.

Charlene nodded, willing to share since he was being so forthright himself. "I found out that Darren Shultz had a vasectomy."

Sam's head rocked backward in amazement, and she sensed their friendliness had just flown out the window.

"When? Where?" Sam crossed his legs and smacked his palm to his thigh. "How did that conversation come about, Charlene? And don't tell me it's just talk, because a man doesn't bring that up in casual conversation, like, how are you today; oh, fine—I had a vasectomy."

She laughed at his reaction.

Sam glowered at her, his brows drawn.

Her heart thrilled.

"It was just conversation." Charlene rose and stepped toward the fireplace, unlit, but with cinnamon pinecones stacked in a basket as a room freshener.

Sam stalked her around the yellow armchair. "Explain it to me, please."

"Well, Avery and I stopped in to give our condolences to Patty."

"Patty Wagner, Elise's sister." Sam's jaw clenched.

"Yes." Charlene bit her lower lip, trying not to laugh at his predictable overreaction.

"And?" Sam tucked his hand into his slacks and stared at her.

Charlene didn't look away, though she was tempted to duck her head. Sam could be so intense. "We asked if there was anything we could do to help her, and Patty said yes." Much to Charlene's shock.

"Go on." Sam's left brow twitched.

"We were in luck because her assistant at the bakery doesn't drive, so Avery and I made the important daily deliveries for Patty, who was much too upset to do it herself." Patty had been a mess, and Charlene was glad to have helped.

"That doesn't explain how you got Darren to tell you such very personal information, Charlene." Sam leaned toward her, gesturing with his thumb toward the kitchen. "With Avery present."

"We asked if there was anything else . . ." Charlene let the sentence draw out. Avery had been safe upstairs with Klara for that conversation.

"Of course, you did."

Sam sounded so annoyed with her for just being nice. She might reconsider and have Minnie cut off any future treats when he arrived at the house. Uninvited.

"And Patty said yes, that if we could go to Darren's to get a dress for Elise that would be appreciated since Darren wasn't answering her calls. Patty would take it to the funeral home, so he didn't have to handle that chore. People help one another in times of trouble, Sam." Charlene lifted her chin.

"It's starting to make sense," Sam said, eyeing the ceiling.

Charlene hiked a brow at the detective. "Darren knew Elise wouldn't want a dress, but he had a special outfit in mind, which he put together. The man is in torment, Sam. Agony. He didn't kill Elise."

"I still don't understand the vasectomy info dump," Sam's voice rumbled between them.

"Well, Darren knew Elise wanted a family. Hence the big house with all the bedrooms that he didn't even like, but he bought it for her." Charlene glanced at Sam from the corner of her eye.

Sam shrugged a broad shoulder. "And now he can sell it. If he's not guilty of murder."

"I don't think that's the plan," Charlene said. "It

sounds like he wants to stay in Salem. Spellbound was something he and Elise worked on together, and Darren doesn't want to let it go without trying to make it a success."

Sam rubbed his chin, his strong jaw shaved, his gaze inward. "And yet, Darren's procedure prevented him from giving Elise children."

"Yes." Charlene pivoted to face Sam.

"They can have those things reversed," Sam said.

"Darren wouldn't." Charlene held Sam's gaze. "He mentioned something in his genetics that he didn't want to pass on as a reason."

"Not good, Charlene. Several sources say Darren and Elise were arguing loudly that afternoon at the theater."

"It was about the vasectomy," she said.

Silva meowed and brushed up against Sam's calves. He refused to be distracted and continued to study her as if she was an alien from another planet.

"He didn't do it!" Charlene said.

Sam blew out a breath, maintaining his patience by a thread. "Did you learn anything else while you visited Darren?"

"Klara is staying at the house right now." She liked Klara and understood her brash, no-holds-barred personality. She was a loyal friend to Darren. Did that make her dangerous?

Charlene thought it might. What would some-one like Klara do, if pushed into a corner by Elise?

"The same Klara who is supposed to be having an affair with him?" Sam tucked his thumb into his belt loop. "That's convenient."

"And not true," Charlene said softly. "Klara has a girlfriend, DiDi, who lives in Pittsburgh. It's an hour away from Saint Mary's, where Elise and Darren lived."

"Ah." He nodded speculatively.

"What kind of poison was used on the popcorn? Was it wolfsbane, or aconitine, like the flowers?" Darren had said the petals might cause nausea, but the seeds could kill.

"Yes." Sam sighed and shifted his weight from one loafer to the other. "It was in the canister with the roasted garlic salt. So far, that was the only one that had the poison added to it. Darren's popcorn tub was empty, but you said Elise had gotten him a fresh one. There is a trace amount of the roasted garlic salt on the tray with Darren's name. The popcorn was all gone, but it matches what was in her stomach."

Charlene bowed her head. "Elise was the target."

"Yeah. Darren will remain a person of interest. He didn't get sick from the salts. He probably knew not to eat the roasted garlic."

"He didn't eat it because his favorite was the herb and chili! Both Darren and Elise had full trays of popcorn with their favorite salt, while the rest had sampling trays."

"You could have been in danger—you and Avery," Sam said.

"We didn't eat enough to get sick." Charlene reached for his hand but then dropped hers. "Klara isn't the one who moved the wolfsbane from the office, but she suggested Franco might know who did. He was acting weird. Worried that he and Matthew both might get fired by Elise."

"Charlene. I will question Franco Lordes. I will question Matthew Sinchuk. I will question Seth Gamble." Sam swiped his hand through his hair. "I will question Klara Maxwell, and Patty Wagner. I am questioning *you* right now. Darren Shultz lied to his wife about his desire for a family. He had a vasectomy he didn't tell her about. Instead of thinking he's innocent, Charlene, it makes him appear more guilty!"

Sam rattled off the names of the people around the concession counter as if he'd memorized them. He was an excellent detective. But this time, she feared he was focusing too much on the husband. "Why would he want her dead? Sam, this was their project."

Sam stepped closer to Charlene and put his hands on her shoulders to stare into her eyes. "What if Darren decided it was easier to find a new wife than divorce this one, who would want half or more of his millions? You know as well as I do that most murders are committed by someone the victim knows. They are often committed out of passion, and everyone heard them argue."

Jack appeared in a blast of cold, and Charlene jumped.

"I hate it when Sam has a point," Jack said, completely disgruntled.

# CHAPTER 10

The front door of the bed-and-breakfast slammed open before Charlene could digest what had just been said; as in, Sam had a valid point on why Darren might kill Elise, to save himself a bundle of cash. Jack agreed with the detective.

But Darren wasn't just about the money.

Charlene hurried across the living room, her hand to her chest as her heart sped rapidly in alarm. Sam stepped in front of her, protectively, to keep her safe from danger.

It was a little sexy, she thought, grateful when it was Georgio and Maria Lopez in the foyer instead of a mad popcorn killer.

Georgio's arm was in a blue cloth sling, and Maria hovered at her husband's side, lines of concern wrinkling her brow.

"Are you all right?" Charlene asked with concern. She moved around Sam.

Georgio's dark hair was damp. Maria's sundress,

light yellow, appeared slightly wet from where she'd stood so close to her husband.

"Fine, fine," Georgio said, sounding embarrassed.

Minnie arrived with Avery from the kitchen, Avery carrying a stick of butter for her cookies. Minnie fluttered her hands as if wanting to help but not knowing how.

Charlene felt the same way. What to do and how to assist? "What happened?"

"Georgio forgot that he is sixty-five and not thirty anymore." Maria *tsk*ed. There was worry behind the sharp remark.

"I was going for the biggest fish of the competition." Georgio used his good arm to stretch out to his side.

"Georgio!" Maria said in exasperation. "The doctor told you to relax. *Por favor*, could we get a towel?"

"I'll get it!" Minnie slipped into the laundry room and returned with a big, fluffy towel. "Here you are, Maria. Why don't you and Georgio go to the living room? I'll bring you some refreshments."

Avery followed Minnie into the kitchen while Charlene and Maria escorted him to the sofa. Charlene spread the towel over the cushions, though she could see Georgio was mostly dry. Maria got an ottoman for his feet and then adjusted a pillow for his side. Jack manifested by the mantel to observe.

"Are you in pain?" Charlene asked.

"It's nothing," Georgio said. "Just a slight sprain of my elbow." He sighed with a forlorn expression. "I won't be able to fish in the competition tomorrow."

"Oh, no! Your vacation." Charlene stepped back with a shake of her head.

"He can walk just fine," Maria said in a tart tone. "We can still do all the tours on our list. Didn't I warn you to be careful?"

Georgio gingerly settled his arm on the pillow. "I'm glad the vacation isn't ruined, but what a story, Maria, if I'd caught the fish and not lost the reel into the ocean!"

Minnie hurried in with water and little round cheese puffs on a tray. "Just rest awhile. I'm so glad you weren't hurt worse!"

"He'll be telling this story until he dies, only he'll have caught the fish." Jack smiled at their injured guest. "He seems fine."

"I should get going," Sam said, heading toward the foyer. At the last minute, the wily detective switched directions and went down the hall to the kitchen, where Avery was baking all alone.

Charlene rushed after him. Would he question the teen?

Avery stirred the batter of peanut butter. "Hey, Sam!"

"Hi." The detective rested his weight against the threshold where the pocket door was slid back. "I just wanted to touch base with you about the visits you went on this morning with Charlene. I hope she's not being a bad influence?"

Charlene sucked in a breath. Of all the nerve! That was it—no more scones or croissants, no more coffee with key lime pie . . .

"Charlene's great, Sam." Avery placed the bowl and spoon on the counter. "She gets people to open up like you wouldn't believe."

"Oh, I would," Sam drawled. "I do. Were you a part of the vasectomy conversation?"

"Huh?" Avery asked.

"Sam!" Charlene said in a loud voice. "I think you should go and stop badgering Avery. She's working."

"You should also be working. Both of you," Sam instructed, "please stay away from the theater until this case is closed. All right?"

Avery nodded, uncertain. Wanting to please but also having her own agenda. She was just like Charlene in that regard.

"He's like a broken record," Jack observed from his usual spot by the fridge. "When you have a second, can you talk with me? It's not urgent, though, if you want to make sure Georgio is all right."

She smiled for Jack, and Sam. "Let me walk you out, Sam."

They reached the porch, the door open at her back.

The detective turned to her with a warm, yet wolfish smile. He thought he'd won, but the ladies in this house had minds of their own.

"Sam." Charlene crossed her arms. "I want you to know that I understand why you ask us to be careful. I promise I will do my best."

His smile turned to a scowl. "I can't win here."

She shrugged. "We can't be wrapped in Bubble Wrap or locked away from danger."

"Too bad." Sam stood on the porch, peering down into her eyes. He brushed a loose strand of her hair back, his touch gentle yet electric. "What brought about the 'understanding' part of your speech?"

·"Avery." Charlene recalled how the teen had stopped Klara in the Tesla with her body. "I worry for her, but I have to bite my tongue."

Sam's expression turned thoughtful. "I'm glad you guys found each other. You're a family. Really cozy, Charlene. You should be proud of what you've created here."

"Thanks. I am. Thank you, for being there." Her voice lowered. "I know that I can always call on you, and that means a lot."

Sam gave her a two-finger salute and a wink, then departed down the stairs. She pulled her gaze from him and hurried inside for a big drink of water to quench her sudden thirst.

After she finished, Charlene rinsed her glass.

Avery studied her closely, wiping her hands on a towel. "I think you should date Sam."

Charlene gave a quick look around, glad that Jack was not in the kitchen, but he was probably in her suite. Or wherever he sometimes went to rest. "I'm not going to date him, or anyone. I have my reasons."

"You used to say it was Jared," Avery said. "Is it still?"

Avery was observant, this young woman she'd allowed into her heart.

"Some of it." Coming to Salem had helped with the healing process so much. Jack's friendship, and Sam's flirtation. Jared was her soul mate. Could there be more than one great love in a person's life?

It seemed almost selfish to even dream of it.

"Are you scared to move on?" The tray of peanut butter cookies in the oven smelled amazing. Avery had the next tray ready to switch as the first cooled.

"No." Charlene put the glass in the dishwasher, answering honestly. "Not scared. It's just that I really like the way things are right now. Who knows what the future will hold?"

"Ask Kass to do a reading for you," Avery suggested.

"I'd rather be surprised," Charlene said. "Now, let me go check on our injured guest."

Avery cleaned up a dab of butter on the counter. "Should I cancel my dinner at Seth's to help here tonight?"

"No, sweetheart—you go and enjoy." Charlene murmured, "I want to hear all about the ghost."

"Okay." Her nose crinkled. "I might be out late. His friends are doing another summer bonfire, and Seth wants to go."

"Sure. Send me a text is all, so I don't worry."

Avery nodded and smiled at her.

Charlene hurried out to Georgio before she started bawling like a baby. How could one person make your heart so darn full? And then Avery was going to college to have her own life, and hopefully, Charlene would still be part of it.

She also understood her mother so much more.

Minnie refilled Georgio's water.

"It's half past one in the afternoon," Charlene said, heading toward the bar in the corner of the room. "Would you like something stronger than water?"

"Now we're talking," Georgio said. "I don't drink alcohol, but do you happen to carry orange soda?"

Charlene nodded. "I do. It's in the pantry, so I'll need to put it over ice for you, is that all right?"

"I told you I was going to love this place," Georgio said to his wife. "That'd be great, Charlene."

Making her guests happy made her so happy too. "Why don't I fix a tray of snacks for you, and you can enjoy it on the widow's walk? The oak tree provides a little shade and there's usually a nice breeze from the ocean."

"That would be wonderful," Maria said. "But too much trouble."

"It's not any trouble," Charlene reassured the woman. "I know you'll love it. It's so relaxing, and you can use the telescope to see the boats on the water. Are the stairs going to be okay?"

"No problem," Maria said, patting her hip. "We play tennis."

"Not well, but we play," Georgio seconded.

Avery helped the couple bring everything up, and then ran the vacuum on both floors. While Minnie did laundry, Charlene went into her suite.

Jack waited for her, relaxed in his armchair, a documentary about herbal medicine on the TV. He paused the show with a snap of his fingers.

"What are you doing?" Charlene asked. He was an avid documentary viewer.

"Brushing up on natural remedies for illness." Jack's turquoise eyes sparkled. She wasn't sure how he managed to make them do that, but she loved that he did it for her. "As you said earlier, you want that certified doctor who will prescribe medicine. I did my part for the pharmaceutical companies. Now I'm learning there is so much more."

"Your quest for knowledge impresses me, Jack."

Jack's image wavered at the compliment. "How is Georgio? His color seemed fine to me."

"I sent the Lopezes up to the widow's walk to relax and still feel like they're on vacation. It amazes me that people like orange soda." She pursed her lips as if sucking a lemon. "I never have, and never will."

"What about cream soda?" Jack asked. "Root beer?"

"Root beer is good, over vanilla ice cream," she conceded. "Why did you agree with Sam about Darren's motivation to murder Elise?"

He gestured to the love seat, so she sat down. Jack emanated cool air from his spectral energy, but in the summer, it was quite nice, and she didn't need the afghan.

"Sam has a point, that's all. It doesn't mean Darren is guilty, but they must not have concrete evidence, or he wouldn't be out of jail," Jack said. "I saw on the news he was released."

"Klara bailed him out." She snuggled back into the cushion. "It seems like last week. You won't believe what has happened since, Jack."

"Start at the beginning, and give me all the details," he said, patting the side of the love seat closest to him. This was what she liked best about their friendship, the easy camaraderie that came with total acceptance of another person. Being one's true self.

"All right," Charlene said. "Avery and I arrived at the station as Klara was leaving in Darren's Tesla. Darren had jogged home so he could burn off some energy after being confined. Avery jumped in front of the car to stop and question her."

Jack disappeared with a *pop* before returning. "Jumped where?"

"You heard right!" Charlene laughed, able to see the humor now that time had passed. "Klara was just pulling out. I think Avery's going to make a terrific cop."

"If I had a heart, it would have stopped," Jack said. "She's obviously fine."

"Avery is completely okay. I asked her not to do it again." Charlene patted her chest. "Anyway, Klara suggested we go bother Patty, so we did, to see if we could help with the funeral since Darren is taking this so hard. Patty asked us to do her bakery deliveries to the businesses because her assistant doesn't drive. And then she wanted us to drop by Darren's to pick up a funeral dress for Elise. Darren wasn't taking her calls."

"Why didn't Patty go over to Darren's herself?" Jack relaxed back into the chair, his fingers on the armrest.

"She's upset about her sister, really devastated, and it was just as well that she didn't go. Darren kind of had a meltdown after being in jail. He says he didn't kill Elise. He still wants to keep the Spellbound open."

"What?"

"Darren is riddled with guilt." Charlene glanced at the television on pause, then at Jack. "He'd had a vasectomy. He refused to have children with Elise, and a family was all she wanted. Well, not all, but it was a big deal to her."

"I only heard a little bit of the conversation you had with Sam," Jack said. "Did Darren tell you why he wanted the vasectomy?"

"He had something genetic he worried he'd pass on to his children. He was kind of vague." Charlene wished she had Silva to pet while they were sitting so quietly, but the cat wasn't around.

"Genetic." Jack narrowed his eyes in thought. "A maternal serum screen is a standard procedure, which would show if the pregnant mother's baby was at risk of neural tube defects, or a chromosomal disorder like Down syndrome."

Science amazed her.

"Then again, not all genetic disorders would be visible from the outside, and he was teased, correct?"

"Yes." Darren was of average height. Muscular build. Dark brown hair and eyes. "Darren looks fine, right?"

"I thought so. Then again, I never studied him like I would a patient. It's different." Jack shrugged.

"I understand the nuance," Charlene said. "Darren feels very guilty over not being honest with Elise, combined with his loss. Klara said he drank a bunch of tequila yesterday and was at it again this morning before Avery and I arrived." He'd probably sobered up while in the cell.

"Sam had a good point." Jack sighed. "It could be that Elise was going to ask for a divorce after she found out about the procedure. Especially if he wouldn't get it reversed."

Could Darren have poisoned his wife? He didn't seem to be about the money. He felt so guilty that he probably would have given her everything she wanted and more. "They were in the office before the premiere arguing loudly about it, according to Seth. But Klara didn't bring the wolfsbane flowers until later."

"The flowers would have had to be dried and powdered to be mixed in with the salt, so I agree it would not have happened from Klara's bouquet." Jack's image went in and out of focus as he lost concentration on maintaining his manifestation.

"Darren said that as well." Charlene spread her arm to the side. "Then why would someone get rid of the flowers? It seems like hiding evidence."

Jack rubbed his jaw. "Maybe the person who removed them fears it will lead to them? What did Darren or Klara say about the bouquet?"

"Klara suggested we talk to Franco, who was acting 'weird' because he was worried about getting fired, just like Matthew," Charlene said. "Seth shared that Elise had threatened Matthew, and Franco figured he was next on the list."

"Well, maybe you should go visit Franco and ask," Jack suggested. "See for yourself if he heard anything unusual. Get his opinion of Darren and Elise and their marriage."

"I'll go tomorrow." Charlene tilted her head toward the computer behind her. "Do you mind working your magic and finding his address for me? Matthew's, too. Their last names are Lordes and Sinchuk . . ."

"Happy to help, Charlene." Jack leaned forward with a charming smile. "Any chance you can invite Darren over so I can examine him?"

"Sure, I'll ask, but I don't know if he will be accepting invites anytime soon. He's broken up."

Charlene sighed. "He wants to open the theater this weekend as normal, but people will come for the wrong reasons."

"Grief affects folks in different ways," Jack said.

"I was in bed for a month after Jared died," she admitted. "It took all I had to get up and shower. Go to work. It was awful."

"I'm sorry, Charlene." Jack fluttered her hair to make her smile. "Things are better here, aren't they?"

"Yes. In great part due to you," she said. "You keep me on my toes."

After a moment of companionable silence, Jack said, "I heard our Avery is having dinner with Seth's family?"

"She's excited about it. I wish I could go too, actually. I'd love to know if I could see their family ghost."

Jack burst out laughing. "It would be strange for Avery to bring her boss along on a dinner date."

"It's tacos, though!" Charlene stood up with a grin. "Just kidding."

"I'm curious, too. Someday, Charlene, we need to find a way for me to leave the property." Jack rose, as well, in a motion that was more immediate.

"And just where would you go?" She raised a brow at him and smiled gently. No matter how hard he willed it, Jack was bound to this site.

"Wherever you went." Jack held up his hands at her mutinous expression. "Fine. Guess we need some boundaries," he said with a chuckle.

"I appreciate it." She looked at her watch. "How did it get to be half-past three? I have work to do!"

Avery knocked on the door that connected Charlene's suite to the kitchen. "Can we talk for a minute?"

"I'll be right there!" Charlene said to Avery. "See you later," she whispered to Jack. "Back to your studies on herbal medicine."

She left her bedroom and joined Avery at the kitchen table.

"Hey," Avery said. "Sorry to interrupt, but Seth just texted that Darren called him into work tomorrow for matinée hours, on a freaking Tuesday!" She crossed her arms, disapproval of this decision clear in each bone of her body. "I disagreed already with the weekend opening, but now? Seth and the others could get hurt if a mob shows up wanting to make sure Darren is behind bars."

"It's no problem, hon. What do you want to do about it?" Charlene propped her elbow on the table, hating to see Avery so upset. "You saw for yourself that Darren's not listening to reason right now."

Avery shifted on the kitchen chair. "You need to talk to him. He can't open the theater."

Charlene held Avery's concerned gaze. "At the end of the day, it's Darren's business to do with as he wishes. Maybe I can remind him of the budget that he and Elise created together." The weekend was prime time for cash to come in, the weekdays not as much. Elise had been very quick to understand profit and loss.

Agitated, Avery rose from the table and packed the cooled peanut butter cookies into a plastic box. "You'll try, though?"

"Yes. Of course." Charlene sighed. Grief and sorrow were mountains to be climbed after you'd already run a marathon and had no strength left. "What does Seth think?"

"He's got a weird feeling about it, so he's still gonna check around for a different job," Avery said. "He liked this because it was weekends only, which would have fit his schedule once college started."

"True." Like Avery, Seth seemed to be on the more mature side of teenager. Maybe being raised by a hardworking single mother had something to do with it.

"Well, whatever he decides will be cool with me. If we stay friends after summer. Who knows?" Avery filled a second plastic tub with the cookies. "I'm looking forward to college myself. Like, dorm decorating?"

Charlene perked up. She'd found out while furnishing the bed-and-breakfast that she very much enjoyed interior design. "I am happy to help."

"Cool." Avery gestured to the hall with a wave of her hand. "You have excellent references for your work. I'd want something more modern, though."

"Smart aleck," Charlene said. She couldn't wait to go shopping. "How are those cookies?"

"Delicious." Avery patted the second tub. "I saved a dozen for your happy hour."

"So thoughtful!"

"All right, I'm outta here. Didn't hear anything from Officer Bernard about the shoes beneath the curtain." Avery put the first box of cookies into a paper bag with a handle. "Honestly, I checked again, and it could be out of focus. It was dark, and I was in a hurry."

Charlene laughed. "It's all right. Maybe you can score a spectral photo at Seth's."

They'd tried to take pictures of Jack, but it hadn't worked. But who knew? She'd learned to keep an open mind.

"Bye!" Avery left with a smile.

Charlene called Darren as she'd told Avery she would and left a message about Elise and profit and loss. Maybe he could honor her by sticking with her plan. He didn't call back, and she hoped it was enough.

At four, she and Minnie had everything set out for her guests. Quesadillas, chips and salsa, and miniature taquitos.

The twins galloped down the stairs, followed by their parents, Bob and Joanie. Everyone had a little bit of a sunburn from being outside on this lovely summer day.

The Lopezes descended at a slower pace from the widow's walk, Georgio earning sympathetic comments on his sling.

Sheila, Cora, and Dustin all sat together on the sofa and had made dinner plans at Sea Level. Dustin suggested a full moon party on Tuesday night to take advantage of the telescope. Charlene couldn't wait to put that idea in motion.

Lastly, Spencer, Natalie, Lara, and Christopher arrived, not sunburned, as they'd spent the day inside the museum.

"And Charlene," Lara said. "We had ice cream, just like you said!"

"The Peabody Essex Museum was wonderful." Natalie offered a juice box to Christopher. "I could spend the whole week there."

"Where's Avery?" Lara asked, tapping the museum sticker on her T-shirt. "I want her to push me on the swing."

"How about tomorrow? She's out with friends tonight," Charlene said.

"I'm her friend!" Lara's lower lip pouted.

Spencer rested his hand on her shoulder. "All right, my dear, may I tempt you with a quesadilla? Or a skinny taco?"

"Or," Charlene said, "how about a peanut butter cookie Avery made herself?"

Lara allowed herself to be pulled out of a bad mood. "Can I have two, please?" she asked sweetly.

"Absolutely." Spencer winked at his wife, acknowledging they'd just averted a crisis.

Charlene poured wine, and Minnie topped off iced teas and lemonades. She put an orange soda in the fridge for Georgio so it would be cold when he was ready.

"So, what are the plans for dinner?" Charlene asked from her position by the bar.

"Turner's Seafood," Maria said. "I'm ready for a whole lobster with all the trimmings. And a side of corn. I'll even wear the bib. I don't care."

"Nor should you—we are on vacation." Georgio flapped his injured arm. "I'll have the scallops tonight. Easier to eat."

"You mean to say that Maria won't crack your lobster for you?" Natalie teased.

"No, ma'am," Georgio said. "When we agreed to come to Salem, it was with the promise of lobster three nights and no sharing. Usually, we do, after forty years together, but my lady loves her lobster."

Maria nodded. "It's not my fault a certain someone got overly enthusiastic about that fish he wanted to catch."

"But it was going to be thiiiiissssss big." Georgio laughed.

"I like that rule." Natalie turned to her husband, then the others, bouncing Christopher on her hip. "That was one of the reasons we wanted to be in Salem as well. We've heard such amazing things about the lobster."

Charlene raised her hand in a sacred pledge of a hostess to her guests. "I have eaten at every restaurant that sells lobster in Salem, and I promise you, my friends, you can't go wrong at any of them."

# CHAPTER 11

That evening after the guests were all out to dinner, Charlene poured a glass of wine and took her phone to the back porch to watch Silva chase butterflies while she called Patty to make sure she'd gotten the outfit for Elise.

"Thank you for dropping it off," Patty said, sounding exhausted. "It's not what I would have chosen for my sister's final foray into the afterlife. Something a little more demure would be more appropriate to meet God, don't you think?"

Charlene didn't want to argue with the poor woman but actually thought Darren had put a lot of consideration into the clothing. "The pink is very pretty," she temporized.

"Our father would not have approved." Patty heaved a sigh. "But he's gone. Mom's gone. And I am left all alone, just as I always feared."

"Were your parents strict, growing up?" Charlene sipped her wine and set it on the porch step, the phone on speaker in her palm.

"John Wagner's belief system could have been genetically coded from our ancestors on the *Mayflower*. The Wagners have been Protestant for generations. My grandpa could laugh and joke, but my dad had *no* sense of humor. No lightheartedness."

Charlene had gotten a glimpse of that from the picture on the wall. "What was your mother like?"

"Mom was Christian and went along with Dad's ways of discipline. If the meek do inherit the earth, she'll be first in line," Patty said wryly. "We weren't beaten, but Dad could be cruel in other ways. A spanking would have been easier on us."

"I'm sorry to hear that." Could that be the reason for the invisible scars Darren had sensed in his wife?

"I'm afraid my outburst earlier left you with the impression that my sister was all about the money," Patty paused, then said, "but in her deepest heart she wanted to raise a family so she could do things better."

Charlene and Patty shared a moment of silence, each lost in thought. Charlene wondered if it was an unbreakable cycle of children wanting to do things the opposite of their parents. How Mother Nature had it planned.

"Patty, do you need us to help with your deliveries tomorrow?" Charlene couldn't take away Patty's pain, but she didn't mind assisting in other places. She and Avery had gotten the system down.

"No, thanks," Patty said, the gratitude in her voice clear. "What you did today was so kind. Each day will get better. I don't know what to do about the pretzels . . . the movie theater. Darren left a crazy message about opening on Friday. I hope he quits and that he and Klara go back to Saint Mary's."

"I don't think so. Just so you know, Klara has a partner she loves. Darren plans on making the theater a success so Elise would be proud of their effort not going to waste."

Patty's breath exploded through the phone. "Darren is an *idiot* to think people will want to come to a movie theater where someone was poisoned eating the popcorn—and he's under the microscope."

Well, that was certainly a factor, Charlene thought, sipping her wine. Silva gave up catching a yellowtail butterfly to doze in a ray of sunshine through the tree leaves. "He said they put all their money into the house and theater."

"Not all," Patty said with confidence. "It's why I'm surprised Darren is even considering keeping it open. He's a smart businessman. He's got a couple hundred thousand in the bank to ride for the first year. No matter what else was going on, Elise was impressed by his acumen. She told me she knew she never had to worry about not having enough money."

Charlene thought of the closet full of clothes Elise had never worn. "Was that a problem for her?"

"Our mom didn't work, well, she did at the bakery, but it wasn't as if she had a salary. Dad was strict and didn't think we needed extras, especially not makeup or designer clothes, like this Dior outfit Darren packed for her." Patty seemed judgmental.

"If she wanted those things, maybe it was a struggle for her not to have them." There was nothing the matter with beautiful things so long as they weren't an obsession. Or as long as you didn't have to steal to get them.

Patty sighed. "I hear your pity for her. Well, Elise was sly. She got very good at stealing what she wanted and hiding it so that our parents didn't see it. Started with lip gloss and went up to her prom dress for high school. Don't feel so sorry for little Elise Wagner."

If Elise had that much baggage, what did Patty carry around? How had she handled the strict upbringing?

By *not* wanting . . .

"I should go," Patty said. "I'll call as soon as I have funeral information. I'm torn about going to buy a plain black dress. I'm so worried about what our dad will say in heaven. More so than I am about God. God actually forgives."

Patty hung up. Charlene finished her wine in a contemplative mood. Elise, a thief, or Elise, a pitiable woman who wasn't allowed pretty things as a child? Like the wolfman, struggling with his dualistic nature. Elise and Darren had that in common.


The next morning, Avery gushed about Seth and his mom and his brother over bagels and cream cheese.

"They have a nice house, you know, regular—three bedrooms, two bathrooms. Big backyard. Attached garage. I wouldn't mind a house like that one day," Avery said. "When I'm working as a police officer at Salem PD."

Charlene laughed at her enthusiasm. Sheila, Cora, and Dustin were at the other end of the table with fruit and muffins, talking amongst themselves. She hoped Dustin would still want to host the full moon party tonight.

The Lopezes had taken food upstairs, and the other two families hadn't come down yet. So far as she knew, everyone had a very packed Tuesday.

"I could afford it, I think." Avery dabbed her mouth with a cloth napkin. "And have a whole room for my guitars. Can you imagine? A studio of my own! And a dog. I might get a dog. Or a cat. Or both."

"That sounds wonderful." Charlene took a sip of her creamy coffee. "But there's no rush to leave here." Like, ever, if she didn't want to. Was that too much to ask? *Do not turn into Brenda Woodbridge.*

"Whew." Avery swiped the back of her hand across her forehead. "My dream home might take a few years after college to afford."

"I will help however I can." Charlene rested her forearm on the table. "I bet you can take a finance class as an elective to learn how to be financially prepared for your goals."

"That's a great idea," Avery said, drinking orange juice.

Charlene glanced at the other end of the table to make sure the guests were still occupied, then asked, "What about the ghost? Did you see the little girl?"

"Don't tell me you believe in ghosts, Charlene," Avery said, her eyes twinkling.

"What happened to having an open mind?" Charlene stayed in place but raised her brow.

"Well." Avery swallowed a bite of her bagel. "There was a cold spot in the kitchen that Dani, his mom, said was the little girl ghostie. I guess Stephen, his younger brother, can see her sometimes too."

"But Seth can't?"

"No. He feels the energy, though." Avery shrugged and straightened. "It's pretty cool that they all just accept it. Maybe it's a Gamble family thing. It's hard for me, because as a police officer, I will be debunking ghosts and paranormal stuff, as part of the job."

Jack appeared, standing behind the guests with his arms crossed. His dark hair was styled perfectly, his blue shirt the color of his eyes. He *tsk*ed. "Just like Sam."

Charlene drank her coffee, saving her last bite of bagel and cream cheese to be enjoyed last. "Sam is the same way, but I think other officers, like Officer Bernard, might be more open-minded to things of a different dimension. He seemed that way at the theater."

"You're right. And he was cool about the photo." Avery finished her juice, then placed her napkin over her plate. "Well, I don't have to decide anything now, just experience the world so I can bring my own unique outlook to the force."

"The force? She sounds like a *Star Wars* character," Jack said with a quirk of his mouth.

"Whatever you want to do, you will achieve." Charlene knew that from personal experience.

"How can I not, with support like you've given me?" Avery blew Charlene a kiss.

Just then Lara Cohen raced into the dining room with a grin. "Avery! You're here! I have *so much* to tell you."

Avery laughed and scooted her chair so there was space for the little girl to sit next to her. The dining room table easily sat twelve, and Charlene had one end, and Dustin the other with lots of seating in between. Today was Minnie's day off, so Charlene and Avery would split duties, though it would be a light day.

"Good morning, Lara. How did you sleep?" Avery asked.

The rest of the Cohens arrived, Natalie and Christopher on one side, Spencer on the other. Charlene had a booster seat for the chair that she could buckle in, and that's what Christopher sat on. His auburn curls were so precious it was hard not to tug them.

"We went to the museum and had ice cream and I got a special sticker, and my favorite thing was the scary, old witches." Lara curled her fingers like claws.

Spencer went to the sideboard and filled plates for Natalie and Christopher first, bagels and fruit, and a softer banana muffin for Christopher.

"Here you are, Natalie." Spencer placed it before her. "Coffee?"

"You know it, please and thank you," Natalie said.

"Pwease and t'ank you," Christopher repeated.

Lara, the helpful big sister, shook her finger at her brother, "*Pl*ease and *th*ank you."

Christopher ignored her and reached for his muffin.

"Lara, muffin or bagel, sweetheart?" Spencer asked.

"Bagel, bagel, bagel, please. Can I put the cream cheese on myself? With the knife!" Lara squirmed. "Can I?"

"If you sit quietly," Spencer said.

Lara froze in place. Spencer got his daughter situated, then brought a coffee for Natalie, and another cup of joe for himself, as well as his own bagel and fruit, sitting down at last.

Charlene was exhausted just watching him.

"This breakfast is just right," Natalie told Charlene. "It's fuel for the day and really helps with the budget. Thank you."

"You're welcome," Charlene said.

"Saturdays and Sundays we have huge breakfasts," Avery said. "Eggs, bacon, sausage. Quiche."

"What's quiche?" Lara asked, intrigued by the new word.

She was a smarty, and it was great that her parents encouraged her questions. It was the age of questions. By thirteen, from what Charlene had witnessed, kids knew everything.

"A savory pie filled with egg, meat, and cheese," Avery said.

"It can be hot or cold," Natalie added. "It's popular at brunches. I bet you'd like it, Lara. You are an adventurous eater."

"That's lucky for you," Charlene said to Natalie. "I've had guests whose kids were so picky that it was harder for them to travel unless they had the right food."

"It's true," Avery said. "I like everything."

"Me too!" Lara said. "It's why we're best friends."

Next to arrive for breakfast were the Welches, Bob and Joanie, and the twins, Braydon and Sheridon.

"Good morning, everyone," Joanie called.

The guests all returned her cheery greeting. Joanie had the personality Charlene appreciated best, in that she could talk to anyone and make friends. She was interested and sunny without being fake.

"Hi!" Charlene got up to check the coffee carafe. She shook it and realized it needed a refill.

"Is there enough for a cup before you take that?" Bob asked with pleading eyes. His wild beard had been combed this morning and shone with oil.

"Of course. Joanie?" Charlene poured two cups, then topped off the Cohens. Cora, Dustin, and Sheila shook their heads.

"This is amazing," Sheila said. "Just perfect. I thought I'd spend my days quietly, but I'm having the best time."

"And tonight," Cora said, reminding Charlene, "Dustin is happy to talk about the full moon and constellations."

Dustin quickly swallowed his coffee after being put on the spot. "I am."

"Can't wait! It will be my first full moon party. I'll be right back." Charlene quickly filled the carafe from the pot in the kitchen.

Jack was there waiting. "I have the addresses for you, for Franco and Matthew."

She nodded.

"Are you sure you should go today since Minnie isn't here?" Jack watched her closely.

"Later," she mouthed, hurrying back into the dining room.

"Can't blame me for trying," Jack said with a laugh from the threshold.

Silva meowed by the dining room door as if Charlene had forgotten her. "Your dish is full, Silva."

"That's boring dry food," Avery said, smiling at Lara. "Silva also likes quiche."

"And anything else that isn't kibble." Charlene put the carafe on the sideboard. "So, where are you all going today?" She sat at her place at the head of the table and ate her last bite of bagel.

"We are doing the harbor tour," Dustin said. "And we've talked Sheila into joining us."

"I hope to see some dolphins." Sheila wound the tip of her long braid around her finger. "They're supposed to bring good luck."

"I love dolphins," Charlene said. "I've seen them in Salem Harbor. There is something so special about them in the wild."

"I want to do that too," Lara said to her dad.

"We're doing the witch tours today, but maybe Friday, pumpkin," Natalie said. "You wanted to see the secret staircase at the House of the Seven Gables, didn't you?"

Lara's eyes widened. "Yes!"

"Salem has so much to offer for all age groups," Charlene said. "And the festival this week means there are more kiosks and fun things by the wharf."

"Have you been to the Seafarer's Festival before?" Joanie asked. She had two muffins and an apple on her plate. Braydon was the twin with the shorter-by-an inch brown hair, and Sheridon had a smile that quirked to the right.

"I haven't," Charlene admitted. "I didn't even know they had a fishing competition."

"I'll go with you," Avery offered. "Maybe tomorrow, since Minnie will be here. It's just a blast to walk around. I think Poseidon or Neptune has a booth, if you want a picture with the Sea Lord."

"All right." Charlene would take lots of photos and add them to her website. "Sounds fun. And tonight, we will have a full moon party on the widow's walk."

"I've never been to one before," Natalie said. "Is there a special dress code?"

Charlene laughed. "Definitely casual!"

Wednesdays could be busy if they had families leaving, but her guests, except for Sheila in a single, had all booked suites for a full week. She'd run a special that if they paid for five days, she'd toss in the sixth for free, which meant that most booked for seven.

"I'm all done, Daddy," Lara said. "Can Avery push me on the swing?"

Spencer looked at Avery, his breakfast not quite finished.

"I'd be happy to, Spencer." Avery stacked her dish with Lara's. "Come on, my new friend. Let's soar."

The guests were out the door by ten to their various activities. Charlene and Avery finished the dishes, then Avery vacuumed, and Charlene went into her suite to do paperwork. That is, to talk to Jack.

"You are never happier than when we have a full house," Jack remarked.

"I know." Charlene sat at the narrow desk against the wall and turned on the laptop to check her email. "Here's a couple asking about Christmas."

"It's a beautiful time of year in Salem," Jack said.

"I like it too." And hopefully, this holiday season wouldn't hold the tragedy of a past Christmas, when the manager of her favorite Italian restaurant had been killed in a hit and run while her parents were in town.

No regrets, though, as that was the event where she'd first met Avery.

Jack crossed the room to stand by her chair. "I've pulled up the addresses for Franco and Matthew and sent them to your cell phone, so you don't have to write them down."

"Thank you, Jack." She smiled at her handsome assistant, who was so much more.

"What is the plan today, Ms. Morris?" Jack floated her cell phone to her from where it was charging and tucked it in the side pocket of her purse, setting it on the coffee table. "Besides the full moon party, which is genius. I can't wait to learn more about the constellations from Dustin, an actual astronomer."

Charlene nodded, very pleased. "Don't let me forget to take tons of pictures." It could be a new monthly celebration.

"But first?" Jack prompted.

"The guests are all out, and Avery is fine at the bed-and-breakfast. I'll run to Franco's before he goes into work at the theater to ask about the flowers." She tapped her fingers on the desk. "Then, if I have time, Matthew's."

"What will you ask him about?" Jack relaxed his posture, arms crossed loosely at his waist.

"The same—the missing flowers, and if he felt like he was in danger of losing his job. Klara said Franco was worried too. What if either of them thought to keep their paycheck by killing Elise?" Charlene raised her brow at Jack.

"It's as plausible as Darren poisoning the love of his life. Or Klara." Jack spread his arms to the sides. "What do you want to prove?"

Charlene reached for the pen by her landline. "Darren's innocence. He never called me back, or Seth, so I'm assuming he's going to be at the theater today. Not a good idea at all."

"True."

"I'm good at conversation, Jack." She doodled a pentagram. Not only was it a sign for the werewolf, it was also used in witchcraft. "I need to speak with Franco, face to face. He was friends with Darren and might shed some light on Elise and Darren's relationship."

"Be careful, Charlene. Bring your pepper spray."

Charlene checked her watch. Half past ten. "I will." She went to her closet and grabbed the pepper spray, then put it in her purse. She had to discover more about the Shultzes. Hopefully, knowledge would lead to the true killer.

Could it be Franco? He had his quirks.

"What are you going to do about the theater, since Sam asked you to stay away?" Jack air-brushed her hair off her forehead.

"I never promised. I said I'd try," Charlene said with a clear conscience. "Sometimes Sam can be too protective."

She didn't dwell on the fact that there were times she liked it.

# CHAPTER 12

Charlene shouldered her purse and walked through the kitchen toward the foyer, passing Avery, who whistled as she dusted the books on the shelf built into the wall. The bed-and-breakfast had so much character, from the wine cellar to the hidden nooks, to the widow's walk, and this gem was just one of a hundred reasons it was unique.

Avery straightened, feather duster in hand, as Charlene went by. She was very cute in her short coveralls, freckles, and ponytail. "Hey! Where are you going?"

Charlene turned, her back to the front door. "Franco's, to ask him what happened to the flowers."

"I want to go too!" Avery said.

Recalling Sam's reaction to her bringing Avery to Darren's, she said, "You'll help me best by being at the bed-and-breakfast and holding down the fort with Minnie not here today."

"I'd rather go with you!"

Avery resembled Lara Cohen at the moment, and Charlene hid a smile. "I won't be gone long, and I'll bring home lunch if you'd like. Your choice."

Crossing her arms, Avery sighed. "I don't care about lunch. Just make sure your ringer is on, all right? I worry about you."

"That is sweet, and not necessary. Franco is so skinny I could take him out with one finger push." Charlene demonstrated this by flexing her index finger.

Avery crossed her arms, the feather duster tickling her nose, and she put it on the shelf. "Don't be too long, and text me right after you meet with him. Seth is freaked out about going to work today."

"Darren never returned my call. I'm sorry, hon."

"I wonder if Patty will bring the soft-baked pretzels? The specialty salts should be off the menu, maybe forever."

"Patty hopes Darren will keep the theater closed for a while," Charlene said. "I spoke to her last night, and she was very grateful that we'd helped yesterday, but she was good for this morning."

"Okay." Avery walked with her to the porch, where Silva sprawled on the railing, too lazy to chase a spider within her paw's reach.

Charlene couldn't resist a tug of Avery's ponytail. "Why don't you grab a book and relax on the porch?"

"Nah. If I'm not cleaning, I feel like I should be studying." Avery stuck both hands in her pockets. "It's weird to relax."

"You've earned it, sweetie. Enjoy the break before school begins." Charlene remembered the whirlwind of starting college and how exciting it had been, but it was overwhelming too. "Maybe scroll social media for dorm-decorating ideas."

Avery's eyes lit up. "Sounds good. I'll get some iced tea and wait for your call. I'll be on pins and needles until I hear back from you."

Charlene waved at Avery and got in the car, pulling up the address Jack had sent her and putting it into the GPS.

According to the map, she was only fifteen minutes away. Franco didn't live near the water, but toward Boston. She listened to the radio and soon arrived at a colonial-style town house. So many older buildings were split into condos as the price to maintain a large house was astronomical.

Franco lived on the second floor, which she could reach via an outside staircase. It was eleven when she knocked on his wood door. If his hours were like Seth's, he needed to be at work at two.

This was the opposite of Darren's shiny and new, modern place.

Franco's was run-down and worn with plywood used as patches on the porch. She heard someone shuffling from behind the door, then it was opened a few inches, locked with a chain.

"Hello?"

"Franco?" She stepped closer to the door so he could see her better. "Hi, it's me, Charlene Morris."

"Who?"

This was the greeting she was used to getting when she arrived uninvited. Bless Patty Wagner for being friendly.

"Charlene Morris. We met at Spellbound Movie

Theater? I'm a friend of the Shultzes and helped with the new business plans."

"Oh." The door didn't budge. "What do you want?"

"I just had a few questions," she said. "Can I take you out for coffee? My treat."

Franco realized she wasn't going away. He sighed. "Hang on."

The door closed. She texted Avery that she was ready to go in and would text when the visit was over.

Five long minutes later, Franco opened the door. Charlene had braced herself for squalor, but the interior was clean. Dated, but on purpose, at least as far as the movie posters on the wall went. Hardwood floors were covered in throw rugs. A sofa and coffee table were to the left and the kitchen to the right.

A corridor lit with red light, like the movie theaters, probably led to a bedroom and bathroom. Pleasant and homey.

"Come on in. I have a Keurig if you'd like coffee. I don't often entertain visitors," Franco said. "I had to pick up a little."

"I appreciate you letting me drop by unannounced."

His groomed brow lifted at her remark. He was thin but attractive with brilliant green eyes. Family pictures on the wall showed two plump boys and two obese parents.

Verdant houseplants were on a windowsill to catch the light. A lizard was in a cage sunning beneath a lamp. Crickets chirped, waiting to be eaten.

"That's Larry Talbot," Franco said, showing a

dimple. "From the movie? I used to have a Gwen, but she died."

Gwen had been the love interest for Larry in *The Wolf Man.* Charlene had no idea what the life span of a lizard was. Until Silva, she hadn't been a pet person. "I can't believe how many posters you have in here."

Franco smiled modestly. "I've been collecting a long time. I lived in the movie theaters and would ask for the posters when the run was over. Coffee? Tea?"

"Tea would be great—anything herbal is fine."

He stepped into the kitchen and waved her to the couch. "Have a seat. This will just take a minute."

His manner seemed welcoming. On a shelf by the television was a framed diploma. It was a master's degree in film.

Interesting. "I didn't realize you needed a degree to work at the movies," she said, sitting on the sofa. The lizard flicked his tongue toward her. She shivered.

Franco returned with two mugs. "Here you go. Lemon zest for you, and Earl Grey for me. My parents gifted me the Keurig, and I never thought I'd use it. I can't live without it."

"I love mine too." Charlene accepted the hot mug and put it on the table before her. "Instant gratification."

Franco snapped skinny fingers. "That's it. That's why." He sat on the opposite end of the couch from her. Knobby knees rounded his jeans. He wore an open flannel over a T-shirt as if cold—he had zero body fat. The pentagram pendant was visible today.

"Thank you," she said.

"I need to run to the grocery store after work today. I'm afraid the cupboards are bare and I'm down to my worst flavors of soups." He inclined forward to share. "I don't know why I buy things I don't really like, except they're on sale. French onion." His nose flared. "Split pea."

Charlene took another look around, wondering if he was poor. Could she help? Drop off groceries? Anonymously, of course.

"Before you say anything you might regret, I'll admit to you that I'm just lazy," Franco said with a wry laugh. "I don't know if I should be insulted or amused, Charlene."

Her cheeks flushed. "I have a curious nature," she said. "I don't mean to be rude."

"It's fine." Franco gestured to the pictures of his family. "That's me and my brother, Mom and Dad. They both died of heart disease. My brother is a diabetic. I decided I wouldn't let food be a priority. So, I eat when I need to and don't worry about it."

Was that healthy? She'd have to ask Jack if there was anything they could do. "Again, I apologize. It's not my business."

"True." Franco tapped his fingernails to his mug. She was reminded of a praying mantis.

He regarded her expectantly, and she pulled her thoughts away from buying Franco a grilled chicken sandwich on whole-wheat bread.

"Why are you here?" Franco asked bluntly. "I assume it has to do with Elise's death."

"Yes! I wanted to ask you two things—and forgive me if this is prying, but I'm just trying to understand what happened. The Elise I knew wasn't like how others saw her."

"You mean to say that she was nice to you and not a be-yatch?" Franco watched her from over the rim of his mug. "You must have met her exacting standards."

"That's a little harsh," Charlene said. "Klara mentioned you might've been worried about getting fired."

"Klara is a gossip." Franco sipped his Earl Grey. "That's the thing with her."

The sales rep did seem to have the lowdown on everyone and didn't mind sharing. "Was she right?"

"Yeah. Unfortunately. I heard how Elise tore into Matthew about the freaking office door not being closed. I knew if anything went wrong, she'd clean house. She made fun of me and Darren for knowing the lines to the movies by heart." Franco shook his head. "I don't think she liked Darren having any other friends."

"Who was your boss? Darren, or Elise?"

"Well, Darren hired me. He said we could get paid weekly and we worked for two weeks getting the theater ready. That was nice. He signed the checks."

"How did you get hired?"

"Matthew recommended me," Franco said. His gaze was clear and not evasive. "He was the manager for the last two businesses in that space, one of which was a movie theater for several years. I'm thirty-eight, had a late start from college but had my master's in film by thirty. Like Darren and Matthew, I love the dark atmosphere of the movies."

Charlene nodded. "I didn't even realize it was a degree. I graduated in marketing," she said. "Chicago."

"Windy City," Franco said. "Home of deep-dish pizza."

"I am a fan," she said. "But I like New York style too. Anything with cheese, really."

"Pizza is not a food I'll eat these days." Franco sounded sad. "I used to love it as a child. Now I want to be healthy."

"Moderation is key," Charlene said softly.

"Problem is, I am still that fat kid who, if I sat down for a slice of pizza, I'd eat the whole thing, and heaven help you if you got in my way." Franco slanted his head toward the photos on the wall.

His laugh held pain.

Charlene didn't join in. "That's why you went to the movies?"

"To hide from bullies. Me and Darren have that in common. I don't think Elise liked that he might not be perfect." Franco shrugged. "Well, *perfect* isn't the right word. He might be defective in some way. Girls like that home in on a man's weakness."

She wondered if Franco knew about Darren's childhood spent in the orphanage. One way to find out—keep talking. "That seems critical."

Franco touched the pentagram pendant. "Nobody else is going to understand getting the crap kicked out of you just for being who you are like another kid who had the crap beaten out of him for being different. Elise was all about the shine. It would be too big of a risk for Darren to show her his underbelly."

"Do you know what his *difference* is?" Whatever it

was had prevented Darren from ever wanting his own children.

"No. I heard about the fight in the office from Matthew, where she wanted kids and he told her no. He'd had a certain"—Franco crossed his legs—"surgery and wouldn't get it fixed."

"Darren never said why?" Plenty of secrets at Spellbound Movie Theater.

Franco sighed softly. "I didn't push. I'm just glad he's given me a job. I have a skill in reel film when everything is digital now."

That would be a problem. "How long were you out of work?"

"The building was empty for a few years. I play online poker but mostly live off my parents' inheritance." Franco sipped his tea. "As you can guess, it wasn't lavish, but I get by."

"You have a comfortable home." Charlene meant her words. "It's nice that you don't worry about not having shelter."

"I agree. My brother and his fat wife bought a boat. A boat." Franco glanced at the pictures on the wall with dismay. "To each their own."

Charlene reached for her mug. "Hey . . . Klara suggested you might know what happened to the wolfsbane flowers?"

"Weren't they pretty? Elise was sure wigged out, wasn't she?" Franco grinned, then clamped his lips closed as he realized it was probably not an appropriate response now that she was dead. "You saw for yourself how she acted."

"It did seem like an overreaction, but then again, she *was* poisoned." Charlene tilted her head.

Franco's eyes widened. "With the flowers?"

"The police are looking for the bouquet to rule things out," Charlene said. "Wolfsbane is also known as aconitine."

Franco wouldn't meet her gaze. "I'm familiar. It's used for anxiety or fever. It's funny how in nature that what is poison can also cure. I use herbal remedies rather than over-the-counter stuff."

"Why is that?" Charlene asked.

"I think it's healthier. Even vitamins are loaded with sugar. People think they're being healthy by popping their gummy once a day, but not really, you know?"

"You have a good point," Charlene said. "Do you currently use aconitine for anything?"

"No! No." Franco denied it, but she detected a tiny bit of fear. She'd have to ask Jack about common uses since he'd watched that documentary on herbal medicine. "Everybody takes something, Charlene. What's in your medicine cabinet?"

She laughed at his pointed question. "Those sugar-filled daily vitamins."

Franco shrugged as if to say, *See?*

"So," Charlene said, "you were hired on by Darren, through Matthew. You were afraid Elise was going to fire him, and then you."

Franco cupped his tea, his foot jiggling with nerves. "Yes, I suppose so. Geez, it doesn't matter now, does it? I can't imagine Darren will keep the movie theater going. How could he? Matthew thinks the building is haunted." He shook his head. "Hopefully ghost Elise will be nicer than alive Elise."

Charlene wondered if all ghosts changed in the afterlife, as Jack had done. "Do you believe in ghosts?"

"Of course, I do. I live in Salem." Franco shuddered on the couch. "But I am not afraid of the dead, Charlene."

"Oh?" She placed her tea on the table.

"No. It's living people who are jerks—trust me on that one." He peered into his tea mug, and she thought of Kass, who also claimed to see ghosts.

Charlene could see Kass and Franco being friends. "If you like custom tea, you should check out my friend's store at the pedestrian mall. Fortune's Tea Shoppe. You can make your own or get a reading from your tea leaves."

Franco brightened. "How interesting. I didn't think you would be into the paranormal. You seem a little straitlaced, if you don't mind my saying so."

"No." Charlene shrugged, guilty. "I'm from the Midwest, and Salem was culture shock. Since moving here, I've learned to enjoy the differences in people."

Franco nodded with approval.

Charlene decided to press ahead and risk alienating Franco, who was adept at avoiding a direct answer. "When I left that evening, I looked into the office. The door was open."

"Oh?" Franco wouldn't meet her eyes, again. "Matthew or Darren must not have locked it on their way out."

"I bet Matthew would make sure it was locked after Elise yelled at him the way she did," Charlene said. "Darren said he did lock it, on his way out."

Franco strummed his fingers against his mug.

"So, I went to shut the door and noticed the bouquet was gone. The wolfsbane you'd put in there to keep the peace."

After a moment, Franco asked in a rush, "Was it

wolfsbane that killed Elise? I've been so afraid it
will come back to those dang flowers." He placed
the mug on the table, brows drawn. "I was only trying to help."

He did know about the bouquet! *Thank you,
Klara.* "What did you do with them?"

Franco snuck a furtive glance at her before ex-
amining his thumbnail. "I threw them away in the
Dumpster behind the theater in the alley. I didn't
want them around, and I worried it would cause
another argument between Elise and Darren.
Trash pickup was this morning. The wolfsbane is
long gone."

"There was aconitine in the roasted garlic seasoned salt," she said, dismay in her veins. It didn't
matter, really, because the flowers were a dead end.
Not only had they been trashed, but they hadn't
been what had poisoned Elise.

"I didn't do it on purpose." Franco raised his
chin defensively. "I certainly didn't poison Elise."

Charlene realized he was mentally retreating
and lifted a palm. "I was just curious about what
happened to the flowers, that's all."

Franco settled down. "I would never harm a
soul. I have a no-violence policy in my daily life
after how I grew up. Other than fiction, I like stories that show the underdog overcoming all odds.
You just can't do it as well in color as you can in
black and white. That is the tragedy of *The Wolf
Man*, I think. You don't see his comeback. But Darren is right—the first movie sets up the hero's journey for the franchise."

Charlene sipped her tea, which had cooled con-
siderably. Franco was intelligent. His life was the

movies. Despite his words, would he want to protect what he'd found at the theater? Not just a job,
but a friend?

"Darren will need his friends in the upcoming
days and weeks. I've lost a spouse, and it's something that takes time to heal from, though you
never really do." She placed her hand to her heart.

Franco studied her with empathetic green eyes.
"I'm sorry to hear that."

"It's been over three years now," Charlene said.
"It's more manageable, but the emotions have
been brought to the fore these days because of
what's happened to Darren. I knew them as a couple. What can you tell me about their relationship?"

"Over the last two weeks, Darren and I just
clicked. Elise was in the office more while Matthew, Darren, and I hung posters and chose the
movies. We watched them from the projector
booth many times as we worked." A small smile
hovered over Franco's mouth. She got the impression he didn't have many friends outside of work.
"I didn't see them interact much together."

The movies constantly running would have kept
the lines fresh in their minds and probably drove
Elise crazy. "Because of the argument before Elise
passed, Darren is feeling all kinds of guilt. I hope
you can be there for him, as his friend."

"The police are trying to say he did it. I don't
think he did," Franco said loyally. "For the same
reason that I wouldn't hurt someone. We know
how much it sucks to be on the receiving end of a
fist, or worse. Being different makes you a target."
He shifted on the sofa. "Unless you're beautiful,

like Elise, then the rules of the script change."

Franco and Darren's lives were both all about the movies.

Charlene finished her tea. "I suppose that what was so terrible as a child for him doesn't matter anymore, especially with Elise gone." She met his gaze. "You hid because of your weight. Do you know why Darren might have hidden from bullies? Could it be related to who killed Elise?"

Franco abruptly stood and checked the time on his phone. "Have to get ready for work. Darren sent a text to dress in comfortable clothes, so I guess we're going to do some cleanup."

That was better than opening to the public. "I'm glad he changed his mind." Franco was done talking, and she hadn't learned if he knew about the orphanage. Charlene started to take her mug to the sink, but Franco gestured for her to leave it on the table.

"I don't mind," she said.

"I'll do it. It's no bother."

Franco walked Charlene to the door, peering into her eyes. He had three inches on her. "If I had to make an educated guess, I'd bet it had something to do with his time spent working in a circus."

With that, Franco nudged her to the outside stoop, closed the door, and locked it.

Charlene's mouth gaped and she snapped it closed. *Circus?*

"Franco!"

He didn't answer the door, no matter how loud she knocked.

# CHAPTER 13

Charlene called Avery on her Bluetooth as she headed away from Franco's house. She couldn't believe Franco had teased her like that before shutting her out. The man had learned all about how to end a scene while earning his diploma.

If Franco didn't have a job at the movie theater, what else could he do? Or did he make enough money playing poker so that Spellbound Movie Theater would be a social outlet more than money?

"Hello?" Avery answered on the second ring. "How did it go? I was starting to get worried it had been so long."

"Franco was a wonderful host and offered me tea, even though I was pushy." Charlene drove toward Salem at about five miles over the speed limit.

"You?" Avery said as if shocked.

Charlene ignored Avery's sarcastic reply and checked her mirrors before switching lanes, then raised her foot off the gas pedal to keep from

going close to ten miles an hour over. It was her
weakness to speed. She wanted to be at her desti-
nation already and would welcome the invention
of teleportation, in real life, with all her heart.

"Be nice."

"Just kidding!" Avery giggled. "Did you find out
what happened with the wolfsbane flowers?"

"I did—Franco tossed them out, thinking to
help his pal Darren avoid an argument with Elise."
The pair had let their true colors shine at the theater, or maybe the stress from the launch had
stripped the nccd to be polite.

"Oh, no. Where are they?" Avery asked. "Can we
tell Sam and get them back?"

"The Dumpster has already been emptied." Charlene reached for her sunglasscs in the console and
put them on. "The flowers are a non-issue."

"Well," Avery said, "did you find out about his
relationship with Darren?"

"They were friends." Charlene smacked the
steering wheel. "You will never believe this—Darren was in the circus!"

"No way," Avery said. "Wow. What do you think
he was? A trapeze artist? A lion tamer? It had to be
something cool."

Hmm. Darren as a lion tamer? Maybe. He had a
thick body, muscular. "Maybe Seth knows? Franco
didn't say." She'd keep her humiliating exit to herself. Nobody needed to know that Franco had
tweaked her good.

"I'll text him. Are you on your way?"

"Yes. I have just enough time to go to Matthew's
before his shift starts at two. Darren is just having

them do cleanup today, thank goodness." Jack had sent her both Franco and Matthew's addresses to her phone, so she would just need to pull it up.

"Seth told me! I'm glad. So, why go to Matthew's?" Avery sounded exasperated.

"I want to get his take on the Shultzes' marriage. Franco said he didn't really see Elise and Darren interact very much. She was in the office, while they were getting the place ready. Also, to see if he felt like he was in danger of getting fired." Charlene heard her defensive tone and took a breath.

"We know he was because Elise shouted it out," Avery said. "Why don't you come home, and I'll make us chef salads."

Charlene sensed more to that request than hunger. It was Avery's summer vacation before college. "Are you bored? I thought you were going to hunt for dorm-decorating ideas."

"I did that already. It was nice on the porch and all, but it's a beautiful summer day. I want to do stuff."

Charlene thought of the tasks at the bed-and-breakfast and figured it all could wait. "I understand. Why don't you get ready, and I'll pick you up? We'll go to lunch down at the wharf and say hi to Sharon at Cod and Capers. Then, go shopping!" She could pick up a few supplies for the full moon party tonight on the widow's walk.

"Yes!" Avery ended the call after a quick goodbye.

Matthew's house would be a little bit of a stretch anyway, and this was time spent with Avery for fun and shopping before she went to college. When

Charlene arrived a few minutes later, however, Sam's SUV was in the driveway, to the far right by Avery's car, leaving her room.

Uh-oh. What could be wrong?

Charlene rushed inside. Jack was by the fireplace while Avery and Sam talked with Silva, who was between them on the brocade sofa.

"Hey!" Charlene said, her tone breathless from her rush. "Having fun without me?"

Sam stood and brushed cat hair from his hands to his jeans. Oh, she loved his jeans. He wore a dark-brown Henley rolled at the wrists to reveal a leather watch and brown beads on a bracelet.

Jack waved at her. "Hello, Charlene. Can't wait to hear how the visit with Franco went. I found out some interesting things while you were gone."

She turned her shoulder to Jack, who simply shimmered in front of her on the other side of the couch, not to be ignored.

"Hi, Charlene," Sam said. "Do you have a minute to talk?"

"Sure." She noticed Avery's disappointed face. "If it's about the Shultzes, I think Avery should hear too. She was there when it happened and called for help. And she wants to be a police officer someday."

Avery nodded with enthusiasm. "I do."

Sam smoothed his mustache in deliberation, but at last agreed. "Okay. We have news from the forensic team."

Charlene leaned toward Sam. What could it be?

Avery waited patiently, hands folded before her.

"What?" Jack asked impatiently. "The man can draw out a moment to make it scream."

Charlene inwardly laughed. *Jack.*

"Part of being a police officer is eliminating possibilities," Sam said. He waited another full minute as if not sure he wanted to tell them anything. But he required their help, and this was how the interview process went.

"Like?" Charlene also wished Sam would hurry up.

"Like the seasoned salt on Elise's popcorn being *the only* salt that was treated with aconite," Sam said. "None of the other canisters in the theater were affected. Only the roasted garlic that was on Elise's tray. This was a deliberate attack on her."

"Now what?" Avery asked.

"Through years of experience that might lead to a certain conclusion, I believe the facts suggest we need to broaden our search. I have found no proof directly linking Darren to Elise's murder. He is innocent until proven guilty. His fingerprints were on the trays because they shared both trays." Sam paused. "I'd like to make a list of everyone invited to the premiere, and compare to see if our lists match."

Avery darted to the kitchen for the notepad in the drawer.

Jack blasted cold waves to show his annoyance. "And now he has Avery to help him solve his crimes."

Charlene swallowed laughter and did her best to ignore her ghost.

"Where were you, Charlene?" Sam asked. "When I arrived?"

"I was visiting Franco." She put her hands in her capris pockets.

"Franco Lordes, from Spellbound Movie Theater?"

"Yes." Charlene held Sam's gaze without a single flinch. "Klara had suggested I ask Franco about the flowers, so I did. He said he tossed the wolfsbane bouquet in the Dumpster behind the theater, and the garbage truck already picked it up this morning. He said he threw them away to avoid a fight between Elise and Darren, to help Darren."

Avery returned to hear the end of Charlene's sentence. "Elise fought with everyone. Too bad. Did you tell Sam that Darren was in the circus?"

Sam looked from Charlene to Avery, then shrugged as if not sure what to do with Charlene, and now Avery. "Can we please concentrate on the list of people at the theater Saturday night?"

"Of course!" Charlene perched on the armchair, getting down to business. Avery sat cross-legged on the floor, able to write on the side table. Jack watched from near the mantel. Sam paced as they wrote the list.

A half hour later, they had the names of everyone there. The guests, the workers. Charlene quickly calculated the people. "Forty. Most are friends from the new business association," she realized. "Who also had an interest in classic horror movies."

"Or employees, like Seth." Avery retrieved her phone from her back shorts pocket. "Could be forty-one. So, I showed this to Officer Bernard." She handed Sam the blurry picture of possible shoes beneath the hem of the drapes.

"What is it?" Sam narrowed his eyes, then turned the phone sideways in confusion.

"Well, I'm not sure," Avery said, her skin turning pink. "We were at the theater in our seats, and I had the feeling you get when someone is watching you, you know? Where your skin tingles and your belly knots?"

"Sure." Sam made the picture larger, then smaller.

"I had that feeling, but Seth didn't believe me." Avery got up in a single motion. "So, I flashed a picture."

Sam wore a smile that showed he wanted to believe her, but the image wasn't gelling. "Well . . . what did Bernard say?"

"'Thank you'." Avery chuckled self-deprecatingly. "He probably wasn't sure what to do with it, either. I think it could be Crocs, with the rounded toes?"

"Who wears that style of shoe?" Charlene asked.

"Hospital employees, doctors, nurses," Jack said.

"A doctor or nurse," Avery offered. "Gardeners!"

"Also, restaurant workers," Charlene said.

Sam handed the teen her phone. "You guys are way off on a tangent. Come back to me!" He lifted the list of attendees. "Seriously, though, you have been very helpful. Thanks."

"You're welcome," Charlene said. Avery gave him a thumbs-up.

"Hey, do the movie theater employees wear Crocs?" Sam asked.

Avery shook her head. "Nope. Black sneakers. Tan pants and the polo shirts with the *Spellbound Movie Theater* logo."

"All right. I can't think of why someone would hide behind a curtain," Sam said. "Let's move on."

He checked the time. "Shoot. It's two, and I'm supposed to be at the station."

Charlene rose and smoothed the wrinkles from her capris.

Sam pocketed the list. "Avery, how long have you known Seth?"

"Just a few months. Why?" Avery rubbed the tattoo on the back of her neck.

"No reason." Sam cleared his throat to keep Avery's attention. "But until this murder is cleared up, I don't want you to be alone with him, okay?"

Avery's face turned bright red. "Seth isn't guilty of killing Elise. He just wanted a weekend job while he goes to community college for his business degree."

Sam immediately held up his hands. "I'm sorry if I crossed a line, Avery. I care about you, that's all." He turned those eyes on Avery, full of sincere apology, and Avery relented.

"I accept your apology." Avery was stiff, from her posture to her tone. "I will be careful, but I also trust my own judgment when it comes to people. Seth is a good person."

Charlene couldn't be prouder of Avery for not only standing up to Sam, but doing it with such grace.

She could learn a thing or two.

"She's so grown-up," Jack said from behind Charlene.

"I . . ." Charlene bit her cheek, almost agreeing with Jack out loud. "I also like Seth, and I think you've got a brilliant head on your shoulders. Much more so than I did at your age."

"I had to grow up fast," Avery said. "It's made me the person I am right now."

Sam clapped his hand on Avery's shoulder with an affectionate nod. "Pretty cool young lady. I'd be happy to sponsor you when you're ready to come to the department if that is still what you want. Four years of college is a long time. Five, if you get your master's."

"I won't change my mind!" Avery floated on cloud nine to the front door as they all walked Sam en masse outside to the porch. "I want to be a detective like you."

Charlene and Avery waved from the top step. Jack didn't wave but mumbled, "How is it the guy has you do all his work for him and you two think he walks on water?"

With that, Jack disappeared in a snap of air.

Yeah. How was that? Charlene shook her head, still smiling.


Happy hour that day was especially happy as Avery still was on an ecstatic high from the news that Sam would be her advocate in her chosen career. She'd called Jenna, who used to be her best friend; Janet, her chaperone at the teen house, and Minnie. They'd even called Charlene's parents, who'd gushed appropriately.

The menu for this summer day was watermelon cubes in a watermelon boat with melon balls of honeydew and cantaloupe. Cheese cubes, sliced sausage, warm bread, and of course wine from Flint's Vineyard equaled a light repast that was perfect for the lazy afternoon.

Charlene had games in a shed beside the house. Braydon and Sheridon tossed a football on the side lawn while Lara and Avery played croquet. Christopher was thrilled with the swing on the oak tree as Natalie pushed him gently. If she did build a gazebo, it would interfere with this expanse of grass. Something to consider.

Pitchers of lemonade and iced tea along with bottles of cold water kept everyone hydrated. Georgio and Maria Lopez were on the front porch with books, lounging with Silva for company. Bob and Joanie sat on a blanket on the grass. Sheila, Cora, and Dustin were all out on the harbor cruise still. It was the perfect day to be on the water and hope to see dolphins or whales in Salem Sound.

Jack appeared on the back porch with a worried expression. "Charlene, can you come here for a minute?"

She got up from the patio chair with a smile at everyone, placing her iced tea on the grass. "I'll be back in a second. Can I bring anyone anything?"

"This is heaven," Joanie said, sprawled on her side, a dragonfly flitting around her hair. "I don't want to leave." Birds chirped, and a light breeze kept the heat from being unbearable.

"Well, you are welcome anytime." Charlene smiled.

"We will be back," Bob said, dozing, his hands on his stomach.

Charlene went into her suite from the back door. "What is it, Jack?" she asked after it was shut.

"I was thinking about the old building and how the manager claims it's haunted, so I did some research. This is not the first structure, which was built on a cemetery."

"I meant to ask you about the building!" Charlene couldn't believe it. A cemetery? "I'm so glad you checked into it."

Jack's smile meant he'd decided to let the Sam incident go. "There might be bodies still under there. Could that bring on a haunting?"

"What year are we talking?" Charlene pressed her hand to her stomach.

"Seventeen fifty."

They exchanged a look, and Charlene sat down at her desk, scanning the history of the building Darren had bought. It had been a long time since the mid-eighteenth century, but for Salem, it wasn't that long ago at all.

As was true with many buildings in Salem, they'd been torn down for something new or rebuilt to stay standing. Those with significant historical meaning had all been clustered together by the House of the Seven Gables and the Peabody Essex Museum.

Darren's movie theater was on the outskirts of downtown in a building that had originated in the 1750s as a country market.

The market had burned, killing the owner.

Next, the settlers built a homestead with animals and livestock.

It burned as well. No survivors.

In 1900, it was built again—this time as a theater for movies, which had been a lot fancier back in the day with velvet and gold. It had been made for a night on the town.

"Is this the same brick structure?" She tapped the image.

"I think so," Jack said. "At least a part of it."

Charlene kept reading the history of crimes that had occurred in the building. "Oh, no. Double homicide?" In the 1940s, a couple had gone on a shooting spree like Bonnie and Clyde.

"And ten people have jumped from the top floor. Ten is a lot," Jack declared. "What is that about?"

"No idea. It's too bad Darren didn't know all this before he bought it. Aren't Realtors supposed to disclose that kind of thing?" Charlene wondered if that would have stopped the savvy businessman or if it wouldn't have mattered. The price had been right and too good to pass up.

"I believe so. We could ask Darren," Jack said. "There are more than fifty documented cases of ghosts and hauntings there in the last hundred years."

"Like, the office door not closing?" Elise had yelled at Matthew as if it wasn't the first time it had happened.

"Could be." Jack hovered behind her back. "What if Avery really saw something?"

"And captured a blur?" Charlene turned toward Jack. "We tried so hard to get you on film, but it never happened."

When she'd first moved into the bed-and-breakfast, she'd been a doubter. They were trying to figure out what the rules and limitations to Jack were. So far, they knew he couldn't leave the property and that he didn't appear in old-school film or digital photos.

His essence sometimes didn't show for her, and she feared one day he might not come at all. She didn't want to think about it, because he'd grown to be a dear friend.

"Maybe we should try again," Jack said. "Spectral photography."

"What for? It's not like we would want to put it in a photo album," Charlene said, laughing. It had been in her mind since the beginning to have the classiest bed-and-breakfast, not one overrun with paranormal investigators.

It was also why she didn't invite Kass inside her house. What if Kass saw Jack?

Jack was her secret, for now. Maybe forever.

"So," Charlene said, "is it possible one of these documented entities poisoned Elise?"

"Why?" Jack questioned. "What would they gain?"

"Another soul?" Charlene wished for Silva to cuddle but stuck her hands in her pockets instead.

"Darren is in danger if that is the case," Jack said. "They all are if the building has evil spirits out for blood."

"How, though?" Charlene touched her collarbone. "Franco believes in witchcraft and wore a pentagram pendant."

"That's very interesting," Jack said. "Franco is open to the paranormal. He could be a gateway. Did you know he worked at the building when it was a nightclub? Matthew was manager then."

"No!" Franco hadn't shared that part of their history.

"As a waiter while he was going to college, and then again when it was a theater. Franco has a connection to the building."

"Franco told me Matthew was the reason he was hired at Spellbound Movie Theater with Darren. It makes sense, though, if they're longtime friends," Charlene said. "He didn't seem the sort to have very many."

Would Franco have killed Elise to save his job? Probably not. But to save a friendship?

Maybe.

Jack's energy darkened, and he paced the room. "Hear me out, Charlene. We know there is more to this life than what is visible to the naked eye. What if, like some of the lore we've read, Franco was taken over by an evil spirit?"

The idea wasn't as shocking as it might have been a year or two ago. The building being the source of evil.

Charlene drummed her fingers on the desk. "Franco and Matthew were both afraid Elise would fire them." She looked at Jack with a sick feeling in her stomach. Sam believed a crime would always have a human behind it.

"So?" Jack asked.

"What if Franco decided to poison Elise to protect his friendship with Darren? Or hey, maybe he's trying to protect his friend Matthew from getting fired? That makes more sense to me."

Jack nodded. "What if we flip that to Matthew killing Elise to protect Franco?"

Charlene groaned, the wheels in her brain spinning wildly. "What if they did it together? Poisoned Elise so that Darren would be . . ." She trailed off, not coming up with a good reason.

"Nope," Jack said, agreeing with her. "Killing Elise ruins the theater for Darren. Destroys his dream,

which was also their dream, tapping into their childhoods. I just don't see it."

"You're right. Then, who? Who would hate Elise
and not care about the theater being collateral
damage? Klara?"

"Shultz's Seasoning Salts will take a big hit from
Darren being a suspect in his wife's poisoning
murder. Whoever did this is truly evil." Jack's
image dimmed. "I'd rather believe it was the building. I'm going to keep researching."

Charlene settled back. "I can ask Kass and Kevin
what they know about the place. Have them return
to the Spellbound with paranormal investigation
on their minds instead of movie night with friends.
Considering how that turned out, they'd probably
be on board."

"There has to be a way to clear the bad mojo,"
Jack said. "I fear for Darren's safety until that happens. Unless he embraces it? Makes the haunting
public?"

Charlene wanted to protect Darren and give
him the time and space to mourn his wife without
the pandemonium of paranormal investigators.

"You are a good friend," Jack said, reading her
face correctly. "If it's about making money, though,
think of the Whaley House, or more to the evil
point, the Winchester House—that place was supposedly filled with bad spirits. All the souls of folks
killed by the Winchester rifles."

"Let's try to stay focused," Charlene said. Jack
was practically an encyclopedia with all he'd
learned. "Someone—"

"Or something," he countered.

"Poisoned Elise. Darren is a suspect, but I don't believe he did it. I believe that despite their arguments, he would have given her whatever she wanted. More money, more designer clothes, more houses. Sad as that is, he would have used his money to make up for his lies."

Jack nodded. "I can see that."

"Which means we need to find the real killer before Darren winds up in jail."

"Or," Jack said, "before the theater kills him."

# CHAPTER 14

"**D**on't be so dramatic, Jack!" She hated that it might be a possibility, the building being responsible for Elise's death.

A knock sounded on her back door, and Charlene opened it a crack. This was her private space, and she didn't invite the guests into it.

Avery's sweet smile greeted her, her ponytail loose and allowing strands around her face, nose freckled from the sun.

Charlene relaxed. "Hey, hon. Everything okay?"

Shrugging a slender shoulder, Avery said, "Yep! The guests are all getting ready to go after an amazing, relaxing happy hour. I know you like to send them off with a special Charlene 'have fun' speech that I don't have down yet."

Charlene chuckled and went out, shutting the door behind her on Jack's laughter. "You're very thoughtful. Also, you're right."

Avery descended the wooden stairs to the lawn. "I'll have to work on my Charlene-isms."

"Oh, I don't have any," she said, on Avery's heels. She got a whiff of roses as she passed a full rose-bush laden with soft pink blooms.

"We can work on a catchphrase," Jack said, suddenly appearing outside by the tree swing. He gave it a little push that could be attributed to a summer breeze.

Christopher, on Natalie's hip, waved toward Jack. Spencer and Lara swung their hands between them, and then Spencer spun his daughter around.

A catchphrase might be nice, and she could put it on her business card. They were shiny black and elegant, to match the wooden sign at the front of her property.

They walked together around the side grass toward the front drive. Her guests planned to hoof it in assorted groups to town.

"And don't forget that tonight the moon will be full, and we have a guest astronomer to tell us about the stars." She looked for Dustin and Cora but remembered they were still out on the cruise with Sheila. "I am so excited to learn more!"

This was the first time she'd planned a gathering on the roof to use the telescope for a full moon. She'd imagined it would be popular when she'd purchased it, but to her surprise, it was usually only couples who went up to use it. Or a family with kids, but it wasn't the pull she'd thought it would be. It was a gorgeous antique brass telescope that Archie Higgins from Vintage Treasures had helped her locate.

"I can't wait!" Braydon said, jostling his twin, Sheridon. Sheridon shoved him back. The next thing she knew, the boys were doing flips across the lawn.

Bob and Joanie took it in stride and followed them. "See you later," Joanie called over her shoulder. The last guest stepped out of sight.

Charlene sighed. "And now the party is over."

"There will be another one tomorrow," Avery said, bumping her arm to Charlene's. "I'll get the dishes and meet you in the kitchen." She took off at a run around the side of the house, picking up blankets and toys along the way.

"She makes me tired," Charlene said.

Jack rumbled a laugh. "She's great. She's exactly how she should be—a happy and confident young woman."

Charlene, Silva, and Jack entered the kitchen. She rinsed what was in the sink and had just loaded that into the dishwasher when Avery brought in the rest of the dishes, along with the scent of the outdoors.

Jack sat at his place at the kitchen table, exuding contentment. They'd both come a long way since they'd first met.

"I was researching the ground Spellbound Movie Theater was built on," Charlene said, wrapping up the watermelon fruit bowl. "The plot of land covers a portion of a cemetery."

Avery's brow rose. "That happened a lot in the old days."

"Well," Charlene said, "not all those spaces have a history of crimes taking place in them. The Spellbound has been the scene of a shooting and several fires. Suicides by jumping from the top of the building."

"There's bad energy in places." Avery turned to Charlene and made her fingers into claws. "You can feel it like fingernails on your spine. Poor Darren. What if that's the case here?"

Jack chuckled. "Avery is from Salem, so she doesn't question it. I hope she doesn't forget her common sense when she joins the police force."

"I think it's worth checking out," Charlene said.

"Charlene, can you encourage Darren to sell the theater?" Avery crossed her arms. "Maybe he should go back to Saint Mary's and forget all about Salem. Cut his losses. What if whoever is after him—human or ghost—doesn't stop?"

Charlene hit the *Start* button on the dishwasher. "I've considered that."

"I'm with Avery," Jack said, ruffling the napkins in a stack on the table. "Darren should unload it quickly."

Charlene pressed her fingers between her brows to stop a stress headache. "If he was to sell it, without full disclosure, even with those facts, what would happen to the next unsuspecting Joe who bought it?"

"Matthew would manage it, I'll bet," Jack said in a dark tone.

Maybe Franco would work there too.

Avery's gaze grew troubled. "I'm worried about Seth being there. I'm going to text him to just quit and get a different job."

"Go ahead, Avery." Charlene understood wanting to protect those you cared about. "You know he was already thinking of leaving anyway."

Avery pulled her phone from the front bib pocket of her coveralls and shot off a text. "In hindsight, I wish you wouldn't have gone to see Franco by yourself today."

"I wasn't in any danger—the man is a walking skeleton," Charlene said.

Jack and Avery spoke in unison. "It was *poison.*"

"The killer doesn't need to be strong," Avery continued. "He just needs a reason to want Darren dead. And maybe you, if you get too close to the truth."

"I had my pepper spray in my purse," Charlene said, "and I had my cell phone."

Avery arched a brow. "And you drank his tea, which could have been doctored without you noticing."

"She's right," Jack said. "You need to be more careful, Charlene."

Charlene nodded to appease them both. "I will be more careful. We know how Elise was killed. I think we should focus on why."

Avery sat down in the kitchen, subconsciously avoiding Jack's seat, but choosing the one across from him. "It's good that Sam is seriously looking at other people now, not just Darren. I really respect him."

Jack flashed neon blue, not that Avery could see. Silva, dozing by her bowl in the event of more delicious treats, could, and she meowed at the light show. "Respect! Sam had you make his list for him!"

"Iced tea?" Charlene asked, opening the fridge to explain the extra chill in the kitchen from Jack's display.

"No thanks." Avery drummed her fingers on the table.

Charlene sat with a full glass and sipped, arching a brow at her ghost so he would calm the heck down. "Darren is well-liked. It was Elise who grated on people. Maybe she just ticked off the wrong one."

"Yeah," Avery quipped. "Elise would like you if you had money and style. Patty isn't like that at all. I like Patty lots better. Her soft-baked pretzels are so good, and her croissants. She's a regular person."

"Patty. Hmm." Charlene reached for a napkin and placed her glass in the square to absorb the condensation. "Klara and Darren both said Elise felt cheated that Patty had inherited and Elise got nothing when her parents died. Patty never moved out of the family home."

Jack controlled his emotions enough to maintain his usual image. "It would be strange to be cut out completely. I wonder what the rest of the story is."

Charlene gave a single nod. She cursed her curiosity because, of course, she wondered too.

"It's a cute gingerbread house to match the bakery," Avery said. "Maybe it has something to do with Patty holding down the family business while Elise traveled away from Salem? Leaving it to Patty, the one who stayed. She's the 'good' sister."

"I could see that happening," Jack said. "With the bakery. But the house too? Unless her parents were angry that Elise had left home."

"Their dad, John Wagner, was a very strict Protestant. Patty said her mom just kind of went along with his rules." Charlene sipped her iced tea. "Oh! Did I tell you she said Elise stole things? And never got caught. Darren also told me Elise used to steal, until he gave her carte blanche to buy what she wanted."

"No way." Avery's phone dinged a message, but it was turned over while they were talking. "When did I miss this?"

"The other night on the phone. Elise was very sneaky, Patty told me. She loved her sister, though, faults and all." Charlene swiped a droplet from the glass.

"Extreme love is not that far off from extreme hate," Jack said.

"I feel bad for Elise and still don't like her at the same time." Avery's phone trilled several more messages in a row, and the teen turned it over to see what was happening. "It's a full moon tonight. I've heard there's scientific proof that the pull of the moon affects the way our brains work. Cray-cray. As if Salem needs any more crazy." She dropped her gaze and read.

"It will be beautiful tonight, though. And the movie referred to an autumn moon. This is summer. We're safe from a werewolf attack." Charlene laughed.

Avery stood, and her chair fell back to the floor with a *smack*. "Charlene! Seth texted that Darren was just trapped by the heavy drapes at the theater! They called nine-one-one. They're on the way to the hospital!" Her eyes were round with fright.

"You can't just run into the thick of things," Jack advised, accurately reading her response.

"We need to stay calm," Charlene said, taking in Avery's words. Darren trapped, Darren on the way to the hospital. She righted the chair, putting her arm around Avery's waist.

"Seth rode with Darren in the back of the ambulance and needs a ride home. I'm going, Charlene." Her lower lip trembled.

"All right." Charlene could only do what she did best—offer to help and be there. "I'll drive you there. Come on."

"This might be an attempt on Darren's life, Charlene." Jack rose, his essence levitating. "Be careful!"

"We will."

Avery looked at her funny.

Charlene didn't care that she'd answered Jack. "Grab your purse, Avery. And a water bottle. I have granola bars in the car. I don't know what we might need, but we will make sure he's all right. Seth and Darren both."

Jack followed them to the end of the property before he disappeared in her rearview mirror like a shadow in the sun.

They reached the hospital in eight minutes thanks to Charlene's lead foot. She tried to keep it a hair under ten miles over because getting a ticket would only slow them down.

She lucked out with a parking space near the entrance of the emergency room, and she and Avery hurried in. Seth sat on a chair with a *Spellbound Movie Theater* concession towel to his forehead, thick with blood.

"You didn't say *you* were hurt," Avery cried, rushing to Seth's side.

"Head wounds bleed a lot, but it will probably need a stitch or two," Seth said. "Not a big deal. I'm worried about Darren, though. The thick rod of curtains crashed on him in the upper balcony. Right on his chest. It was so heavy!"

"Oh, no!" Avery said.

Seth winced. "Yeah, and while me, Franco, and Matthew were trying to pull it off, one of the wires came loose and thwacked me good."

He could have lost an eye.

Charlene couldn't get the building's history out of her mind. Was it taking its price out in flesh and blood?

While the Midwestern part of her thought that was silly, the Salem part—the part aware of things beyond the normal—wondered if it could be true. "Where is Darren now?"

"In the back room. He was howling in agony and didn't want to come to the hospital. But the curtains and rod landed on his shoulder." Seth gulped and pressed the towel to his head. "We thought he was dead. He must have fainted from the pain."

"How awful," Avery said, squeezing Seth's hand.

"It was scary," Seth admitted.

Charlene heard a loud shout, followed by cursing in German.

"Should I call Klara? Or Patty?" Charlene paced by the reception desk, answering her own question. "We should probably wait until we know something." The nurse was busy typing on her keyboard, gaze on her computer monitor. "Did you already give her your insurance information, Seth?"

"Yep," Seth said. "I'm on my mom's plan."

Just then, a harried doctor, about fortyish with dark hair and glasses, came out of the back room, slipping off plastic gloves and jamming them in his white coat pocket. "Seth Gamble?"

"I'm here." Seth stood and walked toward the doctor. Avery stayed beside him.

The doctor noticed the bloody towel. "Let's get you back there. I didn't realize you were injured too."

"It's probably nothing," Seth said.

"Let me decide that, all right?" The doctor shook his head. "Full moon tonight, and things are nuts already. So, your boss was trapped by a curtain rod?"

"He owns a movie theater," Seth explained. "It was one of the big heavy poles with velvet drapes. A couple hundred pounds."

"That explains the injury." The doc patted his arm. "His shoulder was dislocated, but it's back in now. You have a ride?"

"We're here and can take them both home," Charlene said, staying in their group. "Charlene Morris."

"Hi. I wanted to keep Mr. Shultz overnight for tests and X-rays, but he's refusing. My hands are tied. I'm concerned about internal bleeding, but he's not, so . . ." The doc's expression said it all.

The doctor led the way back into the emergency room, passing cubicles with patients in various stages of distress, until they reached a vacant one. The doctor slipped on fresh plastic gloves and took the concession towel from Seth's temple.

The doctor studied the wound. "That will need some stitches."

Avery peered at the injury with steady eyes, though Charlene's stomach clenched. The girl was amazing.

"You okay?" Avery asked Seth softly.

"Yep." Seth gave a half smile as if it was no big deal. "I was an accident-prone kid, so I was here a lot."

The doctor cleaned the wound and applied four neat stitches, then covered it with a bandage. "Done. Now, wait here while I go check on your boss."

"Nice work," Avery said after the doctor left. "He gave you a Batman Band-Aid."

"He knows my secret identity," Seth said playfully. "Want to be Robin?"

"I'm Wonder Woman." Avery smiled. "No sidekick status here."

"Understood." Seth grinned.

Charlene thought their banter was adorable. She stepped out of the cubicle, looking for Darren. She followed the sound of grumbling in German and went into a room as he was shrugging into his button-up shirt. He had thick dark hair on his chest, and she saw stubble growing on his arms as if he'd shaved.

The only reason she noticed was that in high school she'd had a boyfriend on the swim team who had shaved his arms, legs, and chest, claiming it made him faster in competition.

Maybe Darren was a swimmer, or used to be. Could that be a circus activity? All she could think of was the water tank with the mermaid. Darren was no mermaid. "Hey, Darren. How are you?"

He spun and quickly buttoned his shirt the rest of the way. "Fine. I want out of this place. They can't keep me."

"No, of course not!" Charlene's goal was to keep

Darren relaxed so he didn't wind up in jail for his temper.

Darren paced toward her, his eyes red and angry. "Someone is messing with me, Charlene, and I don't like it."

"What do you mean?" Did he realize the theater was haunted?

"First Elise, killed in my theater. And now, the curtains?" Darren rubbed his shoulder. "This was an attempt on my life."

"Should we call the police?"

"No police!" he shouted, watching her face, his expression crumpling with grief. "My wife is dead!"

Charlene patted his arm in empathy. He had a right to be upset—and worried for himself. The movie theater had been his dream come true, and now it was ruined for him.

The doctor peered in. "Please stay calm, Mr. Shultz."

"*Nien.* Don't tell me what to do!" Darren yelled. "I want to leave, now."

"There are insurance forms to fill out," the doctor said. A second, female doctor joined him, the pair a diminutive front against Darren's anger, which they didn't understand. Why should they? They were here to save lives, not get to know the patients or their stories.

Though united, they were no match for Darren.

"Bill me. I'm leaving." And so, Darren strode out into the parking lot with a dazed hospital staff watching them. Charlene, Seth, and Avery followed.

She clicked her fob so the car location would sound and alert Darren where to go. He strode in

jerky movements around the SUV, his fist slam
ming into his open palm.

"Darren?" Charlene dared to touch his shoul
der. "Let me drive you home, all right? Is Klara
there?"

Darren raised his face and snarled, "Klara want
to leave, but the cops think she should stick
around. She doesn't know what to do with my
grief. My rage. I thought she was my best friend
How can she desert me?"

"I hear you," Charlene said in tranquil tones
"Why don't you get in, and we can go to your place
first? I'll drop you off. If you'd like, I'll talk to
Klara for you. Then I'll take Seth home. Don't you
want Seth to get home safely?"

Appealing to his employee's well-being reached
him.

"Yes. *Ja.* Let's go." Darren got in the front pas
senger seat and broke down with sobs of rage and
misery. "Who hates me like this?"

"I don't know," Charlene said. "Maybe nobody—
maybe this is just a random, cruel accident." Seth
and Avery got in the back seat and buckled up.

"Elise was no accident. She was killed, and it wa
made to look like I did it." Darren pounded hi
heart and stared out the window. The sky was blue
the day was beautiful, but he emitted despair.

Charlene wanted to help, but what could sh
do? It wasn't the time to ask if he'd known abou
the building's history of tragedy. It would be salt i
the wound.

A few minutes later, Charlene parked at th
white house with the red door. Klara emerged
wringing her hands. She was dressed head to to

in sleek black, like a panther, her dark hair scraped back from her striking face. Her chunky heels added to her height.

"What happened?" Klara opened his passenger door. "I've been worried sick! I tried to call you, but no answer. Matthew said there was a curtain accident?"

Darren almost fell out onto Klara, and she caught him, somehow staying upright. "Not an accident. My phone was crushed. Like my heart."

Klara pushed him back to glower at him. "Now is not the time for theatrics. We need to go to the police station and let them know you don't think it was an accident."

Charlene exited and rounded the front of the SUV to help Klara with Darren if needed. "How?" Darren demanded. "How can you prove that?"

"Let them inside the theater to investigate!" Klara flung her arm in exasperation. "Matthew said you ordered everyone out."

Seth and Avery had stayed in the back of the car, with the windows rolled down for air, or to hear better.

"For their own safety. No." Darren swung his body from side to side. "No investigation."

Klara drew herself up and glanced at Charlene in confusion. "I don't understand why you are being like this, Darren."

"Darren," Charlene said in a hesitant voice, "were you aware that the building has a . . . dark history?"

"Matthew told me about the ghosts! So what? Salem is famous for ghosts, but this is different. Nobody will attend the theater if they think it's haunted by a murderous spook. Scary is one thing, not deadly." Darren yanked at his hair.

"We can spin it just right, but it needs time." Klara patted his back to calm him down like she would a child.

"Where are Matthew and Franco?" Charlene asked. "Not at the theater still . . ."

"Matthew said they'd lock up," Klara said. "Darren, I know it was your dream, but we need to take a break, all right? The seasoned salts at the movie theater were confiscated. We have more in the warehouse, but we must sit on them for a while. Shoot, maybe do a name change on the salts." Klara's eyes were red-rimmed from tears. "This isn't going to fly on the market."

"No. *No!*" Darren shouted and pumped his fist at the sky.

It was seven at night, and there was no sign of the moon just yet, but Charlene was eerily reminded of *The Wolf Man* movie and the angst Lon Chaney Jr. showed with his gestures.

The torment conveyed with his eyes.

His words.

Charlene had been able to feel the pain—just like now, the angst was too much.

"I'm going to drop off Seth," Charlene said quietly. "Klara, Darren, I want you to research the history of the building, all right? Beyond ghosts. It might explain what is going on."

"What?" Klara shook her head. "I don't have time for that."

"It's very important," Charlene said. "Then decide on whether to delay the grand opening or start over somewhere else."

"I am not starting over!" Darren cried. "I am not leaving Salem."

Klara nodded that she'd heard Charlene.

"Call me if you need anything—you have my number."

"I don't," Klara said.

Charlene walked to the passenger door that Darren had left open and retrieved a business card from the console. "Here you go. Whatever you need, all right? I feel connected to this project, and to them, and I . . . I just want to help." It was her personal albatross, this helping gene.

Klara urged Darren toward the house. "Before you scare the neighbors," she said, "ranting and raving like a lunatic." She eyed the sky. "Full moon tonight."

"The doctor said the hospital is already nuts." Charlene raised a hand. "Night."

They went inside, and the red door slammed shut.

Charlene stepped into the car, then drove to Seth's house.

When she arrived, Charlene parked in the driveway. Avery and Seth exited, their heads together as they said good-bye.

A woman dressed in blue jean shorts and a tank top, her long brown-and-gold hair in a braid, rushed to Seth, flip-flops smacking the pavement. "Let me have a peek, Seth! I knew it had been too long since the last accident." She brushed his hair away from the bandage. "It could have been worse."

Charlene climbed out. "Hi."

"Hi. I'm Dani Gamble." The woman offered her

hand to shake. "Are you Avery's mom? She sure is a good kid."

"She is a wonderful person." Charlene shook, noting the silver rings on several of Dani's fingers. The wedding finger was bare. "I'm a friend."

Dani rolled with the explanation. "We all could use one of those. I sure wish Seth would quit that job at the theater. Hey, want to come in? I've got iced tea in the fridge, or better yet, a cold beer."

Charlene shifted toward Avery, who nodded and smiled. Guess she was going to get her wish!

"I would love to come in. I hear you have a ghost?"

# CHAPTER 15

"We do have a ghost—but she's the quiet type," Dani said. "Come on into our humble abode."

Charlene entered the house behind Dani, subtly scanning the cozy home that was lived in, yet not cluttered. Things that mattered were around the house on shelves. Books, pictures—people lived here, and unlike Franco's apartment, this place hummed with happy vibes. Franco seemed mired in the past.

They passed the living room on the right, moving on to a large and airy kitchen at the back of the house. Fresh herbs beckoned on the windowsill. Basil, chives, rosemary. Parsley. Just waiting to be snipped and added to a recipe.

The house was probably built around the turn of the twentieth century. Solid wood beams supported the ceiling, and Dani had left them as a design element. Plants hung from inside as well as on the back patio, which teemed with greenery and vibrant blooms.

It was welcoming. "I love your home," Charlene said. Her gaze went to the stainless-steel refrigerator, which the little girl ghost supposedly liked to open and close.

She didn't see anything or feel anything. Maybe her senses were just in tune with Jack, *her* ghost, at her property.

Charlene had no idea how this stuff worked. Maybe someday she could write a manual and publish it under a pen name, in a fictitious city.

"My son Stephen is at baseball camp during the day for the summer." Dani waved at the magnet photos on the fridge that showed both brothers in various activities. "That kid loves the sport, and it's good to keep them busy or they find trouble. Right, Seth?"

Seth blushed. "Mom. One time I got busted for smoking after school. *One time,* and I have never been able to live it down."

Avery giggled. "I'm glad you don't smoke."

"It was a try-it-out thing, that is all. Obviously. I can't be perfect all the time, Mom," Seth said.

Dani smirked. "You are pretty good. Just busting your chops." She turned to Charlene. "So, what can I get you?"

"Whatever you're having is fine," Charlene said.

Dani studied Charlene with narrowed eyes, her arms crossed over her waist. "Hmm. I bet you like white wine, or a citrus beer. You have that sort of floral, zesty thing around you."

Charlene burst out laughing. "Actually, I do like both of those, and orange or lemon tea as well."

"It's Mom's party trick she likes to do," Seth said with a shrug.

"She guessed I was spicy," Avery said, "and totally scored on the V8 with Tabasco and celery the other night for tacos."

Dani half-bowed and showed the dimple she shared with Seth. "It's a gift. Silly, but fun. And definitely an icebreaker."

Charlene understood exactly where Seth got his cool factor.

"So, tell me what happened at the theater?" Dani said as she pulled out two beers and poured them into glasses.

Seth chose flavored iced teas for him and Avery, then they all gravitated toward the kitchen table and sat down.

A cute black-and-white dog lounged in the shade of the covered back porch and wagged his tail when he saw her.

Charlene hadn't heard the story of what happened in a calm manner yet either. Just Darren's mania. She sipped. "Thanks. This hits the spot."

Dani smiled and raised her glass in salute.

"At first, Darren wanted to open *today* for movie guests, but I guess Charlene left a compelling message to wait like Elise would want him to, so he decided we could spend the next three days cleaning for Friday." Seth twisted off his plastic cap.

"Ridiculous," Dani exclaimed. "It's a crime scene. No offense, Seth, but your boss is a moron."

"We all agree, but he's signing my paycheck, which I'd like before I quit," Seth said. "I already have another job lined up at the gas station. New boss was cool and said I could only work weekends once I start college, so that was awesome."

"Good." Dani patted the table between them. "I knew you'd find something."

"So. Cleaning the theater," Seth said dramatically, "and I'm looking over my shoulder because I've got Avery thinking someone is watching her, and Matthew insists the place is haunted, and Franco, he just gets very high-strung, so I'm a little jittery myself."

"Don't blame you," Avery said, drinking her raspberry tea. "I caught something in a picture," she told Dani.

"No way! I've tried to get our little creeper on film, but no go." Dani leaned in toward Seth, eyes bright. She glanced at Avery. "At least this friend won't think you're wacko because of the ghost in our house."

"Nope. I don't. As for the picture, it's very blurry and might not be anything," Avery admitted with a sly glance at Seth.

"Now you say that. You've been all over me about not agreeing with you that you caught a ghost on film." Seth grinned at them all. "A ghost wearing *shoes*."

Dani laughed softly. "Well, Lucy Locket, my name for the little girl ghost who lives here, hasn't ever told me her name. She doesn't communicate at all. She just is. In a white pinafore over a blue dress, brown curls held back with a bow, but faded somehow. Can't explain it. Seth doesn't see her, but Stephen can. My grandmother is from Wales and was full-on psychic, to the point she predicted her own death."

Charlene shivered even as she absorbed all this information to share with Jack. He would find it very interesting.

"How did she prove it?" Avery asked, her palm casual on the kitchen table. The Gamble house invited relaxation.

"As a teenage girl, Grandma wrote the prediction down and stuck it in the family Bible. It said she would live to be eighty-five and die in an accident of some sort," Dani said.

"Did she?" Avery asked.

"God's truth." Dani held up her hand. "She was traveling to see my uncle on her eighty-fifth birthday, and the train derailed. She died instantly."

Charlene wondered what Sam would make of Dani and her family. Would he deny they'd seen ghosts or could predict the future? She'd never pressed the issue with him, accepting that they believed different things.

She added a mental note not to invite Dani or Stephen over unless Jack stayed out of sight. Seth had looked toward Jack when he'd been in the kitchen, so maybe he was also sensitive, but not in a visual way. He might have felt the cold.

"Finish telling us what happened, Seth," Avery said.

"Right. Well, I was sweeping behind the counter." Seth raked his hair back and let it fall. "I don't know where Franco was, or Matthew, but suddenly I heard a loud crash. Like, an awful *boom*. It was hard to understand what the noise was, you know?"

"What did you do?" Avery focused on Seth, her body tense.

"I stood there, frozen like an idiot, then realized I heard Darren shouting and moaning."

Dani said automatically, "You're not an idiot."

"It freaked the hell out of me, Mom!" Seth surveyed them all, but he stopped at Avery. "I dropped the broom and ran upstairs—not where we sat, but across to the stage. Darren was trapped by the heavy velvet curtains and the rod . . . it had to be fifty feet long."

They all nodded. Charlene could see it perfectly. Avery scooted her chair closer to Seth as if completely entranced.

"If that was me," Dani said, "I'd have hotfooted it out the front door, not go investigate!"

"I doubt that, Mom. You'd have helped. Anyway, Matthew showed up, then Franco, and we somehow lifted this heavy stuff off him. I called nine-one-one, and they arrived right away." Seth reached for Avery's hand and covered it with his. "I texted Avery from the back of the ambulance. I hadn't planned on going to the hospital at all, but Franco kinda pushed me into the back."

Avery flipped her hand so that she could hold his. "It's good he did."

"I didn't realize I was bleeding." Seth squeezed her hand, then moved to grasp his tea. "Had a concession dish towel in my back pocket and pretty much tried to stay out of the way so the medic could attend to Darren, who was cursing in German. I don't know the language, but I got the gist."

"Oh, Seth. Honey." Dani took a breath. "That's scary. It could have been so much worse." She tapped her temple. "I like you with both eyes, son."

"It might be the building," Avery said. "Charlene found articles online going back a ways where tragedies happened on that land."

Dani drank her beer. "Haunted?"

"This building was built in nineteen oh-two, I think," Seth said. "That's not old at all for Salem."

"But built on the same land from seventeen fifty. There was a cemetery on that spot originally." Charlene drank her beer. "Stranger things have happened, right?"

Seth shivered and rubbed his arms. "I don't mind telling you, now that I won't be working there anymore, that I felt eyes on me all the time. Franco said he did, too, and Matthew, well, he's always believed it's haunted."

"I'm glad you're getting out of there, Seth," Dani said in a serious tone. "It's not worth the money."

"I know." Seth finished his tea.

"I could always put you to work cleaning houses," Dani said. "It pays very well, and I have an in with the boss."

"I did it through high school." Seth rolled his eyes. "I can clean a shower to make it shine."

"I told him it will impress the right girl." Dani laughed and smacked the tabletop.

"I agree," Charlene said. "A man who can pick up after himself and do laundry? That's pretty great. Jared was hopeless."

Avery sent her a sad smile.

Jared was on her mind more than he had been, thanks to Darren and the loss of his spouse. "Do you see ghosts outside your home, Dani?" Charlene asked.

The woman scrunched her nose and drained her beer. "None as clear as Lucy Locket. Not that I go looking, either."

Would Charlene be able to see the other ghost? She was curious, no doubt about that.

"Well, how about we all have dinner?" Dani suggested. "This has been fun."

Charlene read the time on her watch. It was after seven. How did that happen? Time flew these days. Jack was hopefully waiting for her with information about the Spellbound Movie Theater property.

"I run a bed-and-breakfast, so I should get back." Charlene wished she could stay, but she had a full moon party to prep for. "Avery, you stay and have dinner, hon, if you want. I can pick you up later since you didn't drive."

"I'll bring her home," Seth said, smiling at Avery.

Young love. Was there anything as cute?

Charlene stood and carried her tall glass to the sink to rinse. "This was such a treat!" She placed it on the counter. The herbs on the windowsill begged to be plucked, and she imagined doing an herb garden in the back of her own place, next to the roses.

"Well, a rain check, then, for another night. We can plan something that way," Dani said. "My life is very much run by a schedule. Kinda boring."

"You love it that way, Mom." Seth also got up from the table. Avery too.

Dani chuckled. "Yeah. I know."

"This would have been perfect except that I have guests at the B-and-B, and I like to stick around in case they need something." Charlene laughed at herself. "They rarely do. Also, one of my guests is an astronomer from Berkeley, and he's offered to do a presentation tonight because it's a full moon."

"I forgot about that!" Avery frowned.

"I can handle it—you stay and have fun," Charlene said. "This is your summer before college starts to be with your friends. A bonfire on the beach sounds terrific."

"Are you sure?" Avery asked, side by side with Seth.

"Absolutely." Charlene moved away from the sink.

"Full-moon craziness," Dani said. "I am glad to stay home with my dog and a great book. I love to read."

"Me too!" Charlene said. "Romance and mysteries are my favorite."

"I like those, but I devour historical fiction." Dani smiled. "We should talk books sometime."

The foursome stepped out of the kitchen toward the living room, Dani and Charlene, Avery and Seth. Behind them, the refrigerator door squeaked open on its own. Goose bumps raced up Charlene's spine, and she whirled around.

"Hello, Lucy," Dani said. She'd pivoted on her heel and pointed to the refrigerator door.

Seth pulled Avery forward. "Mom says she shows up right there. Charlene, what do you see?"

Charlene squinted toward the fridge. Was that a girl shape? Nah. She was imagining things because she wanted to see them. "I'm not sure."

"Nothing!" said Avery.

A *pop*, like when you put your finger in your cheek and pull, sounded.

"She's gone," Dani said. "She might have been startled by a new voice."

"Darn it!" Avery sounded bereft. "I didn't mean to scare her."

"Who knows what they think for sure? Trust me." Dani patted Avery's arm. "She'll be back."

Charlene left with promises to return soon, which she hoped happened for numerous reasons—Dani seemed like someone who would make a terrific friend.

Once in the car, she saw a missed call from Sam. She plugged in her phone and dialed back via Bluetooth.

"Hey, Sam," she said when he answered.

"I heard you were part of the full-moon craziness at the theater." The detective had the nerve to sound somewhat accusing.

"First of all, I wasn't at the theater, but I did pick Darren and Seth up from the hospital. Would you like to discuss it in a friendly manner? I'm in the car and can pass by the station if you're there. Where are you at?"

"The station." Sam paused, and she could practically hear the wheels turn in the detective's head. "Yeah. Drop by. I'll meet you at the front."

At a stoplight, Charlene applied lip gloss and smoothed her long dark-brown hair so she didn't look like she'd been at the ER or playing taxi for Darren.

"Vanity, thy name is woman," Charlene intoned, hearing her mom's voice. That tone was replaced by the new and improved Brenda Woodbridge, who might not be so snarky.

She had to circle twice before finding a spot to park. Though Tuesday wasn't normally busy, not only was it a full moon, but the Seafarer's Festival was in town.

Salem was so vibrant in the summer, and like in Chicago, people appreciated the sunshine a lot more because of the blustery winter weather.

Blue skies equaled bright smiles—she was no exception.

Charlene got out, locked the door, and walked with that happy feeling up the stairs to Salem PD.

Sam waited for her and opened the door. He wore jeans and a snug, muscle-fitting polo shirt loose at his waist. His hair was sexily unkempt.

"Well, hello, Charlene." He smoothed his mustache, and his eyes warmed with appreciation. "Won't you come back to my office?"

Her stomach fluttered. "Nice to see you, Sam."

The inside of the department was a bustle of noise and activity. They didn't talk until they reached his office. It hadn't changed since the first time she'd been inside almost two years ago.

The NY Rangers coffee mug she'd given him for Christmas one year was on the corner of his desk. Sweet.

"Have a seat." Sam gestured to a seat on one side of the desk, and he took his office chair on the other as if deliberately keeping the desk between them.

Hmm.

"So," Sam said, rocking back in his chair, the wheels squeaking.

"Yes?" Charlene didn't like to make things easy for him, though she knew he wanted to know about the theater and Darren, and she would tell him, but she'd make him work for it.

It was the small joys, she thought. He was the law and right most of the time.

Not that she would share that.

"I heard there was an emergency at the theater." Sam laced his fingers over his flat stomach. "Lennox was the officer on call."

Officer Lennox was the one who had instigated Darren into losing control, Charlene recalled, instantly raising her guard. "I wasn't there, so I can't tell you too much."

"Thanks for that." Sam straightened and placed his elbow on his desk, observing her from around his computer monitor.

"I had no reason to be there, so it wasn't a problem at all," she said. If she'd needed to be at the theater, she'd covered her bases earlier by only telling Sam she'd do her best to stay away.

"Good." Sam cleared his throat and tapped a file folder. "I was reading the report, and it's a little confusing. Muddled."

Charlene sat on the edge of her seat. "What did the officer say?"

"She reported an accident with a curtain rod?" Sam's brow rose. "I don't understand how an ambulance would need to be called for that."

The doctor at the ER hadn't understood either. "It was a fifty-foot rod with velvet stage curtains that have to weigh a lot—hundreds of pounds, according to Seth."

"Got it." Sam nodded and waited, watching her.

She squirmed on the chair like a fish on a hook. At last, Sam asked, "How's Seth?"

"Good!" Charlene hated the relieved tone in her voice, but if Sam hadn't spoken, then she would have and lost this little game they played. "He needed stitches on his temple, but he's okay."

"Nice, nice." Sam steepled his fingers. "Darren? Lennox says he was howling like a wolf. I was sure she had to be mistaken."

Charlene scooted forward a little. "Darren had a dislocated shoulder. I hear that's painful."

"It is. And again, explains a lot." Sam rubbed his shoulder in commiseration. "It's happened to me more than once."

Charlene couldn't tell him about the evil building theory—Sam wouldn't give it credence. "I drove Darren home to Klara. She'll make sure he rests, if possible. He was very upset." Darren didn't want the cops in the theater, which meant she didn't disclose that Darren feared it could be an attempt on his life, now that Elise was gone.

"He's got a reason to be," Sam said. "In cases like this, the widower, if innocent, hasn't had time to grieve because of the nature of Elise's death."

"Murder," Charlene said.

"Exactly. Seth called in the emergency. Lennox arrived on the scene." Sam knocked a knuckle to the file folder. "Matthew Sinchuk and Franco Lordes locked up the theater and went home."

Charlene nodded. "That's what I understand as well."

Sam sat forward, both elbows on the desk so he could look her in the eye. "Thanks for stopping by to clear things up—it helped."

"Welcome." She glanced at him instead of studying her hands in her lap, noting his primal gaze on her.

"Charlene, Avery had mentioned that you knew Darren had been in the circus. In what capacity?" Sam relaxed backward.

"Franco had mentioned it, but I never found out more." Charlene wished she knew, but Darren wasn't easy to question due to his grief, compounded with the realization someone wanted him dead.

"Have you eaten dinner?" Sam's voice was low and deep and downright sexy. How could she possibly hold him at bay?

Charlene was glad she'd taken the time to freshen up in the Pilot. "No."

His brow rose, and his lips curved in a half smile that did things to her belly. "Wanna step out for a slice of pizza?"

She considered this. It would be fun.

It was kinda against the rules—his rules.

Would he think she was leading him on? She didn't want that.

"I can see smoke from your ears," Sam said dryly. "It's pizza, not a commitment."

Charlene laughed out loud. "Busted—yes, I would love to get a slice of pizza with you. I can't stay too long." She had a party to prep for.

"Great." Sam got up and pocketed his phone. "The officers frequent a spot around the corner where you start with a basic slice—a NY slice, not that ridiculous deep dish like you have in Chicago."

She smirked, her stomach filled with butterflies.

They made it as far as the front door before Officer Jimenez called his name.

"Detective, we have a shooting." The officer's expression was unreadable, as she didn't so much as glance toward Charlene. "Domestic violence."

"Damn." Sam stopped and chucked her gently with his finger under her chin. "Rain check?"

"You got it, Detective."

Charlene meant it.

As she returned to her car, she reflected that she hadn't had two rain checks in one night before. On the way home, she stopped at the party supply store for full moon paper plates and napkins. She also picked up a party pack of star-shaped sunglasses. And just for fun, she bought bubbles with a moon-shaped wand.

Charlene hurried home, excited about the party, and to tell Jack about the little girl ghost in the Gamble house that she hadn't seen but heard.

She got out of the car where Silva waited on the front porch. Picking up the cat, she went inside and paused in the foyer, listening and sensing the house was empty.

Charlene went into her suite. The computer was closed, the television on low, but there was no sign of her roommate. "Jack?"

Nothing.

She worried as she always did that he might not come back. Would this be the end of their journey together? *Stop it, Charlene. He will come back.*

Charlene turned on the radio in the kitchen and made her and Silva chicken salad with a baguette. She poured a glass of wine and went to her suite.

"Jack? Jack!"

She could tell in her bones that Jack wasn't around.

"Strike three!" Charlene murmured to herself. It was a good thing she had prep work to do for the full moon party or else she'd feel at a loss. She prepared snacks and sang along to the radio.

Jack's absence bothered her, but she realized it was because of Darren, losing Elise, which had brought her feelings so close to the surface regarding Jared's death. She was more sensitive today, that was all.

Jack had filled in the loneliness for her after she'd moved here, and it was because of their friendship that she'd healed her broken heart.

Charlene sipped her wine. As Darren would realize for himself, there would always be a scar.

# CHAPTER 16

Ten o'clock was normally when Charlene was winding down in her suite, but not tonight. Tonight, she had snacks and drinks and a real live astronomer to give them the lowdown on the full moon and the constellations that Jack had always loved.

It was understandable that the widow's walk was no longer his favorite part of the house, as it had been instrumental in his death. Since Charlene had bought the mansion, she'd had Parker create cushioned benches so there was plenty of seating and little tables. The railing and floor were painted brick red, the cushions deep blue.

The antique telescope stand had an aqua patina from weather and age. The replacement telescope she'd bought from Archie for a steal at five hundred dollars was an Ambassador Executive Celestron with fifty-millimeter glass optics and 45x magnification. It was brass and copper with leather bindings, and quite beautiful.

All of her guests had returned from their outings to listen to Dustin Miller expound on the spectacular features of the full moon. Cora watched her husband with pride. The moon was round and gold in the dark sky.

Dustin, in shorts and a polo, flip-flops on his feet, clasped his hands together as he faced them. His bald head glistened. "Does anyone know how long a full moon lasts?"

Spencer Cohen raised his hand. "Two days? Three?"

"It appears that way to the naked eye," Dustin said, shaking his head but in an inviting way that Charlene could see him using in the front of a college classroom.

"A week?" Braydon Welch guessed. He and Sheridon were both drinking root beer and eating carrot sticks with ranch dressing. They hadn't been interested in the bubbles or sunglasses she'd bought.

"No, sirree. It's one night only." Dustin hooked his thumb over his shoulder to point at the moon behind him. "It is *precisely* when the moon is at exactly one hundred and eighty degrees opposite the sun. Ecliptic longitude."

"Huh?" Bob tugged his bushy beard with confusion. His boys laughed.

"Ecliptic longitude," Dustin repeated. "What it means is that this is the time when the moon is directly opposite the sun."

"Ohhh," the Welch guys said together.

Joanie laughed at her brood and sipped her red wine. "Way to make me proud," she said. "Sheridon, you just did a school report on the constellations."

"I forgot!" Sheridon said. "It's summer."

"Vacation tends to empty the brain," Spencer said. "Happens to my students too."

"And mine," Dustin admitted.

Her guests all laughed good-naturedly.

There were very few clouds in the night sky. Charlene could not have asked for a nicer night. The stars twinkled.

Jack appeared, and she grinned as he asked, "What's going on?"

She didn't answer him, but she watched him, watching Dustin. Charlene was so happy to see Jack that she almost greeted him. Almost.

"We are very fortunate the sky is clear tonight," Dustin said. "There are many planets visible to the naked eye—Venus, Mars, Jupiter, Saturn. We can also use Charlene's telescope to zoom in and get details." The astronomer pointed to various objects.

"Can we see the man on the moon?" Lara asked, very serious. She was on her second bottle of bubbles and had put the star-shaped sunglasses in her room.

"Want to try to find him?" Natalie asked.

"Yes, please!" Lara looked through the telescope's glass lens. "I can't see him," she complained. "Is he hiding?"

"He's not real," Braydon whispered.

Joanie gently popped her son on the back of the shoulder. "Hey, now."

Natalie took a peek through the lens. "Maybe he's sleeping."

"Mr. Miller, does anybody live on the moon?" Lara asked. "For real?"

"Because there is no water on the moon, there are no living organisms," Dustin said. "As of now, it is not suitable for human habitation, but who knows what the future will bring. It's why I like science so much. We are constantly learning."

"I want to be a scientist," Lara decided.

Cora smiled with encouragement. "It's a great career. I especially love to research the stars in the sky."

Dustin sipped from his bottle of beer. "Does anybody here know the name of our galaxy?"

Sheridon said, "The Milky Way!"

"Excellent," Cora said. "Now, how about some constellations?"

"The Little Dipper," Braydon said.

"The Big Dipper!" Jack said.

"The Big Dipper," Bob echoed.

"Also known as Little Bear, in the Ursa Minor constellation," Dustin said. "Ursa Major holds the Big Dipper, a larger version of the Little Dipper. The brightest star in Ursa Minor is called Polaris."

"The North Star!" Sheridon said, his memory probably jogged by the recap from Dustin.

"Exactly." Dustin nodded. "Sailors used it as a marker to find their way at sea. In the old days, people had to use maps for navigation."

"What do we use now?" Cora asked the group, obviously at ease in feeding questions for Dustin to answer.

"GPS!" Spencer answered. "Thank God for Siri."

"And what does that stand for?" Dustin asked.

Charlene's mind went blank. It was just *GPS*. "Something, something . . . satellite?"

There were many guesses, and finally Dustin put them out of their misery. "Global Positioning System. This is information derived from a group of satellites"—he gestured to the sky above them—"to provide information to your navigation system in your car, or on your cell phone."

Lara scuffed her sandal to the deck floor. "I want to know more about the moon."

"I've got you," Dustin said, allowing the seven-year-old to keep them on topic. "Do you know what the full moon is called in June?" He was good at keeping the conversation flowing, Charlene thought.

"Do the moons really have names every month?" Sheila asked.

"They do. I am not kidding!" Dustin put his hand to his chest and raised the other in an oath. "This particular moon is called the Strawberry Moon."

"Will it turn pink?" Lara asked, her tone excited.

"No, ma'am." Dustin took another drink of his beer. "Last month's moon would have been spectacular with the lunar eclipse. It was a blood flower moon, and it did turn an amazing orange and red. Did you see that, Charlene?"

"No. I'm usually tucked in bed by now," Charlene said with a laugh.

"True," Jack agreed. "Or watching movies with me."

"'Blood moon' sounds way cooler than 'strawberry'," Braydon said.

"Agreed." Dustin put the bottle down by his feet. "But it got the name because June is when we pick strawberries. Now, what is a full moon famous for?"

"Werewolves," Braydon said right away.

"Yep, werewolves." Jack gestured to the moon. He sat on the railing without fear that he might fall backward. *"Even a man who is pure at heart and says his prayers at night, may become a wolf when the wolfsbane blooms, and the autumn moon is bright."*

Bob groaned and smacked a palm to his forehead. "Not real, bud. Not any more real than the man on the moon."

"They might be, Dad!" Sheridon came to his twin's defense.

"How many of you have seen *The Wolf Man?*" Charlene asked, spurred on by Jack's quote from the movie.

Four hands raised. Not surprisingly, they all belonged to the Welches.

"We have horror movie night every Saturday," Joanie said. "We love them. I like *American Werewolf in London* better than the black-and-white movies, though."

"We were hoping to go to the Spellbound Movie Theater, but then that murder happened," Bob said. "Do you know anything about that?"

"Not much." *That I can talk about,* Charlene finished under her breath.

Dustin pointed to the sky. "June is amazing. We can see all kinds of planets. Hey, boys, do you have the NASA stargazing app? If you use your camera lens, your phone can tell what you're looking at."

"Instead of the telescope?" Spencer didn't seem convinced. He and Natalie taught middle school rather than college but also had a thirst for knowledge.

"I am a man of science," Dustin said. "I will use whatever tools necessary to document, record, and learn."

Sheila twisted the tail of her long red braid. "I appreciate the science, but this is magical too. I can see how people in the olden times worshiped the sun and the moon."

"The moon goddess," Joanie said. "She was a major foundation of our religion growing up. My mother practices the craft to this day."

"What is that?" Natalie asked. "The craft? Do you mean modern-day witches?"

"Yes, that's right. Mom believes, and I suppose I do, too, in the triple goddess." Joanie sipped her wine. "The maiden, the mother, and the crone. Each symbolizes a phase of the moon and of the female life cycle." She reached for Bob and tugged his beard with a wink. "Her consort is the horned god."

"But that's make-believe," Dustin said.

Charlene realized this could go wrong quickly.

Jack did, too, and murmured, "Did you know Joanie was Wiccan?"

Charlene didn't answer but sucked in her lower lip. Joanie had a lot of like-minded folks in Salem. She might recommend the couple head to Flint's Vineyard to meet Brandy and Evelyn at the winery.

"I think all religions have a faith base that requires a leap into the unknown," Bob said, not rising to the possible insult, but letting it go. Not his first foray into defending his wife's beliefs against science.

She liked the Welches all the more for it. The Millers also rebounded and returned to the subject of the moon. "I hate to be a myth-buster," Dustin said, "but despite all the hype around full moons, and the word *lunacy* coming from the word *luna*, Latin for *moon*, there is no scientific proof this is true."

Jack gave a thumbs-down at that.

Dustin chuckled. "People are crazy, just because."

Charlene thought of Darren and his out-of-control behavior. It would be nice, in a way, to have an explanation.

At midnight, just as they were all headed downstairs to bed, Charlene thought she heard the faintest howl of a wolf.

Jack laughed. "Don't fear the werewolves, Charlene. It's not autumn."

Breakfast Wednesday morning was boisterous and filled with fun energy as everyone relived the glorious full moon party on the widow's walk. It had been an evening loaded with laughter.

It was their first full moon party, and she could see making it a summer thing. Charlene brushed crumbs from her blueberry muffin into her palm and dropped them on her plate. She'd dressed for a casual day in shorts and a sleeveless, flowing top.

"The boys want a telescope for their birthdays in August," Joanie said. "But we don't have the view you do. Our roof is a boring A-frame with shingle tile."

She'd brought yogurts to the sideboard for additional choices to the cold cereal, bagels, and muffins—English, banana, or blueberry.

Sheridon spread peanut butter on his English muffin. "It will be so cool to see the stars and planets. Maybe a UFO!"

Braydon sipped orange juice. "Aliens rock." He made the rock-and-roll horns with his fingers.

Lara, again next to Avery, said, "Do you like aliens, Avery?"

Charlene had heard the teenager come home around one and gone to sleep herself soon after.

"I've never met an alien," Avery said. "They might be nice."

"Not in the scary movies. They are *not* nice," Braydon said. "If you see one, you should run for cover."

Lara studied Braydon across the table with smug superiority. "You don't know, though."

"You're also twelve, almost thirteen. She's seven," Joanie said patiently. "The ones she watches probably are nice."

Bob groaned and drank his coffee. "Teenagers. How are we old enough to have teenagers in a few months?"

Joanie laughed, peeling an orange. "I don't believe it."

"Time just speeds by," Spencer said, gesturing with a cereal spoon to his kids. Christopher was making a mess of the yogurt as he tried to feed himself. This kid was so cute he could be a poster child for healthy living.

"Sounds like I missed a fun rooftop party last night," Avery said.

"Where did you go?" Lara demanded in a half

pout. The star-shaped sunglasses were next to her plate.

"I was with my friend Seth, and we went to the beach for a bonfire with our friends. Things got a little wild when some of the guys pretended to be wolves. I was able to quote that movie, *The Wolf Man*, since we just saw it at the Spellbound Movie Theater. They were impressed," Avery said.

"You were at the theater? Did you know about the murder that happened?" Bob asked. He turned to Charlene for confirmation.

Avery clamped her lips closed, eyes as wide as a deer in the headlights, before glancing at Charlene.

Charlene patted Avery's hand. "It's okay." She cleared her throat and murmured, "We were there, but we can't talk about it because there's an ongoing investigation."

There. That sounded just right.

Bob seemed impressed.

"We understand," Joanie said, scooping a spoon of yogurt. She raised a brow at her hubby, who was literally about to burst with questions. "Right, Bob?"

Bob ran his fingers through his beard, exhaled, and halved a blueberry muffin with his thumbs. "Right."

Natalie finished her banana nut muffin and her coffee, then reached for Christopher's hands. "Come here, hon. I'll help you."

"I do it!" The toddler screeched loud enough to bring Silva from wherever she'd been dozing to investigate the dining room. The cat blinked golden eyes at the little boy.

Maria and Georgio Lopez, Georgio still in his sling, exchanged a look—the same one Cora and Dustin did, as if to congratulate themselves on not having kids.

Sheila laughed down the table, on a different page, probably because of her many siblings at home. "He's so cute. How old?"

"Three," Natalie said.

"Terrible twos over with?" Sheila's hair was loose today and wavy from her braid of yesterday.

"No. He just got louder," Spencer admitted.

Charlene enjoyed the lazy vibe the group had this morning over breakfast. Nobody's tours started for the day until well after ten.

"How was the harbor cruise?" Charlene asked. "We were so entertained last night, Dustin, that I forgot to ask you all how it went."

"I saw three dolphins and a whale," Sheila said, her green eyes bright. "They are gorgeous, and the whales are inconceivable in size."

"Can we do that, Dad?" Lara asked. "Go on the boat ride?"

"I think so," Spencer said after a nod from Natalie. "Maybe Friday."

"You might want to buy those tickets today," Charlene suggested. "They sell out quick for the weekend."

"Good idea," Natalie said. She half-tilted her head toward Spencer.

"I'm on it after breakfast," Spencer said, picking up on the couple-shorthand often used in long-term relationships.

"Thanks—maybe we can switch the Plymouth

Rock tour, if necessary," Natalie said. "It would be a nice addition to our vacation."

Spencer nodded.

"Thanks, Daddy," Lara said, hugging his arm. She had cream cheese on her upper lip.

Avery reached over with a napkin and wiped it off Lara's face.

Lara, embarrassed, giggled and hid under the table.

A knock sounded on the front door, and Minnie went to answer. Charlene followed, alarmed by the intrusion of their quiet breakfast. Klara stood on the porch, her dark curls untamed around her head. Her jeans, with stylish rips, were skintight, and her orange T-shirt was too. Her heels were orange wedges that matched. "I tried to call you. Charlene. You have to help me!"

"What is it?" She heard Avery in the foyer with Lara.

Charlene quickly shut the door on her audience as Klara didn't appear well. "It's all right," she murmured. "What's the matter?"

Klara grabbed her forearm. "He's gone."

"Who?" Of course, Charlene knew who, but the question had just popped out.

"Darren. Gone. I was worried when I didn't hear from him—we had a huge fight yesterday, and well, this morning I wanted to clear the air. I don't want to return to Pittsburgh with him in this state, you know?"

Charlene nodded. Had Sam cleared Klara to leave town? Klara would have had access to all of Darren's salts, and she hadn't liked Elise.

"I knocked on his bedroom door for twenty

minutes straight, and he still didn't answer. I finally used a hairpin to trigger the lock, fearing the worst, like he was dead." Klara pressed her hand to her chest, her brown eyes filled with fear.

Charlene patted Klara's upper arm. "That must have been some fight." Had it been about her wanting to leave him, as he'd said yesterday?

Klara blinked. "A doozy." She gulped. "The room was freaking empty, and Darren was gone. His window was wide open."

Remembering the howl of the wolf at midnight, Charlene had a bad feeling. "Did you call the police?"

"That would be a big no." Klara moved an inch away from her. "There were muddy footprints on the white floor. God, I hate that white. And then on the windowsill. Like he'd gone out, and then come back, and then left again. Thank heaven he was on the first floor. What is he doing?"

Charlene's thoughts whirled and settled. "Last night was a full moon." Dustin, the scientist, had said there was no proof that it changed behavior. And yet. The doctor in the ER had seemed to credit it.

"What if Darren has gone crazy?" Klara asked. "What if not only losing Elise, but being a suspect in her murder, has made him nuts? He's as conflicted as the wolf man!"

Jack materialized on the porch. "Ask her if she knows about the circus? It could be a clue to the genetic trait that Darren was so ashamed of."

"Klara, did you know Darren was in the circus?" Charlene asked.

Klara winced in surprise, her eyes narrowed. "How did you know? He never talks about it, ever. I don't think even Elise knew. He was so private about his past."

Franco had told her. Charlene hedged, "He must have mentioned something about it."

"Well, he was part of the circus troupe in Munich." Klara shook her head. "See, he tells partial stories. I never knew he had a sister who'd died."

Charlene waited, listening with compassion as Klara dealt with the onslaught of emotion caused by her friend's pain.

"Then, he tells you about her, so casually, like it was no big deal, while sitting in his kitchen. I think being abandoned at an orphanage with your sibling is pretty damn important, but he acted like it was nothing. *Acted.* I know he was hurt."

She ushered Klara toward the railing to sit and calm down. Charlene sat on the opposite side.

Jack paced the porch with concern. "*The Wolf Man* movie is about a man possibly dealing with schizophrenia, according to everyone around him. What if that is happening to Darren? Stress can cause a break with reality. I wish I could see him, Charlene. Can you bring him back here?"

Charlene had to find him before he hurt himself. "I'll help you find Darren," she said to Klara, but also Jack.

"Thank you." Klara drew in her breath.

"What did he do in the circus?" Charlene asked, thinking of his broad shoulders and thick chest.

"Trapeze. Sold popcorn and peanuts. Greeted folks." Klara met Charlene's gaze. "While the troupe traveled, he was the chef. They tried to be home over the winter to keep the shows locally in Munich."

"The chef! Is that where he discovered his affinity for seasoning salts?"

"Yep. He has an amazing palate and could discern herbs and spices blindfolded. It's what made him think of starting a specialty salt company."

"I can see him welcoming people too," Charlene said. "Darren is very outgoing."

"He is. He's genuine. Where is he? Why is he losing his mind like this?" Klara grasped Charlene's hand and clung to it tightly.

"He's had a huge trauma," Jack said. "If he can get help soon, then it might be contained as a short-term lapse in reason."

Charlene said, "We can find him and get him some medical help to handle this trauma resulting in his behavior."

"You're right." Klara released Charlene to brush tears from her cheeks. "Before he does something stupid. Or more stupid?"

"Did you know he was raised in the orphanage?" Charlene asked. Klara had been his closest friend since moving from Munich.

"It was such a small mention, more as an explanation as to why he'd joined the circus. The job paid very well, but it was all a stepping stone to owning a movie theater."

Charlene nodded. "That goal made him a millionaire."

"Yes. Money to help others motivated him." Klara sighed. "It was never for himself. Darren left the orphanage at twelve to seek work, and the circus didn't care he was underage. He was big for his age, strong."

Child labor laws might be different in a foreign country. And in this case, it had offered Darren freedom. "I see."

Klara swung her leg against the railing, her hands over her knee. "I asked him after you left the other day about his sister. After much prodding, like pulling freaking teeth, he said he went to work to get money to get her out of there and provide her with a nice home. He wanted to protect her, but he was just a kid himself. Twelve!"

The Welch twins were twelve and fumbled footballs. Charlene couldn't imagine them saving anyone. But then again, when pressed, people could do astounding things—and they did, all the time.

"Darren saved every cent, and at the age of fourteen, he went back to get her, but the nuns said she was dead. Died in a fire, so there was no place for him to mourn her loss. Can you imagine?" Klara swiped another tear off her cheek. "He left and toured with the circus, cultivating his palate as the chef, saving for his dream of a happy life. That culminated in retirement with a movie theater. He had a Midas touch with money, but he would have given it all up for his sister. By donating what he does to the orphanages, it's like he's still trying to save her."

"I think it's very kind." Charlene blinked back tears at Darren's loss. "I don't understand why he left Germany. To start selling seasoning salts?"

"No. He was miserable in Germany and wanted more than the circus life. He did his research and decided on Saint Mary's, Pennsylvania, because of the large Bavarian community there. He taught himself English and bought property right before it would go up in price. His investments turned into big profits. He's thirty-six now, and I met him when he'd just turned thirty-one. Selling his salts at a vendor's booth and getting excellent reviews. I knew I could help him reach his dream of becoming a millionaire."

"And to support those orphanages." Charlene nodded. "That's special."

"He's a great guy and never thought he deserved someone as pretty as Elise." Klara pursed her lips. "He wanted to be happy."

Charlene bowed her head at that observation. Love was love.

"It's like a modern-day beauty-and-the-beast kind of thing, only the beauty isn't—*wasn't*—worthy of the beast." Klara sniffed and patted her heart.

"I'm sorry," Charlene said. "This must be so hard."

"Come with me to find him, Charlene." Klara speared her with her brown-eyed gaze. "You are a steady person. I need that."

Avery cracked open the door. "Everything okay?"

"It is!" Charlene looked at Avery, who appeared understandably curious. "Hon, would you bring me my purse, keys, and phone?"

"Sure! Back in a sec." Avery shut the door.

Jack shimmered with apprehension. "I don't like this. Call Sam. You can't just go off with this woman, who has not been cleared of suspicion."

Charlene bit the inside of her cheek. Jack had a point.

Avery returned and handed the items over. "Where are you going?"

Charlene gestured to Klara to explain how much she was willing to share with the young lady.

Klara exhaled. "Darren has lost his mind. He went out last night and never came home. Hey—" She got up from the railing and stepped toward Avery. "Can you call Seth? Maybe he's heard from Darren."

"I can do that," Avery said. "What about Matthew and Franco?"

"I tried to call and had to leave messages." Klara tugged her orange tee over her hips. "No answer from either of them, but it's still early."

"What about Officer Bernard? Or Sam?" Charlene suggested.

"God, no. No police," Klara said. She ran her fingers through her wild curls. "He hates that woman who put him in jail and hasn't stopped being angry about it."

Officer Lennox was not winning points toward Officer of the Year. "Okay. Do you want me to drive?"

"Sure." Klara pointed toward the sleek black car next to Charlene's. "I'll get the Tesla later. You know the area better than I do."

Charlene nodded at Avery. "I'll be in touch— call if you hear anything, all right?"

"Yep. Be safe," Avery said. "Don't forget—a murderer is running loose in Salem." And, as her subtle chin gesture at Klara inferred, Charlene was riding around with someone who had a motive.

Jack put his hands behind his back and scowled. "Very safe. I wish Avery would call Sam anyway."

And say what? They were missing a suspect in a murder case? It probably wouldn't go over well.

"Bye." Charlene checked that her pepper spray was in her purse from when she'd visited Franco. It was within easy reach in the side pocket. She and Klara both got in the SUV, and Charlene drove carefully away from the bed-and-breakfast. "Where should we go first?"

"I've driven all around town looking for Darren, but he's not anywhere." Klara sucked in a sob. "He loved Elise so much. Too much. It zapped his reason."

Where would Darren go if he was trying to make things right? Not for himself, but for Elise? "Let's go to Patty's. She might have seen him. He was very upset about Elise not being part of the Wagner inheritance."

Klara curled her upper lip. "Really? Patty is not my favorite person, either."

Charlene focused on the road ahead. "Why is that?"

"I don't like Patty any more than I did Elise. She was angling for Darren's attention behind Elise's back." Klara tried to tame her wild curls by smoothing them down. They *sproing*ed defiantly.

Charlene's stomach sank. "Do you mean, for the bakery business?" Patty had told her that Elise had had the salts and pretzels in mind since Elise and Darren got married.

"No, I don't think *just* the business," Klara said slyly. The tone made Charlene wary. Though Klara had said she wanted to return to Pittsburgh, Charlene didn't know if Klara had actually been cleared to go by the police. Could she have killed Elise?

"Before I change my opinion about a woman who seems fairly decent to me, tell me what you saw, or heard, exactly." Charlene slowed for a light, but then pressed the gas pedal as it turned green.

"Hey, I thought 'poor Patty' myself at first, but then . . ." Klara stared out the window as they went down the hill, and didn't finish her sentence.

"Yes?"

"Never mind." Klara kept her gaze on the passing traffic.

They passed Brews and Broomsticks and continued toward town, which reminded her of Kevin. "Hey, did you get a chance to read about the history of the Spellbound building?"

"I started to research it, but honestly, my focus was on keeping Darren from hurting himself," Klara said with a bit of snark. "Priorities."

"Got it." Charlene relaxed her shoulders, thinking that Klara would keep her Patty gossip to herself.

She was wrong. Klara said, "I came here for a short visit two months ago. The four of us were all drinking, celebrating the movie theater having an opening date. A launch. Celebrating the seasoned salt flavors Darren was working on. The house, everything. Just, life being great."

Life had been magical while she'd known the Shultzes, seemingly unstoppable in their good fortune. "Yes?"

"We were out on the town, dancing, drinking champagne, acting like big shots. It was fun, I won't deny it." Klara rested her hands over her knees, covering the stylish holes in the denim.

It didn't seem like Klara really wanted to share the story but felt she had to. Charlene said, "Drinking lowers people's inhibitions."

"Tell me something I don't know." Klara rolled her eyes. "Patty kept touching Darren, you know, like, his arm, then his back. When Elise went to the ladies' room, Patty kissed his mouth. Darren retreated so fast. That's why I know he would never cheat on Elise. Can't believe Patty even tried it."

"That's awful. Did Elise find out?"

Klara shrugged. "I acted like I saw nothing, and Darren didn't bring it up either. Guess we both just attributed it to her drinking."

How terrible for Elise. Charlene braked at a *STOP* sign, scanning the streets for Darren in the passing vehicles. Silly, but she did it anyway. The man was on foot. "Hey, does he have another form of transportation? What about Elise's car?"

"Elise didn't drive—they just had the one." Klara nodded at Charlene. "Good thinking, though. I knew you'd help me. You give off that impression."

Charlene half-smiled. Some people liked it, others not as much. "Does Darren have a phone?"

"Nope. His was smashed at the theater, and he didn't have a spare at the house." Klara put her hand on the door. "Stop!"

"What?" Charlene checked her mirrors and pulled to the side of the road.

As soon as the car was in PARK, Klara said, "That's him! Darren. Coming from Patty's?"

Klara jolted out of the car like a lightning bolt and zigzagged across traffic. All Charlene could do was hold her breath as her stomach lodged in her throat.

*Please don't get killed in Salem!*

# CHAPTER 17

Charlene exhaled, her body trembling with tension and adrenaline, unable to look away from Klara until she'd made it safely across the road and out of sight. The bright orange of her top and heels made her visible, thank heaven. She gripped the wheel. Had Klara seen Darren?

Charlene inhaled and then breathed out, her thoughts calming. Or maybe Klara didn't want to visit Patty after sharing what she'd seen. Could Klara be exaggerating what happened as payback for Patty accusing Klara of sleeping with Darren? Franco had mentioned Klara was a gossip, and this might be a prime example.

What should she do? Go after Klara or continue to Patty's in her search for Darren? Shaking her head, Charlene drove toward Wagner's Bakery. People were complicated beings, and she'd learned from her bed-and-breakfast as well as the occasional venture with Sam, that there was more than one truth.

Like Joanie, being Wiccan, and the Millers scientists—they'd managed to get along and not make it about that, but they found common ground. Moon and stars. The night sky.

Turning right, Charlene followed the tree-lined road until she arrived at the bakery. She parked on the side street. The big, open window showed Patty behind the glass case and counter. The gingerbread-style roof matched that of the house. Patty saw her coming but didn't wave or even smile as Charlene opened the door.

"Morning," Charlene said.

Someone hummed beautifully in the back room out of sight. Wagner was a German name too—so was Maxwell. Was there more to Klara and Darren's friendship? Glorious smells of fresh-baked goodness welcomed her far more than Patty did.

Patty crossed her arms and narrowed her blue eyes as if Charlene had offended her somehow.

"Hi," Charlene said. "I was wondering if we could talk?"

Patty pursed her lips and then nodded, coming around the corner and untying her apron to drop on the counter near the register. "I'll be back, Mila."

The woman kept humming.

Patty shook her head, her brown hair back in a tight bun covered in a net. "I've never met someone so shy in my life, and my mom suffered from every phobia you could think of. Made her an easy target for my dad."

They left the shop, the wood-and-glass door swinging shut behind them. Charlene glimpsed their image together when she turned to the side—both brunette, Patty shorter and dressed in a Wagner's Bakery shirt, over slacks. Charlene's sleeveless top flowed in the breeze, and she was glad to be out of the warm bakery.

They stopped at the sidewalk near Charlene's SUV.

"What do you want?" Patty asked in a curt tone.

"I was wondering if you'd heard from Darren recently?"

"Oh, yeah," Patty said in a furious voice. "I sure have."

That didn't sound good. Well, Charlene was here for answers. "When was this?"

"Darren showed up here this morning right before dawn." Patty's upper lip curled. "I was awake and getting ready to walk to the bakery to start the donuts. He scared the daylights out of me, and I don't like it. I shouldn't be afraid on my own property!"

"Oh, no." Charlene didn't share that Darren might be having a manic episode of some kind brought on by Elise's death and the attempt on his life.

What if Patty was responsible for them? She'd been by the pretzels at the counter that day and could have easily put the poison in Elise's seasoned salt. Maybe in her hurry, she'd sprinkled some by accident on Darren's tray. But why? Could she have set up the drapes to fall on Darren?

Patty was not her friend in any case, but Elise's sister, whom Charlene had liked, at least on the surface. The baker glanced back at her shop, eager to return to work.

Charlene shrugged her purse up to her shoulder as it had slipped. "I wonder why Darren was here so early?"

"He must've been out all night. I don't think he realized the time at all." Patty arched a brow to convey how ridiculous that seemed to her. "Who loses track like that? He smelled like tequila."

His drink of choice definitely would lead to a lapse in time and reason. "Do you know what he wanted?"

"Yeah," Patty admitted brusquely. "I'd called him yesterday and told him I'd bought a black dress for Elise that I felt was more appropriate than the pink Dior number with the price tag still on." She vibrated self-righteous anger.

That could be a problem. "Darren said Elise had picked that out. It was her favorite outfit."

"I believe it."

Charlene waited. And was rewarded.

"She was no better than a whore," Patty whispered, "marrying for money." She glanced around as if to make sure no neighbors were watching.

Charlene bowed her head. It was difficult to keep quiet when she had so many opinions, but she'd learned that if she was silent, people talked.

She thought the Wagner sisters had both been abused by their religious father, and now Patty was left on her own to handle it. "I hope you didn't say that to him?"

Patty's skin turned a mottled red. "I did."

Charlene breathed in through her nose to keep from reacting. She could imagine Darren's reaction on a good day, let alone when he was in emotional agony. "What happened then?"

"He called the mortician and forbid me to be in

contact. Over my sister's body!" Patty looked up at Charlene with disbelief. "The nerve of that man really burns me up. How dare he?"

Her lip quivered, and her eyes were glassy—not with regret, but anger.

"That's too bad," Charlene said in a neutral tone. "Maybe if you apologize, he will change his mind. You're both overwhelmed."

"It's worse." Patty peered over her shoulder as if praying for someone to intervene, but there was nobody to come to her rescue.

"How? You can't see your sister before her funeral."

"Darren's going to have her cremated and spread her ashes over the sea." Patty crossed her arms. "We have a family plot at Salem Cemetery. We have five generations of Wagners there."

"That's quite a history." Of abuse? Religion could get fanatical, as evidenced by the Salem witch trials. She could hear the pride of family in Patty's words.

"Darren told me Elise didn't want to be there, but I just don't believe it." Her chin quaked. "I don't. He's lying!"

Charlene patted her shoulder.

Patty cried and dabbed her nose with a tissue from her pocket. It wasn't the first time she'd needed it today, obviously. It was so sad.

"Was Darren welcome to be buried in the cemetery with Elise?" Charlene shifted her weight from her left to her right, wishing there was a place to sit down—she didn't think suggesting the shady porch of the house would go over well.

"No." Patty's nose hiked. "Of course not. He wasn't family."

"Technically, he was." Charlene didn't see remorse on Patty's face any more than she'd seen regret. "He married Elise. Maybe that's why Elise didn't want to be there either."

Shrugging, Patty said, "I thought he was the perfect man for her, until . . ."

"Until what?"

"It's not important."

Patty regarded her shoes, just visible beneath the full hem of her slacks. Crocs. Black, rounded toes of hard plastic.

Charlene's nape tingled. "I like your shoes."

"Thanks." Patty's eyes narrowed as she stared at Charlene. "They're the best for being on my feet all day."

"I've heard that." Charlene pulled her phone from the side pocket of her purse, wishing she could get a picture for Avery. She backed up a step, glad they were on the sidewalk in broad daylight after all, though the street was quiet this many blocks away from downtown and the wharf. Could Patty have killed her sister by accident, while trying to kill Darren? She hovered her thumb over the call screen, in case she needed 911.

"Why are you looking at me like that, Charlene?" Patty demanded.

"Patty, you accused Darren of straying. With Klara."

"So?" Her brow furrowed.

"It wasn't true." Charlene shook her head, trying to understand. "Why would you do that to your only sister?"

Patty defaulted back to being mad, ping-ponging like Darren had. "What are you saying?"

"Did you make a move on Darren? Did he turn you down?" Charlene repeated what Klara had told her she'd seen. "You kissed him. On the mouth."

Patty's face turned bright red with shame and humiliation. "No. Never."

Charlene raised a brow at the obvious lie. "Did you want payback against your sister?"

A tear slipped free from Patty's eye.

"The one you love so much." Charlene gestured to the family home with its fairy-tale gingerbread trim.

Patty placed her hands before her in a prayer position, her attention on the sidewalk.

"You said she stole from you all . . . Did you get your revenge by somehow coercing the house from your parents?"

"How dare you accuse me of such things?" Patty asked, guilt clear in her gaze.

Charlene could see she'd hit the nail on the head. "Did Darren realize what you'd done? He said your sister had invisible scars and guessed it was from how you were brought up. You must carry those wounds too."

"I don't know what you're talking about. My father was a pillar in this community. A pastor. Always giving." Patty's mouth trembled. "Setting an example of how to be a good man."

"He's gone now, Patty. You don't have to protect him anymore."

"I'm not." Patty sobbed and brought her hand to her chest.

"Darren was right. Is that what he was telling

you about this morning at dawn?" Charlene pressed. Had Patty poisoned her sister?

Patty fell to her knees on the sidewalk, her head bowed in supplication. "Darren asked if I'd killed my parents like I'd killed Elise. To get the house away from Elise."

Charlene swayed at the words coming from her mouth. Was this a confession?

"Killed?" She gripped her phone tight, ready to call for help.

"I didn't do that." Patty rocked back on her heels and pleaded with Charlene. "I told him I didn't do it. He kept howling outside my window like a demon. Like one of those wolf monsters from the movies he likes to watch. I warned Elise he was a monster too."

"Because he told you no?"

"He didn't even care, which is worse." Patty stayed on the sidewalk, her hands before her. Tears slid from her closed lids.

"I'm going to call the police," Charlene said. "They can sort this out."

"No!" Patty scrambled to her feet. "I didn't kill anybody. Not my parents. Not my sister. Darren's wrong. I convinced them to leave me the house because Elise stole everything else from me."

"That's not true," Charlene said. She wanted to believe Patty so much. Could she? The woman was desperate.

"It felt like it." Patty swayed on the sidewalk, side to side. "When she left for Pennsylvania, I had nothing. I had no defenses against our dad. I was so miserable without her here in Salem. At our house."

"You are an adult woman," Charlene said. "You're an incredible baker. Your parents are dead. You can't blame anybody but yourself for your unhappiness."

Patty turned toward the path leading to the shaded house. The fairy-tale home that wasn't. "You have no idea what my life was like, always in Elise's shadow. Always second."

"It's the past, Patty. Change it if you don't like it. Sell the bakery. Sell the house. Go to Hawaii. I moved from Chicago to Salem to start over, and it's been the best thing I've ever done."

A police car drove by, with Officer Bernard behind the wheel. He pulled over and got out of the vehicle, a man sworn to protect and serve Salem. "Everything okay? Got a call about a possible disturbance."

Charlene narrowed her eyes at Patty. "I'd like it if you shared with the officer what you just did with me, and then I'll be on my way."

Patty curled her upper lip but told the kind Haitian officer her side of the story—from Darren to Elise, and then her parents. "Darren refuses to bury her in the black dress I bought," Patty said, still angry on this point.

"Darren is her husband," the officer said. "Maybe when things cool down, we can all have a conversation together."

Patty nodded, chin jutted stubbornly.

Officer Bernard focused on Charlene. "When was the last time you saw Darren Shultz?" he asked.

"Yesterday, when I drove him home from the emergency room," Charlene said. She didn't mention that Klara was searching Salem for him. She didn't want another incident where Darren might get tossed in jail.

Officer Bernard nodded. "Take care, Charlene."

She smiled her thanks and gestured slightly toward Patty's feet and the Crocs. She left as the officer questioned the baker on her footwear. It was clear he recalled Avery's picture. Charlene didn't know whom to believe, but she trusted that Officer Bernard would get to the bottom of things.

Charlene drove toward Darren's home, checking for missed calls. Nothing. She dialed Klara, but it went to voice mail.

She parked in the driveway of the gorgeous, white four-story home. Charlene knocked, but there was no answer. Where was Darren—or Klara? She left a note for Darren to call her, or just drop by her house, putting it under the red front door. The Tesla was parked, so Klara must have brought it back. Or Darren had. Her head ached as she imagined Klara chasing Darren around town as Darren imagined himself to be a tequila-swilling werewolf.

Before returning to the bed-and-breakfast, Charlene decided to stop at Brews and Broomsticks to talk with Kevin about the haunted building. Kevin and Darren had been friendly during the Salem business association meetings, chaired by Brandy. If anybody knew about Spellbound Movie Theater's history, it should be Kevin Hughes.

She went into the dim bar—it must be a prerequisite to have low lighting in the places, she thought—and chose a stool at the corner of the counter.

"Charlene!" As a bartender, Kevin was a font of information.

He was also good at gaining information, so she had to be careful only to give away what she didn't mind sharing.

"How are you, Kevin?"

"Great." Kevin smoothed back his blond locks, the broomstick tattoo visible on his inner forearm in his black T-shirt. "Sunny days, lots of tourists at night. I can't complain."

"Good to hear." She placed her purse on the stool next to her.

"How is it with you, Charlene?"

"All right." Charlene smiled over the counter and settled in for what she hoped would be a productive chat.

"Any news about the movie theater?" Kevin murmured, his tone pitched invitingly. "How is Darren, with Elise gone? Are the coppers easing up on him now?"

"That's one of the reasons I'm here, actually," Charlene said. "Have you seen Darren at all today?"

"Nope." Kevin poured a glass of water and passed it to her. "You want something with a kick to drink?"

"Tempting, but I must get back to my guests. I was hoping you'd seen him. He's not feeling great, which is understandable, but his friend Klara is especially worried."

"She was a hottie," Kevin stated, no flirtatiousness about it as he was firmly attached to his girlfriend, Amy Fadar. "Amy wondered if they used to be a thing. In Pittsburgh?"

"Saint Mary's," Charlene corrected. "No. She has a girlfriend of her own."

"Ah. Got it." Kevin nodded. "So just great friends, then."

"Klara helped him build his salt business up to what it is today," Charlene said. "Though, Elise also took credit."

"It's a sucky time." Kevin leaned back against the counter behind him. "What rotten luck for the guy."

"Yeah." Charlene sipped her refreshing water. "So, Kevin, what do you know about Spellbound Movie Theater? The building itself?"

"What are you asking?" A blond brow hiked.

She murmured, after a glance around, "Is it haunted?"

Kevin laughed and slanted toward her. "Charlene. *Every* old building in Salem is haunted."

"I mean"—Charlene also scooted forward—"by bad energy. Evil spirits, maybe."

Smoothing his bare upper lip, Kevin asked, "What do you know? I could add it to my paranormal tour."

"The grounds used to be a cemetery." She splayed her hand on the counter.

Kevin paled. "Never good, unless the ground has been consecrated. Was it?"

"I doubt it." Charlene sniffed. "There've been fires and murders. Suicides, people jumping from the roof."

Kevin's gaze dimmed as his excitement was quelled by the awful truth. "I'll dig into it. I mean, Kass and I each felt things during the premiere, but that's normal for us, you know? I'll give her a ring and see if she wants to help me research. She's got much stronger paranormal radar than I do."

"Thanks. I'd like a solid plan to convince Darren not to reopen the theater the way things are right now." Charlene finished her water.

"Got it. Was there anything else on your pretty mind?" Kevin wiped down the counter with a bar towel.

Charlene looked around to make sure they were still alone. "Do you know Dani Gamble? She owns a housecleaning business. Two boys—her son Seth worked the concession stand at the theater."

"No. Why?" Kevin dropped the towel into a bucket of soapy solution beneath the sink.

Charlene held his gaze and spoke softly. "She has a little girl ghost at her house."

Kevin rolled backward on his heels and grinned. "No way."

"Yep." She shrugged. "I was wondering if you knew, but since you don't, I guess you can't answer my questions about it."

"No." Kevin crossed from the sink to the counter in the blink of an eye. "Charlene, I have more questions now for you. Like, I want to meet this woman and this ghost for myself. Did you see the little girl?"

"No!" Charlene waved her hand dismissively. "I did not. Avery didn't either, but I guess the refrigerator door opens on its own."

"That is incredible. You know that stuff rocks my world," Kevin said. "What was the woman's name again?"

Charlene shook her head. "Slow down. I'll talk

to Dani to see if she is okay with it all. I mean, maybe she doesn't talk about it because she doesn't want her place crawling with paranormal investigators." Which she could relate to.

Kevin put his hand to his chest as if she'd shot him point-blank with an arrow. "You wound me, Charlene."

"Have you been taking acting lessons from Amy?" Charlene held in a laugh.

"Maybe." Kevin straightened. "Dang it. I was so excited, and now, I'm bummed. You'll talk to Dani?"

Just then, three folks in summer clothes walked in, the sunshine illuminating their happy faces. The smell of sun and the sea clung to them.

"Promise," Charlene said. She put ten dollars on the bar top. "For the tip jar. I didn't mean to keep you away from other customers."

"Have a good one, Charlene," Kevin said. "Let's touch base tomorrow about the building."

She waved and headed out, back to her SUV. Kevin's bar had been a bust. She called Klara again, but there was no answer.

There was a phone call from the Salem PD. She had a feeling it was Sam, and he probably wasn't happy with her about talking to Patty, so, since there was no message, she decided to wait to call him back.

"Home sweet home," Charlene mumbled.

Avery waited for her, as did Jack, though Avery didn't know it, on the front porch with a magazine and a glass of lemonade. Silva curled up in her lap, so large she took up the whole thing.

Charlene parked and skipped up the steps. Silva

slowly stretched and jumped down to greet her with a meow. "How's it going?"

"Good," Avery said, not quite meeting her eyes.

Jack shook his head to warn her that wasn't the whole story. He sported a gold Rolex and a golf shirt tucked into slacks and loafers on his feet sans socks.

Charlene braced herself. "Anything special happen while I was gone?"

"Well, Seth said that Franco isn't answering his phone, so he called Matthew." Avery glanced up at Charlene.

"Okay . . ."

"Matthew isn't answering, either." Avery stared at her with worry-filled eyes.

Charlene didn't feel good all of a sudden. "So, why would all three people be MIA? It has to be connected to Darren, and his manic behavior."

"Exactly." Avery stood and gripped her phone. She bravely held Charlene's gaze. "Seth asked me to go with him to the theater to check things out."

This was exactly what Sam would not want them to do. It was probably why Jack had looked the way he did as well. "Sam asked us not to go."

"But this is important," Avery said.

"It could be dangerous."

Avery shrugged. "Maybe it is, but these are Seth's friends. Co-workers. What if they're in trouble somehow?"

Charlene couldn't forbid Avery to go, or Seth for that matter. "Why don't we call Officer Bernard to check on things at the theater? I just saw him at the bakery with Patty." She nodded at Avery. "Patty was wearing Crocs."

"Patty was?" Avery's eyes widened. "Klara said she didn't want any cops around, though."

Charlene paced the porch, setting her purse on the rail. She had to make the right decision for them both. "Sometimes we need to make the safe choice even if it isn't popular. Do you understand?"

"No." Avery shook her head. "I take it you didn't find Darren?"

"I did not." Charlene stopped and held her arms out from her sides. "Dang it." Where was the man?

Avery reached for Charlene's hand. "Seth says he really wants to go. I don't want him to go to the theater alone. Can you come with us?"

Charlene exhaled. Was she setting the wrong example for Avery?

Her phone rang, and she answered without looking at who it might be. "Hello."

"Charlene? This is Sam."

Her skin tingled. "Hey, Sam. Just the person I wanted to talk to."

Avery shook her head and put her finger to her mouth, while Jack applauded and pumped a fist into the air.

"Anything to do with Officer Bernard and Patty Wagner earlier today?" the detective drawled.

"No. That was handled. Officer Bernard is a wonderful policeman."

"Charlene," Sam growled.

"Sam, you can lecture me later. The kids are really worried about their boss right now, and the other employees at the theater. I was wondering if you could—"

"Darren Shultz evaded arrest this morning at eight thirty. He was around Patty's house, and Patty claims he threatened her."

"There was more to the story than that, as Officer Bernard can tell you."

"Why don't you come down here and tell me your version of what happened?"

"I can't right now. Sam, it's important that you, very casually and nonthreateningly, go by the movie theater."

Avery watched her avidly, trying to understand what was happening from Charlene's part of the conversation.

"There are two cops there right now."

Charlene glanced at Avery. "Did something happen at the theater for officers to already be there?"

Avery sighed.

"Clever," Jack said.

"Nothing yet, but where else does Darren have to go?" Sam said. "We have a patrol unit at his place, as well. Now, do you mind coming down here?"

She realized she didn't have much of a choice unless she risked ruining the relationship she had with Sam.

"Fine. But I can't stay. I have guests to take care of."

# CHAPTER 18

Feeling like a reprimanded child, Charlene deliberately took a deep breath, aware that Avery watched her and would learn. She had to be respectful of Sam, and the Salem PD. She couldn't let her emotions take over.

"You heard there are already two officers at the theater?"

"Yes." Avery swallowed hard. "I'm glad. Why?"

"Nothing happened yet, but Sam is looking for Darren, who evaded arrest this morning. Sam has an officer patrolling his house too."

Avery nodded. "Do you think Darren really poisoned Elise?"

Charlene bowed her head. "I don't think so, hon, but I don't know for sure, and until we do know, with proof, Sam is right. We have to be careful and not blindly trust."

Jack stood behind Charlene, and she could feel his essence as he tugged a lock of her hair out of sight of Avery. "I know it hurts, but well done, my friend."

She grabbed her purse off the railing, climbed back into the Pilot, and rolled the window down to tell Avery, who waited, with Jack, on the porch, "Don't go to the theater, please. Let Seth know there are policemen handling things."

The teen nibbled her lower lip, hands at her sides, phone clutched in her left palm. "Maybe I'll go to Seth's and keep him distracted. If officers are already searching for Darren, and hopefully Franco and Matthew, then we shouldn't be anywhere near the theater."

"She sounds very sensible," Jack said from the passenger seat of her car.

Charlene gave a *woof* of alarm at his sudden appearance and somehow kept her focus on Avery. "Thank you, Avery. It's one less thing for me to worry about. I'll go talk to Sam and be right back, okay?"

"If I'm not here, I'm at Seth's." Avery raised her hand. "Promise."

"She's a good girl," Jack said.

Her ghost disappeared from the SUV when she hit the property line. "Bye, Jack!"

She was annoyed with Sam for being so high-handed as she drove to the station. Air-conditioning blasting against the heat, she blared the radio to sing herself into a better mood, so she wouldn't yell at the detective right out of the gate.

As she reached notes Adele had never intended, her phone rang. It was her mom. Ignore her? That wouldn't work.

She sighed and clicked the *Answer Call* button on Bluetooth. "Hey, Mom!"

"Charlene, sweetheart, how are you?" Brenda Woodbridge asked. Her tone was pleasant and curious, not accusing or guilt-laden.

Made her glad she'd answered. "I'm all right." But she couldn't tell her mother any of what was happening, or her parents might just hop on a plane to surprise her. They'd done it before with not-so-great results.

Juggling a business and her personal life was fine—add in the occasional crime, and her mother wanted to be a part of it. Her mom's friend at the church, Annabeth, had been instrumental in changing Brenda's sour-grapes attitude into one of sunshine.

"Is Avery enjoying her car?"

"She is! Being independent is the best—thanks, again, Mom."

"Our pleasure," her mother said. "Michael was certain Avery would like the blue color."

"She does." Traffic grew more congested as she neared the police station. "The Seafarer's Festival is happening this week. One of my guests tried to catch a giant fish and landed in the ocean instead."

Her mom laughed. "Oops. Are they okay?"

"Yep. Georgio sprained his arm but can still enjoy his vacation—just no more fishing." Charlene decided to park in the lot after cruising by the front of the station with no luck in finding an open spot.

Everything was jam-packed with tourists, which was great for Salem but a bummer for finding parking.

"Your father and I are wondering when a good

time to visit would be. And we are serious about buying a second house. Not right away, of course."

Just then, Sam sped by her at least fifteen to twenty miles over the posted speed limit. His dark-blue SUV was familiar to her, as was his dark mustache. He wore reflective shades as he passed her and was so intent on reaching where he was going, he didn't see her.

"Dang it!"

"What? You don't want us to come?" Her mom sounded hurt.

"It's not that." Charlene hurried with an excuse. "I'm driving, and some *turkey* just blocked me. I should probably go. I'll call you later, but I think November might be nice."

"All right. Love you!"

"Love you both," Charlene said and ended the call.

That Sam! Charlene considered waiting in the station for all of two seconds. How rude that he'd ordered her to his office, only for him to take off. Now, she understood it was his job to catch bad guys, but did he even bother to call her?

"No, he didn't," she said aloud.

What if he was on his way to the theater? Charlene made a sharp turn and drove the two miles out of the way to see if Sam was at the Spellbound.

No cop cars were there at all—but neither was Avery or Seth. The parking lot was empty. She hoped everyone was okay and sped home, a mere eight miles over the posted limit, to make sure she caught up with Avery before the teen left for Seth's.

Of course, by the time she reached home, Avery's

car was gone, but Jack was there, pacing, waiting, guarding.

"That was quick," he said in greeting.

"Sam had to cancel." Charlene, out of the car, set her purse on the armrest of an Adirondack chair. "Didn't bother calling, but he was chasing somebody all right. Smoking tires in his wake. Where's Avery?"

"Avery took off the minute your taillights were out of sight." Jack shook his head. "I really hope she doesn't go to the theater."

"She wasn't there when I drove by," Charlene said. "You think she'd lie?"

"Not lie, but evade. She's a teenager, and when I was her age, there was a lot of gray area in my critical thinking," he said, a fleeting smile on his face.

Charlene laughed and sank into the chair. "I've never heard it put like that—but yeah. Mine too. It wasn't on purpose or meant to harm, but I wanted my way, and I was sure my parents didn't know what they were talking about."

"Maybe Sam located Darren and that's why he ditched you?" Jack suggested. She was annoyed, but after all this time being his friend, she understood that Sam's job was to catch criminals who didn't care about schedules or interruptions.

"I don't know what to think. I hope Matthew and Franco are okay, and that Darren is in his right mind. People do things they regret when they aren't a hundred percent."

"You hope Matthew and Franco are alive, you mean?" Jack clarified.

"Yes." That Darren hadn't killed them in a rampage. "Is Minnie here? Or any of the guests?"

"We are all alone," Jack said. "Why?"

"Hear me out," she said. "Darren loved Elise. Why would he kill her?" She gathered her thoughts for a cohesive argument as to why Darren would not kill Elise.

"Love is no guarantee," Jack said. "Love and passion lead to expectation and disappointment, and . . . unfortunately, murder."

"You're right, but they were building a dream business together, in the city she chose, to be close to her sister." Charlene tapped her fingers on the arm of the chair. "His baby first, then she wanted children."

Jack levitated some leaves on the porch, making them dance. "He couldn't give them to her. Wouldn't."

Charlene rested her head against the back of the chair. "Not in his favor. What could be so bad that he wouldn't even explain it to his wife, certain she'd leave him?"

"I wish I knew." Jack sat across from her on the railing.

"Darren was furious on Elise's behalf of the treatment she'd received growing up, and he'd rightly deduced that Patty had stolen the biggest thing of all—the family home."

"You didn't tell me that!" Jack said.

"This is the first time we've been alone since I saw her this morning," Charlene said. "Patty even told that to Officer Bernard. Which means that Darren is still protective of Elise, and would he be if he'd murdered her? I just don't think so. My intuition is leaning away from Darren as her killer."

"That makes sense. So, Patty had on Crocs?" Jack asked. "The same as in Avery's picture?"

"She did. I'm going to assume that Officer Bernard will check Patty Wagner out very thoroughly."

"Why would she hide in the theater behind the drapes?" Jack stretched his legs out before him.

Charlene shrugged. "I don't know. I have no idea, actually." She sighed.

"That was a heavy sigh, Charlene," Jack said.

The sky was blue behind him with white clouds playing tag. The sun was golden and warm, the landscaping on the front lawn full of floral splendor.

Charlene regarded the wagon with flowers she and her mother had planted together the time before last when her parents had arrived. "Mom called. She's serious about moving to Salem, a small secondary home for her and Dad."

Jack smiled at her, his eyes crinkling at the corners. "I don't trust that *mean* Brenda won't return."

Charlene chuckled and tilted her head to admire her handsome ghost. "That makes two of us, but I'm just going to roll with it."

He crossed his arms and crooked a knee, his ankle bare. "Probably the best course of action."

"I stopped to ask Kevin if he knew about the building being on a burial ground—he didn't, so he's going to look into it. Call Kass, who is better at seeing actual apparitions. They both felt the theater was haunted, but they are so used to it. They probably just block it naturally."

Jack lowered his arms and braced his hands on the railing behind him. "Do you think they could see me?"

"Probably. Maybe? I don't know. I couldn't see the little girl ghost at Dani Gamble's house." Charlene studied Jack. "Seth can't see her, but I know he felt a chill from you in the kitchen the other day."

"I don't know how it works, and I've spent a lot of my free time researching ghost phenomenon," Jack said. "There are so many sources that can't be verified."

"It's the nature of being a ghost," Charlene empathized.

Jack ruffled her hair from across the porch without moving his hand. "You're too serious, Charlene. Things will be okay."

She smiled at him. "I hope so, for Darren's sake. Kevin didn't see Darren, either. How did your research go on the property?"

"I wanted to show you something about Matthew Sinchuk," Jack said. "His name came up on the computer more than once. Want to see?"

"Sure! I'll pour myself an iced tea and join you in my sitting room." Charlene rose from the Adirondack chair. She hated getting out of them as they were awkward, but oh, so comfortable while sitting.

"Meet you there!"

She went into the house the regular way, through the front door, while Jack did his ghost thing and just snapped from one place to another.

Not a bad mode of transportation if one was in a hurry. They didn't know how it worked, and it was one of those things she just put under the Jack file in her head. There was no explanation, and that had to be enough.

Silva waited by her bowl, and so Charlene gave the fluffy cat a few chicken treats shaped like fishes, then poured her iced tea. Minnie had gone for the day, as she often left by noon after the breakfast was cleaned and chores caught up. With a full house midweek, there wasn't a lot to keep up with. Most guests didn't require sheets every night, just fresh towels.

Wednesdays were often when she did her office paperwork or hung out with Jack. He was curious about everything and absorbed it. They had the curiosity thing in common.

Happy hour's menu for today was already put together in the fridge with spicy feta and home-made pita she'd warm later. A hummus platter with fresh vegetables to dip, and to continue the Mediterranean flair, they were having souvlaki, otherwise known as pork skewers. She loved them in Minnie's tzatziki sauce—yogurt with cucumber, garlic, and dill.

She knew her guests would enjoy the lighter fare as they all had plans for dinners out at fancy restaurants tonight; even the Cohens had made reservations at Sea Level rather than the more casual dining they'd done so far. The Millers, and Sheila, were going to Turner's Seafood, and the Lopezes had plans for an upscale steakhouse near Boston. The Welches were dining at the Hawthorne Hotel, which was supposed to be haunted and the boys were incredibly excited.

If only they knew that this bed-and-breakfast

had Jack. She laughed to herself and entered her sitting room, closing the door behind her and locking it for privacy so that nobody walked in while she and Jack conversed.

He sat at her narrow desk against the wall, the computer monitor showing the brick Spellbound Movie Theater building. The television played softly in the background. Her curtains were open to the view of the backyard and the oak tree, vertical blinds at half-inch slats.

Jack's dark hair had the tiniest bit of silver at the temples but otherwise was thick and luxurious. She herself had found several grays a few months back and had been on guard for more ever since.

"Hey there," she said.

"Hi!" Jack rose and gestured for her to have a seat. "Ms. Morris."

"Thank you, sir." Charlene sat on the edge of the wooden office chair. "What am I looking at here?"

"I hope you find it as interesting as I do." Jack, without moving his body, maneuvered the mouse to click open a Word doc filled with information.

She pulled her gaze from the picture of the brick building to the document.

"So, just start at the top of the page," Jack said, standing behind her to read over her shoulder, "but I think this might get Darren out of the hot seat, with the police."

"That would be great." She read quickly, skimming, and then certain she had gotten it wrong, started at the top of the page again. "Oh!"

"Right?" Jack asked, his voice excited. "You need to show this to Sam, or Officer Bernard."

"Matthew Sinchuk was the manager there for the previous movie theater, and then when it was a nightclub. The movie theater was open for five years. In that time, there were six deaths." She sucked in a breath. "All jumpers from the roof! But wait—didn't you say before there was a total of ten?"

"Yes—six while Matthew was the manager."

"What are you saying?"

"I have a reason to wonder if it isn't Franco as the paranormal conduit, but Matthew. I've done the research, and this isn't listed in a cohesive way. We might be the first to put the information together in this fashion," Jack said. "When the lead detective on the case doesn't believe in the paranormal, he won't connect these dots."

Sam did not believe in ghosts or anything that he couldn't put handcuffs on and toss behind bars in jail.

"Do you think Matthew is affected somehow by the evil in the building, Jack?"

He spread his arms to the side. "The truth is that we don't know very much about the paranormal. There are more unanswered questions than answers for us. This dimension is all about accepting that many things are unknown."

Charlene reached toward Jack but didn't touch him. She'd learned her lesson the hard way that directly touching his essence would chill her to the core.

"Continue reading," Jack said. "I don't think you've reached the shocker yet."

Apprehensive, Charlene turned back to the article and the facts that Jack had pulled from the web. "Matthew was questioned in the paper about the deaths at the theater, which is how you found his name! He said two of the jumpers had claimed to be on fire. Fire?"

"Remember that the original market had burned," Jack said. "The first homestead as well."

Charlene's pulse raced. "Matthew was also questioned about the stabbing death of a teenager at the nightclub he managed—she shouldn't have gotten in at all. Though he didn't know what happened." She leaned in, then gasped. "Jack! Is this right?"

He'd copied a psych ward admission sheet with Matthew Sinchuk's name and picture onto her document. Matthew's eyes were round and wild, his glasses missing. His auburn hair was pulled straight up like he'd been hit by lightning.

"Jack! Where did you get this?" She doubted it would be a public record.

"Don't ask so many questions," Jack said lightly. "What do you think about this information?"

Charlene swallowed over the lump in her throat. She felt compassion for Matthew, yes, but also fear. "He looks so different. Really scary."

Matthew had believed the building was haunted all along and told that to Franco so often that Franco had grown alarmed. Did Franco know Matthew suffered from mental health issues? Was that Matthew's secret, and why he might have been bullied as a kid?

"Franco didn't mention Matthew's mental health, but he could have been protecting his friend. I think he was also protecting Darren. Then, he wasn't at the end, by dropping the bomb about

Darren being in the circus. But he didn't tell me why. Loyal, while trying to get me off his tail?"

"It's possible Franco doesn't know about the psych ward stays," Jack said. "If I were Matthew, I'd want to keep it close—especially if I was the boss."

Sitting back, Charlene turned to face Jack. "So, Matthew was the manager all that time." Could it be the manager who was the tie to the building? She picked up her paper and pen. "Let's go over what we know about Franco before we move on."

Jack rubbed his smooth chin. "Franco isn't desperate for money. He plays online poker and owns his apartment."

"He is a loyal friend," Charlene said. "I don't think he has many. He used to be a really fat kid, which is why he was bullied." People could be so mean to those who were different.

"That would make sense. Friendship among bullied kids is going to create deep loyalty," Jack said. "Nobody knows what that hell would be like except for another bullied kid."

Charlene nodded, her throat aching with sadness that bullies existed and won more often than they should.

"But he was familiar with aconitine for herbal remedies," Jack said. "Can we discount that? That poison killed Elise."

"We can't." She circled the word *aconitine* on the page, then drew a star, a pentagram. "This is a solid list. Now, we know Darren inspired loyalty from his co-workers. Respect at least from his wife. I can't imagine what Darren has that is so bad he couldn't tell Elise, his wife and supposed best friend."

Jack gave a low laugh. "Clothing can hide a lot of things you don't want to share with the world at large. But when you're married, there are no secrets. The lights are on, and you're naked."

Charlene thought of how close she and Jared had been, two people as one. "You're right. And I know Darren and Elise shared a bedroom. I saw it."

"Not every couple is best friends, though," Jack said, fluttering her hair. "Some marriages are competitions."

Jack was probably thinking of his own, to Shauna.

"Darren didn't feel like he was worthy of Elise, that he was not as attractive as she was, though that's common enough between rich men and the women they choose." Charlene sighed. "He is attractive in his own way. Darren is not a beast."

"Is there anything you can think of that could tip us off to his disorder?" Jack asked.

"I wondered if he was a swimmer. At the hospital, I saw him button his shirt, and his chest was hairy, but his arms were shaved. He was quick about getting dressed."

"Interesting." Jack appeared contemplative. "Clothing. Hiding. Getting dressed is covering up, hiding secrets, or something shameful. In *The Wolf Man*, Lon Chaney Jr. was ashamed of himself for what he'd done to Bela, and then again, for his transformation to wolf and beast. The transformation was nothing he could control, but it almost made him crazy."

"That is a very philosophical take on the werewolf movie." The duality of human nature, man and beast. Was Darren struggling with that, in his marriage to Elise? Would he have killed her over it? Charlene just didn't think so.

Jack winked. "Can't be joking around all the time."

"Why not?" Charlene smiled at Jack. "I love it when you make me laugh."

"Life, and death, can be very serious subjects," Jack conceded. "Your smile is so beautiful that it makes me happy."

"Beauty is in the eye of the beholder," Charlene said in a teasing way, looking at Jack straight-on. He was so handsome to her.

"You are exactly right about that." Jack stared directly back at her and put his knuckle under her chin with a tickle.

She laughed softly, feeling very fortunate that her ghost didn't scare her but instead gave her compliments.

Returning to the computer, to the manic-eyed photo of Matthew Sinchuk, she felt as if he could be a wild card. Unpredictable. Dangerous? The word didn't quite fit.

Charlene placed her pen and paper down. "Is this man a killer?" She was unable to break her gaze from the scary picture. "Matthew was there at the building for at least seven of the deaths that you were able to count on the internet." Six jumpers, and the girl who was stabbed. "What do we know about him?"

Could the theater manager's mental state be an opening for an evil spirit? She turned to Jack with that question in her eyes.

"Matthew Sinchuk was raised in foster care and

had many different homes. He has a sealed record that I can't access—yet. He is now forty." Jack shrugged. "Owns his home, never married."

"What could be in a sealed record?"

"It could be criminal in nature, or perhaps something psychiatric." Jack tapped his temple, eyes narrowed. "It doesn't mean Matthew's guilty of murder, but if I were Sam, I'd want to question him more so than Darren Shultz."

# CHAPTER 19

Charlene considered what Jack had said, and it felt right. She nodded at her ghostly roommate. Matthew was definitely someone to question, and maybe allow Darren to catch his breath.

She hoped the Salem PD, Sam especially, was even now realizing that Darren hadn't killed his wife. She'd thought it might be Patty, but now, what if it had been Matthew who had committed the crime? And not just Elise's murder, but the previous deaths as well?

"Jack, what did the articles say about Matthew? He didn't have a criminal record, did he?"

"No. He was never arrested," Jack said. "What happens in these situations is that the police officer who answered the call has to decide whether or not the person is considered a threat to themselves or others, which is the choice between the psych ward at the hospital and a jail cell. Once admitted, the person is evaluated, and the doctor proceeds from there."

Charlene nodded. "So, it's better for the person than getting tossed in a cell, which, as we know from the news, is too crowded."

"Exactly," Jack said. "From what I read online, there are laws against keeping someone who is not competent to stand trial in jail without care for too long, to prevent the jails from becoming holding places for people who shouldn't be there. But sometimes the beds at the psych hospital might be full. It's a conundrum—where should these poor souls go?"

There was so much in the world that wasn't fair, but she couldn't take it all on. Charlene handled what came her way, the best she could. "What did Matthew do to end up at this facility?" The paperwork read *Salem Psych Unit.* Charlene felt compassion, but also fear, for him, and of him.

"Matthew threatened to jump from the roof, like the others who died," Jack said.

"When?" Charlene asked, her nerves tingling with apprehension. "How long after the others?" It was very strange that the building attracted people wanting to leap to their deaths, as it was only three stories high with a crenelated roof. Not twenty stories, where it would be a guaranteed death.

"Ten jumpers, but six while Matthew managed the place." Jack paced the room. "So, when the officer brought him down—this is when it was a nightclub—he thought at first that Matthew was on drugs, as he kept saying he was on fire. The policeman realized his actions were manic and took him to the psych unit. Later, the doctors diagnosed him with schizophrenia."

"Schizophrenia!" Charlene's jaw dropped. She snapped it closed. "Like the wolf man."

"It could be why he also has an affinity for that movie," Jack said. "Franco found a haven from bullies because he was an obese child. Darren hid from bullies too. Matthew, mental illness. They are the three amigos, bonded by awful childhoods."

"How do they function? Franco has super control over his body, as well as an online income, and he has created stability for himself. Darren became a millionaire, using his gifted palate to take him out of Germany, where he'd been abandoned at an orphanage after his mother died. Matthew seems normal to me. Nice, even."

"Pull up the Spellbound Movie Theater website," Jack instructed. "Let's see if they have an employees' page."

Charlene typed *Spellbound Movie Theater*, Salem, into the search bar. Jack clicked the mouse until Matthew's manager picture was on the page. He enlarged it.

"Medication, I bet. His skin is puffy. His glasses hide his eyes." Jack stepped back. "If he went off his medication, then that could have caused a break in his reality. Cause hallucinations, like seeing things in the theater."

"It might not be that the building is evil?" Charlene studied the image again. "Oh, Jack. I'm so worried. Why would he stop taking what makes him better? That doesn't make sense."

"Sometimes people feel so good that they forget they need the meds, so they skip it and start a downward spiral. Also, patients who take the medication sometimes complain it makes them feel dopey."

A shadow passed outside by the tree that she caught from the corner of her eye. Her pulse skipped, and Charlene got up slowly.

She had the blinds cracked open to allow the sunshine into her suite, and she peeked out without being seen. Her heart raced as she saw Darren, who, even though he'd been freshly shaved yesterday, had stubble all over his face, including his forehead. "Jack!"

Jack appeared and hovered near her shoulder. "He looks exhausted. Shadows under his eyes. Is that new hair growth?"

"Poor Darren! What should we do?" Charlene whispered her question.

Darren walked up the back porch stairs and knocked loudly. "Please let me in, Charlene! I didn't hurt anybody! I never would!"

Franco was also anti-violence. Or so he'd said.

It was too dangerous, Charlene thought. His bodily changes were scary. Darren was out of control and resembled the wolfman much more than the millionaire she'd welcomed to Salem.

Jack watched her carefully, then gestured to Darren.

"I'm right here," Jack said. "I will keep you safe, Charlene. Let him in so I can study him. This is very interesting."

"What is?" She detected the clinical note to Jack's tone, which meant he was in doctor mode.

"Just open the door and let him in," Jack said.

Charlene very reluctantly opened the door. This was her private space, and she didn't like that it had been invaded uninvited by a possible murderer.

Only, her intuition said it wasn't Darren.

At that, she stepped back. She'd learned to give her intuition more credit, though she would always have her Midwestern sensibilities. She located her purse, which had the pepper spray in the pocket. Her phone was on the desk.

"Charlene!" Darren moaned at the threshold.

"Come in," she said.

Darren entered in jerking movements that lacked grace. He searched her living room without really stopping to see it. The bedroom door was closed, the adjoining kitchen door as well.

"Darren." Charlene greeted him as if this was just another day when they were meeting to discuss the launch of Spellbound Movie Theater. "Where have you been? Klara is looking for you, and so are the police."

"I know, I know." Darren strode back and forth with a manic air. Jack's sharp gaze seemed to be assessing Darren as he moved. "Hate the cops. Can't stay. Can't trust anyone. Not even Klara."

Charlene's big heart responded to the pain in his voice. "Please, sit down. Let me get you some water. Something to eat?"

"I can't sit. I can't. They're after me. I didn't kill Elise."

His shirt had been torn, revealing the arms that had been shaved yesterday now covered in stubble. "That's not possible," Charlene murmured, to herself and to Jack. "You were clean-shaven."

Darren tugged at his hair.

"He was?" Jack inspected Darren's skin. "This is

very unusual, and so rare, I can't believe it. I need my lab to run tests, to confirm. Though there is no particular test for hypertrichosis, it's a process of elimination. Heightened testosterone. Clinical findings."

Hypertrichosis?

"I wish I'd died instead of Elise," Darren said, crossing his arms—then uncrossing them. He had so much energy it was a heat wave off his skin.

Jack walked around the love seat, studying Darren. Darren didn't notice the chill around him. "Charlene, ask him if he has hypertrichosis?"

"What is that?" she asked.

Darren scowled. "I didn't say anything." He rubbed his chest and bowed his head.

"It's wolfman syndrome," Jack said.

She'd heard of that. Oh, that made awful sense. Terrible sense! Charlene gently tugged Darren down beside her on the love seat and clamped her hand over his on the cushion between them.

"Franco told me you were in the circus," Charlene said. "Klara explained that you were a greeter, and a cook while the troupe was on tour. It's where you discovered your amazing gift for discerning flavors."

Darren nodded, tired.

"But that's not all. Is it?" Charlene didn't let go. "Were you a wolfman?"

He froze like a rabbit before a wolf—but he was the wolf! Could he have hurt his friends? His wife? Did he suffer any sort of mental illness?

Charlene didn't release his hand until Darren jumped up and crossed the room, as if to escape, but he didn't leave. He stared at her, emoting so much pain that she couldn't move from where she sat.

Jack said, "Hypertrichosis. Congenital *hypertrichosis lanuginosa* will cause hair to grow all over his body. It's so rare that only fifty cases have ever been documented. Doesn't account for all the affected who were shunned or killed."

How terrible for Darren. She recalled a recent documentary on Julia Pastrana, who had been exploited even after her death by her circus manager husband in the 1800s. She'd died five days after giving birth to her son, who also had the condition, and he and his new wife toured with the mummified bodies. "Do you have hypertrichosis?"

Darren collapsed into Jack's armchair and gave a low howl.

Charlene patted his leg, leaning toward him. "You are safe here."

"Had it since birth. My sister too." Darren regarded her through half-closed lids. "Our mountain village was so small and backward in their beliefs. My mother lived like a wild woman in the woods as a healer, or witch, depending on what the person darkening her door wanted. She didn't show signs of this curse."

"Oh, Darren."

"She kept us hidden from the villagers, but people talk, and they weren't content to leave her alone. They taunted us and pelted our small cabin with rotten eggs, among other things. It was a nightmare." Darren pulled at his hair.

"I can only imagine." Unfortunately, she had a

very good imagination. People were cruel to those who were different in a way not considered beautiful.

"Worse for my sister, as a girl," Darren said. "Males are expected to shave, and there were ways to hide it with caps and sweatshirts. For her . . . there was no hiding." He stared up at the ceiling.

She glanced at Jack, who said, "He's exhausted, but speaking normally. I don't think he's suffering any psychosis."

Darren sat up. "People can be vicious."

"I'm sorry." Charlene waited for him to gather his thoughts. He was calming down now that his secret was out. She hadn't screamed or reacted adversely.

"I've made my peace with my past." Darren looked out the cracked blinds to the oak tree. "I just wanted to live a full life. For both of us. Was that reaching too high?" He didn't turn toward her but stared outside.

"If he was born with it, and his sister, that is congenital hypertrichosis," Jack said. "Ask how he got to the orphanage, will you?"

"Darren, how did you get to the orphanage?"

"Our mother died." Darren at last faced Charlene. "I think she was killed by a man she'd given a curse to, but I can't prove it. We'd spent a week in the cabin alone. I was five, my sister three. It was winter, so we didn't have food. A kind nun visiting the village rescued us and brought us to the orphanage. Sister Lucinda saved our lives." Darren's body was still as he recalled the past. "The villagers would have left us to starve, but a woman alerted

Sister Lucinda of our pathetic existence, and she rescued us. It was her calling from God to save us."

Tears filled Charlene's eyes. "Oh!"

Darren shrugged. "I remember how scared I was and how I tried to hide my sister. She coaxed us out with food and promises of shelter. We were so hungry that I agreed."

She watched him tell his story, her heart breaking. "You were protecting your sister."

"There have been many times that I've wished Sister Lucinda would have let us die there in the woods, together." Darren's nostrils flared as he breathed in. Out. "I don't know where my sister is even buried. The nuns won't say. Just that she died in a fire."

"You've searched, I'm sure," Charlene said.

"High and low." Darren straightened and put his hand over his knee.

"Poor man," Jack said.

"At fourteen, I came back from the circus for the winter season to bring her home with me, to offer her a luxurious life in the circus as a wolf girl, but she was gone." Darren's eyes were dry, his throat scratchy.

"She lives in your heart," Charlene said, wishing she hadn't. Platitudes didn't help with grief such as his.

"Gone. And I've mourned her since." He narrowed his eyes at Charlene. "You see why I refused to reverse the vasectomy?"

She listened, not wanting to agree, but agreeing wholeheartedly.

"Even for Elise, the love of my miserable life. I

could not sentence another human being to the childhood I had. I know it killed my sister." Darren raised a hand. Dark hair grew on the knuckles. "Indirectly, but still. It counts, and I won't do it. The defective line stops with me, and I'm okay with that."

Jack shimmered with agitation. "There is a family in Mexico who has the condition and has found a way to make a life for themselves," he said. He'd looked it up as Charlene spoke with Darren. Darren was so distracted that he hadn't noticed invisible fingers at her keyboard. "Jesús Chuy Aceves."

She glanced at Jack, who turned around to say, "There is hope in the darkness, is all I mean to say. You and I both know there is more to this life than this earthly existence, but that makes this short time even more precious."

Charlene hadn't realized Jack had felt that way. He'd had plenty of time to think about it, anyway.

Before she said something to Jack, again, she faced Darren. "What do you want to do? I am friends with Detective Holden, and I know he would be fair to you."

Darren, practically boneless, sprawled in the chair. "No way. That woman wasn't listening to me at all. Officer Lennox. I can't trust anyone."

"Officer Bernard is also fair," Charlene said. "I would go with you."

"No."

Okay. Charlene shifted on the love seat. "Klara is on your side. She cares for you and is very worried."

"I thought so too." Darren's lids lowered to

closed, and she wondered if he'd dozed off as he didn't move.

"He's tired," Jack said.

Darren's eyes flashed open, and Charlene sat back with a start, her pulse pounding.

"What happened?" she asked. "Does this have to do with your fight last night?"

"She stole from me, Charlene." His expression held anguish. Like, to-the-soul hurt. She couldn't stand it herself.

"Klara?" Elise stealing from Darren she could understand more so than his companion before Elise.

"Yes." Darren exhaled and closed his eyes once more.

Jack studied Darren closely. "The poor man is tired and emotionally drained. He's safe here and knows he can finally relax."

"Can you explain to me what you mean?" Charlene asked in a soft voice. "I don't understand."

Darren sat up again, pinching his brow. "I do my own accounting. I have a talent for business."

"Klara told me that," Charlene said.

"Well, she should have been smarter, then." He pulled on the hair over his ear, then patted it down.

Jack watched Darren as if he longed for a microscope.

"How so?" Charlene asked.

"We fought last night when she told me she wanted to quit working for me." Darren snapped his fingers. "Just like that. Like I needed another loss. If I was willing to accept the cost of her skimming the profits from her sales accounts, then why should she leave?"

She felt it like a punch to the gut, his pain at Klara's betrayal. "When did you first find out about it?"

"As soon as she started doing it." Darren tapped the side of his head. "Hypertrichosis on the outside, still a functioning brain on the inside."

"How long ago was that?" She just couldn't imagine the betrayal by Klara, but it had happened.

"Six months. It was after Elise and Klara argued about her percentage of the sales she'd earned," Darren said. "Elise didn't understand that Klara had been with me since the beginning. I wanted her on my team. I wouldn't budge on that stance."

"Oh, dear."

"Klara started pocketing small sums." Darren winced. "I told her yesterday that I didn't care. I would have given her the money. She didn't believe me."

"If push came to shove between Elise and Klara, then whom would he choose?" Jack asked.

Charlene narrowed her eyes and studied Darren. "Darren, did Elise threaten to fire Klara?"

"I believe so, but I never would have let it happen!" Darren cried.

Klara would have been threatened. Klara had a lot at stake. Could Klara have killed Elise and tried to set Darren up for the murder?

"She took it as protection just in case Elise followed through with her threat." Darren grimaced. "Offered to give it back. She had it in a special account. The 'if Elise screwed her over' account."

"That is so rough," Charlene said. Her stomach was in knots.

Darren peered at Charlene, his eyes pools of emotion. "She didn't trust me to do right by her. That hurts."

"Could she have poisoned the roasted garlic salt?" Charlene asked. "She was around the salts all the time and understood what they looked like. How to blend them."

Darren groaned and bowed his head. "I want to say no." He stood and paced, going right through Jack without a shiver, he was running so hot.

"But . . ." Charlene began.

"I never thought she would steal from me before she did it. I just don't know." Darren stopped by the door leading from her suite to the kitchen. "What is the point of killing Elise? To make me miserable when I've finally found a sort of happiness? To ruin our dream business? Not just the theater, but the salts. And don't forget about the attempt on my life."

That meant Klara was right back at the top of the list, even more so than Matthew. Or Franco.

"Have you seen Matthew? Or Franco? We've been attempting to reach them, to try to find you," Charlene said. "Seth and Avery have been calling."

"Franco tried to calm me down and offered to watch movies with me at the theater. He and Matthew." Darren shook out his hands as if to release the energy inside him.

"Do they know about your hypertrichosis?" Charlene asked.

"God, no. Some things you don't share, not with

friends, not even with your wife." Darren stomped his feet, a runner at the starting line.

"How do you manage to keep the hair at bay? Usually," Charlene amended.

"Laser hair removal every other week," Darren said. "Shave as needed. The laser is supposed to kill the hair follicles, but with this condition, they are on super-growth warp speed so they don't really die."

"And Elise never noticed?" Charlene definitely would have figured out that something was unique about Jared if he was shaving twice a day.

"Laser hair removal applies heat to the hair follicles to kill them, but new ones come back," Jack said. "Usually, hair removal lasts years, but not for Darren. Modern science does wonders, but in this instance, it can't create a miracle. There isn't enough known about the disease."

"No." Darren gave a self-mocking smile. "Elise could be a bit self-absorbed. Her focus was on the big house, the movie theater, and the money to show off once we were in Salem."

Charlene sighed. "Her parents were already dead, so she wanted to show off to Patty?"

"I think so, since her parents had cut her out of the will," Darren said.

"You were right to question Patty," Charlene said. "She admitted to coercing her parents to give her the house."

Darren shrugged. "Patty is a fool. Elise loved me, in her own way."

Jack watched him carefully, his index finger to his chin.

"I saw that for myself," Charlene said.

"I accepted that it would have to be enough. I was willing to give her everything but children. If she'd pushed the issue, we could have adopted. But she wanted her own."

"I am so very sorry."

Darren walked to the window and crossed his arms.

"Nobody's fault." Darren scrubbed his scruffy jaw. "Not all the nuns and priests were as kind as Sister Lucinda. Several thought we should have the demons beat from us for the good of our souls. I've spent my life building myself up from nothing. Less than nothing."

Charlene rose from the love seat and squeezed his shoulder with compassion. "You are a man to be proud of."

"Why have I survived when everyone else is gone?" Darren turned away from the window to Charlene. "My mother, my sister. Elise. Klara. My best friend is still quitting on me. I forgave her, but she is *leaving* me." He pounded his chest with a fist. "Why can't I be enough?"

Charlene stepped back at his anguish. "Maybe Klara just needs time."

"I don't care about the money. I never have. I care about the suffering it can ease. I care about family, even though I won't procreate. I forgave Patty. I forgave the nuns." Darren scoffed. "I hear the lullaby they would sing us in my head and know that I am not forgiven."

"His pain is overwhelming. I can't stand it," Jack said, popping out of the room with a burst of cold.

She searched the room, but Jack wasn't visible to her. This made her very lonely. "Darren, where is Franco?"

"I went to see him this morning, to ask for his help," Darren said this without inflection, which was odd, since he'd been so emotional just seconds ago. "Franco wanted to turn me in—he was lying about joining Matthew at the theater. He thinks I killed Elise. I heard the fear in his voice."

Her stomach clenched. Had she been wrong about his innocence? "Is he all right?"

"Fine." Darren's jaw set. "I locked him up in his apartment. It's for his own good. I need to find the truth."

Charlene wasn't sure what to believe.

"What about Matthew?" Jack asked, his voice coming all around her though she couldn't see him.

"Darren, did you talk to Matthew?"

"Matthew is a true friend." Darren strode across the small living room from the window to the kitchen door. "He understands the nature of the beast. He knows what it's like to give oneself over to the moon mania."

That didn't sound great at all. "Is he okay?" Charlene asked. "Did you lock him in his apartment too?"

"Matthew has his own house. He was raised in foster homes and bounced around a lot. He didn't fit in. I understand that," Darren said.

"What is Matthew's secret?" Charlene asked. "You, you're the wolfman, Franco, the obese child, and Matthew . . ."

He whirled toward her with gold tinting his brown eyes. "You're clever, Charlene."

At that moment, she wondered if she was harboring a murderer in her suite.

She swallowed and eyed the back door, while Darren tensed by the interior door.

Would he know about Matthew's time in the psych ward? Would it matter?

If Franco wasn't guilty, and Patty wasn't either, then that left Darren or Klara.

Or Matthew.

"Matthew was what the nuns would call a 'troubled youth'," Darren said.

His tone was deep. Mellow. It reminded her of the calm before the storm. Like a wild animal might gather itself before launching from one rock to another.

"Is he still troubled?" Charlene asked.

"Matthew is affected by the moon," Darren said.

She and Jack had just heard Dustin say that such behavior was a myth.

"Charlene, I didn't kill Elise," Darren said. "I can't believe Klara is guilty of that crime in addition to theft. Franco wants to turn me in. What am I supposed to do?"

Charlene spread her arms to her sides. "What do *you* want to do?"

"Matthew asked me to meet him, one on one at the theater," Darren said. "He didn't sound right. He says he sees ghosts everywhere. They talk to him."

"That would fit with Matthew's schizophrenia," Jack said, still not visible to her. "Manic delusions."

"There are patrol cars around the theater," Charlene said, guessing what he wanted them to do. Go meet Matthew and confront him. She shook her head.

"I think we need to sneak inside and ask Matthew, face-to-face." Darren grabbed Charlene's wrist. "I think he poisoned my wife."

Charlene pulled herself free and rubbed the red mark on her wrist, truly afraid of Darren for the first time.

Had she made a fatal mistake?

# CHAPTER 20

"Why would Matthew want to kill Elise?" Charlene's heart raced and her pulse skipped like a skeeter bug across a pond. "Surely the threat to fire him isn't enough of a reason."

It could be that Darren was trying to make Charlene think it was Matthew to get her to lower her guard. But if he wished to harm her, they were alone in her suite. He could have already done so.

She felt incredibly torn, thinking it was one person, and then wait, look over there—it was someone else. Patty, Franco, Matthew? And always, Darren. Front and center.

"Don't trust him," Jack warned. His body materialized in pieces as he smoothed his golf shirt over his waist. The gold on his Rolex was dull as the illusion could only go so far. "We don't know if he's telling the truth. I don't think you should go with him. Until you talk to Franco and Matthew, be careful. Call Sam."

"Elise's threat to let him go affected him very

deeply," Darren said. "Matthew is tied emotionally to the theater."

Thanks to Jack's research, Charlene already knew this. "Did you read about the building, as I'd suggested?" She moved so that the love seat was between them.

"Before Salem, I wouldn't have agreed that a building could be evil, but I do now," Darren said. "I think Matthew is in the grip of madness."

That was more accurate than he could know. "I don't think we should go to the theater," Charlene said.

"I agree!" Jack spun around the room with agitation. Darren, so lost in his pain, didn't notice the blinds move.

"The police still think I killed Elise. I didn't. I need my freedom. Charlene, can you imagine someone with my disease in prison?" Darren rubbed his hand over his thick hair. "I wouldn't survive a week."

"He's right." Jack slowed his energy to examine Darren once more, his expression filled with empathy and concern.

"Let me call Detective Holden," Charlene said. "I know he can help you once we explain your . . . condition. And Matthew's unstable mental health."

"No police!" Darren said.

"You have to trust me," Charlene said.

"I don't, actually." Darren crossed his arms. "Trust is a high commodity right now, and I don't owe you anything."

"Then why did you come here?" Charlene asked.

"I was watching you slip something under my

door—I was desperate. Franco was worthless. It was a mistake to stop at Patty's, but I couldn't help myself. I saw the cop cars around my place and the theater." Darren shoved his hands into his jeans pockets, the fabric at both knees torn, but not fashionably so. Grass stains marked the denim.

"What is your plan?" Charlene gestured to the armchair and love seat. "Hang out with me?"

"I want to confront Matthew," Darren said. "I want you to get his confession on video. Your detective friend won't be able to deny the truth then."

"No, sir," Charlene said. "I promised Sam I would stay clear of the theater until this was resolved."

"That you would *do your best*," Jack said dryly. "I think Darren is right to want a recording of Matthew's craziness. It could become a confession. If the police are there, then he won't get one."

Charlene offered her cell to Darren. "You can borrow my phone," she said.

Darren raised both hands. "Not good enough. I need a witness. You are the only person left who is close to a friend." He pierced her with big brown eyes. "Please."

She hardened her heart. "No."

"Charlene!" Darren held his arms out from his sides, his hand knocking into the desk.

"No." She had to be firm. "I have guests who I need to be here for. I run a business, and I can't be gallivanting around Salem trying to trick Matthew into confessing."

"It won't be a trick. If he didn't do it, then we can go," Darren said reasonably.

Charlene thought of a million reasons why she

should ignore his plea and focus on her own business. "Would you have tried to keep Matthew on staff, if Elise had fired him?"

Darren shrugged. "I could have tried, but there was no guarantee."

He wouldn't have made a stand for Matthew as he would have for Klara. Matthew might have sensed that and gotten scared about losing his job. Unlike Franco, he didn't have other ways to bring in money.

"Matthew was standing by Seth and Patty near the popcorn and pretzels. He was the one to hand out the novelty containers. Your tray and Elise's were filled with seasoned popcorn rather than the sampling trays."

"He knew my favorite was the herb and chili—we'd talked about it. Just like he knew that Elise's was the roasted garlic. As the manager, Matthew has keys to the theater, so he could have doctored the seasoning salt at any time." Darren pulled a key ring from his pocket.

She exhaled, speaking her thoughts as they came. "Logically, with Elise dead, the theater would probably close for a while, if not permanently. Would Matthew risk that? Especially with such a tie to the theater?"

"I don't think so," Darren said. He tugged hard on his hair. "Then who? Don't forget the attempt on my life, with the curtains."

Jack said, "Let's follow the inheritance trail, since Matthew closing the theater wouldn't be in his best interest."

Charlene blew out a breath. "All right. Let's put Matthew aside for a moment. Darren, if you and

Elise are both gone, who inherits your fortune? Klara? The orphanages?"

Darren grew very still. "Patty," he said. "She'd be the last survivor. I have bequests for the orphanages and for Klara, but Patty, as Elise's sister, would receive the bulk of the fortune."

That just amped Patty's motivation. She would need to tell Sam right away. "And if Patty dies?"

Darren scowled. "If she didn't have a will, then me. There is no other family."

"That doesn't help his innocence," Jack said.

"Darren, that isn't working in your favor." Charlene sighed. "You walk away with everything?"

"Patty's going to live a long time, I'm sure." Darren hooked his thumb over his shoulder toward the oak tree. "I don't want anything of the Wagners, trust me on that. Elise pushed for her sister to be involved. Patty is a decent baker, but I find her manner off-putting."

Even now, Darren was a gentleman and didn't rat Patty's deceptive behavior out to Charlene, about Patty making a romantic move behind her sister's back.

"I think we should call the police, Detective Holden specifically. Have him meet us at Patty's." Going to Patty's would be better than the theater, which she never planned on stepping foot in again.

"Patty didn't do it. I'm going to the theater," Darren announced. "Matthew sounded half-crazed this morning. I think he wants to finish the job of killing me."

"Why?"

"I don't know!" Darren cried. "I thought we

were friends. I can ask him to his face. He is strong enough to have messed with the curtain rod. He knew I was going to be working on it. It would have looked like an accident if I hadn't survived."

"So what? You're just going to let him try a second time?" Charlene heard the shock in her tone and lowered it to say, "I don't think that's smart."

"I need your help," Darren said.

"I don't want you to go!" Jack said.

"I'm not going. I told you, I have guests."

Darren arched a bushy dark-brown brow. "There is nobody else here, Charlene. I made sure of that as I walked around the property."

Silva meowed from the other side of the door in the kitchen.

Darren backed up, though there was a door between him and Silva. "Don't like cats. Keep her there." He strode around the love seat, annoyance crackling from him.

Her cell phone rang, and she jumped. She picked it up off her desk and saw that it was Avery.

"Avery?"

"Charlene," the teen cried. "I need your help."

"Where are you?" Charlene couldn't be any more tense.

"At Spellbound Movie Theater. Seth just went to drop off his uniform to Matthew, and Matthew yanked him in. We're at the back entrance. We walked from Seth's so we could sneak by the patrol officers."

Never mind. She'd been wrong. Dread in the pit of her stomach, Charlene put her phone on speaker. "Say that again."

Avery repeated herself, then said, "I tried to get

in, but the door is locked. I'm in the alley by the Dumpster. You have to come."

She glanced at Jack, who wore a stricken expression. "You can't. Call Sam," Jack instructed.

"We're on our way," Darren said.

"Who is that?" Avery whispered.

"Darren. He's here."

"Matthew wanted Darren to be there. He told that to Seth. He convinced Seth to drop off his uniform since Seth was leaving them high and dry with a new job. As soon as the back door opened, Seth was sucked inside. I'm so scared, Charlene! Matthew said if we call the police, he'll burn the theater to the ground." Avery sniffed.

Charlene quickly gathered her purse, double-checking that she had her pepper spray in the side pocket. "I am headed to the car as we speak."

"Be careful! What if Matthew hurts Seth?"

"I'm coming too," Darren said. "It's me Matthew really wants, and I will trade myself for him."

Charlene shook her head. There had to be a different way.

"I don't like this at all, Charlene," Jack said.

As if she had a choice. She would do anything for Avery.

"Be careful on your way here. I've been smelling smoke," Avery said. "Something is on fire already, but I don't know what. One cop went over there, and one stayed here. Officer Lennox."

Darren shuddered.

"Stay hidden, hon." Charlene swallowed hard. "We are on our way."

She ended the call, stunned.

"You are going to drive," Darren said, calming

her down with his instructions. "Park a half block over, then we will sneak by those cops to get inside. We are going to find Matthew and save Seth. You are my witness. Get your phone for a recording."

"You're not going to hurt Matthew?" Charlene demanded. "This isn't revenge?"

Darren shoved his hand to his hip. "What on earth do you think? I am being set up, and I need an ally. My wife is dead, my sister-in-law detests me, my best friend has deserted me after stealing from me." He glared at her. "You are my last hope."

"You have to go," Jack said, his image blurring as he fought to be whole. "Save Seth and do what you can for Darren. The only saving grace is that the police are there. Alert them."

"All right." Charlene sighed. "Come on, Darren."

Darren, a broken man, stayed at her side as she opened the door to the kitchen.

Silva saw Darren, and her back arched as she hissed. Her golden eyes were as gigantic as the full moon had been.

"It's okay, kitty," Charlene said. "Darren, this way please. Do you need anything? Water?"

He shook his head and rubbed the bristles on his face. "I just want to get this over with. I thought losing my sister was the worst that could happen." Sighing heavily, he followed her down the hall to the foyer.

Charlene peered over her shoulder at him, a brow arched in question.

"My wife being killed and being accused of her murder is a thousand times worse than any taunts from cruel nuns or villagers."

"You're right." Charlene led the way to the porch and down the stairs to the Pilot.

"When you look like a freak, it's expected," Darren shared sadly. "When you think you can pass, and then can't, it's terrible."

Charlene didn't know what to say to that.

Jack hovered around the car until they reached the end of the property, then she drove toward the theater, despite Sam's telling her not to do it. This was about Avery and Seth. She hadn't exactly promised, and this was why.

With Sam, she often needed a contingency plan.

"I wish I had a tape recorder." Charlene tapped the steering wheel.

"Using the video on your phone should be enough to catch Matthew in the act," Darren said. "Mine was crushed in the accident."

She peered toward Darren. "When was the last time you talked to Matthew?"

"I called Matthew today from Franco's apartment for his assistance since Franco thought I was guilty. He instructed me to come to the projector room so we could watch all five of *The Wolf Man* movies in the franchise, start to finish—as we should have done on the soft opening night, according to him."

"Why didn't you?" Charlene recalled the meetings about movies and times. "Aside from the poisoning of the popcorn. Five films weren't on your schedule."

"Elise thought it would be too much for one evening. We agreed to split them up for three Fridays—Noir Night."

Saturdays were to be romantic comedies and Sundays, main features.

Charlene blinked to clear her vision. The Shultzes had had a cohesive plan to bring the theater to life, all while promoting their seasoned salts.

Lives taken, destroyed, all because one man had a mental illness. Maybe. If it wasn't Patty. No, it was Matthew. He'd taken Seth hostage. Getting Seth out safely was her first priority, even more so than recording Matthew's confession.

"Matthew encouraged me to become a wolf, to let my wolf free, at the theater tonight. Like I'm not a human," Darren said, his tone hurt. "He wants to enjoy the full moon from the rooftop."

"Last night was the full moon," Charlene said.

Darren scrubbed his face with a large palm. "I don't think he cares!"

"If he's not well, we should call the EMTs." Charlene was desperate to get help for everyone. She was not qualified for a rescue mission.

"After we get Seth out safely!" Darren glared at her. "And Matthew's confession, then, fine. We can call whomever you want."

"All right. All right!" Charlene stepped on the gas toward the theater, which was a few blocks away from the bakery and Patty's home.

Sirens screeched in the distance, and a plume of black smoke was barely visible.

"Where is that coming from?" Charlene had a terrible feeling.

"Not the theater!" Darren exclaimed. "Please not that."

Avery! Seth! She calmed a little as she realized it wasn't the right spot. " No—I think it's the Wagner neighborhood. The house, or the bakery—what if the ovens caught on fire or something?"

She wanted to bypass the theater and continue on to see if Patty was all right, but the sirens reassured her that help—real help, not simply conversation—would be on the way.

"Let's stick with the plan," Darren said. His expression was grim with worry.

Charlene raised her brow at him. "Which is?"

"I have a key for the back door in the alley. We sneak in and grab Seth. Send him out while you and I confront Matthew."

She drove past the theater, but there were no police vehicles, probably drawn from surveillance on the theater to the fire. This meant no Officer Lennox to torment Darren.

They probably thought Darren had set the fire.

Charlene parked a half block up from the Spellbound Movie Theater, and she and Darren walked quickly on the bright summer day toward the building.

She broke the rules and sent Sam a quick text from her personal line, alerting him to where she and Darren were at, and why. Matthew had Seth captive and had to be behind Elise's death. He had a history of mental illness, and an obsession with the theater. Seven deaths had happened while he'd been manager—eight, counting Elise.

She pressed *Send*. The message went into cyberspace without Darren noticing what she'd done behind his back. Keeping her phone in her palm, she made sure the sound was off.

Matthew's car was in the parking lot, but nobody else's. Avery wasn't in the alley. She prayed that Avery was simply out of sight and hadn't tried to enter the theater alone.

Darren took his keys from his pocket at the back exit. "Thanks, Charlene. I know I twisted your arm to help me. I just want to clear my name, sell the theater, and move back to Munich."

She gritted her teeth but nodded, recalling his excitement over starting his new movie theater business in Salem. "This hasn't exactly turned out to be the American dream, has it?"

"Not even close." Darren used his key to unlock the door, went inside, then closed the door behind them. They were immersed in darkness that dried Charlene's throat. Panic set in.

"Just wait a minute to let your eyes adjust," Darren murmured.

The hair on the back of Charlene's neck rose in alarm. She closed her eyes, counted to three, and opened them again.

This time there were shadows against the black-red walls. The panic eased a little.

"Someone has turned off the corridor lights," Darren whispered. "Making it dangerously dark."

She stayed on Darren's heels as they moved slowly forward and spoke very softly, "Should I use my flashlight on the phone?" She had all sorts of things in her purse that might help.

"No," Darren replied in the same quiet tone. "I don't want to let him know we're here. He probably has this place memorized by touch and hearing alone. I liked that he knew the building so well when I hired him, but now, I regret it."

Charlene kept her fingers on Darren's back.

She was afraid of being separated from him. The projector room was on the third floor, and then it was the roof.

People had jumped from the roof, afraid of something inside this building. Ghosts, or spirits. Fire.

Avery had caught a reflection of Crocs in the camera. Patty wasn't the only person in Salem who wore that style of unisex shoe.

Could it have been Matthew behind the curtain?

Or a ghost concerned about his feet getting tired?

Matthew had been in plain sight during the first show and the intermission. Klara hadn't been, though. She'd been with Franco. Franco. Charlene hoped he was all right.

Nurses, restaurant workers. Heck, the "shoes" were probably just a blur of the curtain's hem.

Shivers tickled her back as they passed through the lobby by the concession stand. Fresh popcorn waited in a tub with a sampling tray of Schultz's Seasoned Salts. Would they all be poisoned?

Darren put his finger to his mouth for Charlene to remain quiet.

They went up to the second floor, where Elise had died. She could swear she was being watched. She didn't hear a sound. She worried for Seth. Where was he?

She crept along after Darren, peeking over her shoulder.

Curtains had been drawn tight over the windows to block the natural light. Vintage movie posters were torn from the wall into confetti at the base of the front entrance.

That was odd. It reminded her of kindling for a campfire.

Darren, at last, reached the projector room on the third floor. The door was slightly ajar, but there was no sign of Matthew or Seth.

Charlene deeply regretted allowing Darren to tug at her heartstrings. What if she was being set up? "Darren—let's go. I don't feel good about this." She was very glad she'd texted Sam.

A hand shoved her forward into the room and against the metal stand for the film reels. Darren turned to come to her defense. Charlene saw Seth in the corner tied by the ankles to a stool, his hands in front of him knotted with Matthew's wolf tie. Packing tape was over his mouth. His gaze was focused and alert.

"Matthew, man, let's talk this out," Darren said. "I thought we were friends."

"I told you to come alone," Matthew said, his eyes wild, like in the picture of when he'd been dropped at the Salem Psych Unit. There was no sign of the mild-mannered movie manager on his face. His hair was straight up as if he'd been wrangling with it.

"Matthew," Charlene said. "Please, let Seth go."

"Too bad, so sad, Charlene," Matthew sing-songed. "Actually, this might make Mila happy."

"Mila?" Darren paled, and his mouth gaped.

"She haunts this place," Matthew said.

"What's wrong?" Charlene asked, realizing that

Darren was reacting very strangely. "Do you know that name?"

"Mila is my sister's name." Darren quivered. "She died in Munich. At the orphanage."

"I know all about it," Matthew said. "She followed you here from Germany. She wants you to pay for abandoning her."

"She died in a fire!" Darren said, his hand over his heart.

Matthew's laugh was frenetic. "You abandoned her to the nuns when you joined the circus. Just like your mother abandoned you to the villagers." He clucked his tongue to his teeth. "Shame, shame."

"Our mother died. She didn't mean to leave us. How can you know about the villagers?" Darren asked, reeling. "How?"

"I told you." Matthew shook his head. "Mila's haunting the theater."

Now Charlene one hundred percent believed in ghosts. She hadn't before, but now she knew they were as real as Darren and Matthew. Seth. Just because Jack couldn't leave the place where he'd died didn't mean other ghosts couldn't travel—though she'd never witnessed it herself. In this case, she recalled Mila, in a hijab, working for Patty. Not a ghost.

"Where is she?" Charlene asked Matthew gently. "Mila?"

"I don't know. I can't see her. She whispers things." Matthew peered out the projector room door, then slammed it closed. "She told me to bring you here, Darren. To make you pay."

"Why make him pay?" Charlene's phone vibrated with a text message. She was supposed to be recording the confession!

She glanced at the message from Sam. Patty was dead in the bakery. The bakery was burning, and so was the Wagner house.

Charlene pressed *Record* for the video, knowing she'd be recording the floor, but she hoped the audio portion would be enough to free Darren from all suspicion.

"Matthew, did you hurt Patty?"

Matthew's eyes widened.

He didn't say anything but hugged his waist.

"Did you kill Patty?" she asked in a firmer tone.

"Not me." Matthew's lip jutted. "I didn't."

"Did you put the poisoned seasoned salt on the popcorn?" Charlene kept her manner as calm as possible.

Matthew nodded, his eyes darting from Darren to Charlene. "Mila told me to. She said it would make Elise sick, for revenge for her being mean. I didn't know she'd die. I didn't know, Darren."

"You didn't mean to kill her?" Charlene said, to clarify.

"Mila told me Elise was going to let me go. She saw the future! She leaves the office door open all the time." Matthew rubbed his arms. "Elise blamed me. It wasn't me. I was innocent, but she didn't care."

"It's okay now," Charlene said. "You can stop hurting people. Let Seth go free. We can get you the help you need, Matthew."

Matthew leaned his head back and howled.

Charlene smelled smoke coming from downstairs.

Had Matthew started a fire before coming upstairs, possibly to trap them?

"Matthew, what did you do?" Darren shouted, shoving past the manager to open the door. He widened it, and a shrouded figure screeched and tossed burning red drapes at Darren.

"It wasn't me," Matthew said again. He danced around the flames as Darren and the figure entered the hall from the projector room.

The struggling pair were wrapped in the burning fabric, each punching or ducking. Matthew joined Mila in the fight to subdue Darren.

Charlene skirted them to the fire extinguisher on the wall in the hallway, taking it down to point at the three figures wrestling. The trio fell down the stairs to the second floor. Matthew's clothes were on fire, and Charlene sprayed him down, falling backward from the force of the fire retardant.

The figure lunged at Darren, tackling him down the stairs to the lobby. Matthew raced to keep them in sight, cheering. He circled the pair, throwing punches.

Charlene scrambled up, panting, and practically slid down the carpeted steps to the lobby. Darren was shouting, patting down the woman's hijab to stop the flames. Charlene shot another round of fire retardant.

The hijab smoldered, and Darren pulled it back to reveal dark hair like Darren's, but thicker. Her forehead was covered, as was her face.

The woman was no ghost, but Mila, Patty's baking assistant. She'd hummed that same lullaby as Darren had sung to Elise. Mila. How very tragic for the siblings, separated by a lie.

Darren was stunned, but not his sister—she wanted revenge on the brother who had left her behind in Munich, and she lunged at him with a hot-dog skewer from the concession stand, the prongs sharp as she buried it in Darren's forearm.

"Mila!" Charlene shouted, aiming at the deranged woman's face—she swallowed her empathy for the killer and blasted the fire extinguisher with all her might.

Mila hit the popcorn counter, and the machine full of kernels spilled out to the floor like grains of rice. Blue Crocs fell off her feet.

Darren slipped on the kernels to reach Mila and embrace her, even as she struggled and spewed obscenities like a wild animal.

"Mila. *Liebling,* my sister, shh." Darren crooned to the raving woman. "*Meine schwester.*"

Matthew smacked at the flames on his shirt until they were out.

Charlene hurried to the bottom step, ready to run upstairs to get Seth. She stopped as the door was battered down with a battering ram and beautiful sunlight filled the dark space.

Mila was crying and yelling, shouting. Darren murmured soothing nothings to his sister, smoothing her hair down her back, never minding the blood from his arm.

Sam followed two brawny firefighters, his gaze landing on where she stood, fire extinguisher in her hand. She'd lost her phone somewhere in the mêlée but hiked her purse up to her shoulder.

"Sam! Seth is in the projector room."

She lowered the fire extinguisher as Sam reached her and tugged her none too gently from the Spellbound Movie Theater.

"Hurry. It's on fire," Sam said. "Are you trying to kill me, Charlene Morris?"

# CHAPTER 21

Charlene gulped in big, deep breaths of fresh air as Sam dragged her away from the smoking flames, which were thick and hot. The parking lot had a fire truck, two ambulances, police cars, and spectators on the periphery, held back by police officers.

"Drink this." Sam thrust a water bottle into her hands. "I don't want you fainting on me."

"I don't faint!" Charlene protested as her knees wobbled. She twisted off the top of the bottle and leaned back against Sam's SUV.

"You're pale as a damn ghost," Sam said, then held up his hand. "Wrong word choice. I know Matthew claims the building is haunted. And Avery found shoes."

Charlene swallowed the delicious, thirst-quenching water and sent him a grateful smile. "Thank you, Sam."

"Patty told me she got suspicious of Mila acting strangely at the bakery. She found dried flower blossoms and roasted garlic in the kitchen and confronted her about making poison to kill Elise. Mila immediately charged her and knocked her out with a heavy baking pan. We'll test the dried flowers, but I'm pretty sure it will come back as wolfsbane."

"Patty's alive?" Relief filled her.

"Yep." Sam scuffed a boot heel to the pavement. "She's got a concussion and stitches, but she'll live."

Charlene finished the water. "Did she know Mila was Darren's sister?"

"Nope. Mila was very clever and played on their German ancestry, claiming to be shy. She showed burn marks on her arm to Patty as a reason for her hijab."

Charlene nodded. "Darren said Mila died in a fire."

Sam shrugged. "She's obviously not dead. I'll get to the bottom of what happened, never fear."

She knew he would.

"Better?" Sam asked.

"Yes. I just can't believe this." Charlene wished she had more water as her throat and mouth were dry. She warily watched the front of the building, afraid of the gray and black smoke.

"I was very concerned for you." Sam's brown eyes bored into hers, but the meaning in his wasn't clear. He was too good at hiding his emotions.

"Charlene!" Avery raced across the parking lot, followed by Dani, Seth's mother. "You're okay! I was so worried." She flung her arms around Charlene and squeezed, tears streaming down her face.

Sam lifted a disappointed brow at the teenager.

Avery grew hurt, but Charlene would explain later that you kind of had to get used to disappointing Sam. The man was a saint, and they were mere mortals.

"Is Seth okay?" Dani asked. She was very concerned, but calm—probably from her years as a mom to boys. "You can stand in line, Detective, to thrash my son once I find out he's all right."

Sam didn't smile. "Over in the second ambulance nearest the street. He's just fine."

Dani hurried across the tarmac. Avery wasn't sure if she was welcome to go until Dani looked over her shoulder and beckoned for Avery to join her. She ran to Dani, and the pair continued to the ambulance.

Charlene put her fingers on Sam's strong arm. "I know you're mad, but Seth was tricked by Matthew into coming down."

"I know. Avery told me everything." Sam watched Charlene, and it seemed like he wanted to tell her something but, in the end, didn't.

Just then, Matthew was dragged out of the smoking theater to the ambulance, followed by Darren. The theater owner's head was held high—no cowering from him. He'd learned through his childhood struggles who he was at his soul.

Officer Bernard had handcuffed Mila and taken her to his squad car. He opened the rear passenger door, Darren in their wake.

"I'll get you out, Mila," Darren said. "I'm here for you. I'll get you help. I love you. I've never stopped loving you."

Mila had completely lost her hijab, and she wore pants and a T-shirt, the Crocs long gone. Her hypertrichosis was evident in the hairy patches on her skin, intermingled with scars from a fire. She spat over her shoulder at Darren. "*Bruder*! Why won't you die?"

Darren rocked backward, his hand to his chest.

Officer Bernard maneuvered Mila into the back of his patrol unit. He spoke to Darren, but Charlene couldn't hear what he said.

"How disastrous," Charlene said. "Utterly terrible."

"Family isn't all it's cracked up to be, and cases like this remind me of it." Sam shook his head.

She elbowed him. "Your sister and her husband are amazing people. I know you love Sydney and Jim." The Taylors were a fantastic couple who'd stayed at Charlene's bed-and-breakfast twice.

Sam smoothed his mustache. "Of course, my family is wonderful," he teased. "I was talking about yours."

"Very funny."

Sam put his hand on her shoulder. "How are you doing now? Don't lie."

"I'm ready to go home. Sam, Matthew has some mental health issues, and he's obsessed with this building. Did you know it was built on an old burial ground?"

Sam grimaced. "Don't start, Charlene. Real people committed these crimes."

Just then Matthew burst from the back of the ambulance, trailing a fluid bag and hoses, racing past the firefighters at the front door to the lobby inside.

His screams were unearthly as he shouted that the building wanted blood. "My blood!"

The firemen had controlled the flames, but they weren't prepared to stop a madman from running back into the smoking building.

Charlene watched in horror as Sam ran toward the entrance, calling out to stop Matthew but just then flames blocked the theater entrance, the broken wooden door supplying more fuel to the fire.

A bulky, muscled fireman stopped Sam with a hand to Sam's chest and shook his head. "I'll go. You stay, sir."

The fireman dove in, but his partner pulled him back as flames caused by some form of accelerant made going inside the theater impossible.

Charlene cried out in dismay. Smoke and flames heated the air in the parking lot.

Sam backed up and tracked the building, shielding his eyes. What was he looking for? But then, Charlene knew. Her body braced for an emotional jarring as a flaming person howled from the roof, and then jumped.

Matthew landed on the other side of the building, in the alley by the Dumpster, with a *smack*. Charlene pressed her hand to her stomach, physically sick.

Sam and the fireman hurried around the brick-and-stone structure now crumbling in the place that many had claimed to be haunted. She was glad that Avery and Dani were with Seth and had missed Matthew's suicide. Death by fire. Just as the other jumpers had claimed to feel the fire, Matthew had made it happen.

With all her heart, Charlene believed the building was possessed.

It was time to get this place blessed and release

those souls who wanted to go home. Banish the ones who were simply evil.

She knew Kass and Kevin would know what to do, and she planned on calling them both first thing tomorrow.

For now, Charlene just wanted to go home. To tell Jack the horrifying nightmare at the theater was over at last. Where to start for healing?

Darren spoke with Officer Bernard, then joined Charlene by Sam's SUV.

"I'm so sorry about your sister," Charlene said.

"It's not her fault. I have money to help her." Darren rubbed his palm over his stubbled face. "Mila thought I left her, but I didn't. Why would the nuns tell me such a lie? Tell her such a lie?"

"I don't know."

"I will find out. Officer Bernard said he'd call me once she is evaluated, but they will take her to Salem Psych Unit rather than the jail." Darren dragged in a breath. "He's a reasonable officer."

"That's good for her, better than a cell." Thanks to the research they'd just done at the house, Charlene knew the wicked truth was that unfortunate people in need of care might sit in jail for a very long time.

Darren nodded and peered her way, his face covered with soot though it was hard to separate the brown ash from his hair. "Will you give me a ride to my house?"

"Of course." Charlene clapped her hand on his back.

"I'd call Klara, but she doesn't want anything more to do with me." Darren stared up at the sky, gray with smoke.

Was he lamenting all he'd lost coming here?

"I wish things had been different for you," she said.

"That is a waste of energy, Charlene." Darren exhaled. "I'm grateful to know my sister is alive, and that's what I'll remember about Salem, not the bad parts."

"Can you separate it like that?" she asked, genuinely curious. Chicago for her had been all about Jared, and she'd had to leave.

"I was bullied and beaten. I know how to survive." Darren stuck his hand in his pocket. "I'm going to have this building razed," he said. "And blessed. I'll build a fountain dedicated to lost souls."

"That's a lovely thought." Charlene searched her purse. "I figured you'd want to sell it." She breathed a sigh of relief when she saw her phone next to the pepper spray. She'd assumed she'd lost it while struggling with the fire extinguisher.

"It's too dangerous for that."

They shared a meaningful look, understanding completely. "I have friends in the paranormal community who can help."

"You *do* like to do that," Darren murmured with just a hint of sarcasm. "Thank you."

Charlene searched for Sam, but he was busy with the firemen and medics collecting Matthew's body. "It's a good thing we parked a half block away or we'd be trapped back there with police vehicles."

Darren nodded. "I'm ready when you are."

"Let me check in with Avery to make sure Seth is okay," Charlene said.

"I can't believe Mila was telling Matthew what to do while acting like a ghost," Darren said, wearing a stunned expression. "Or that he believed it. And now he's dead. Mila . . . she didn't know. She didn't understand."

"The doctors will help you with her." Had Mila been crazy, or had she been wily? Making the powder from the wolfsbane flowers to put on Elise's popcorn was premeditated and very intelligent. Setting up the curtain rod to crush him.

That would be for the courts to decide.

Charlene crossed the parking lot. Officer Bernard had left, opening a space that curious onlookers filled with questions. Reporters.

She reached the ambulance. Dani and Avery were talking with Seth, who was being released after a checkup. Seth's eyes were a little wide with shock, though he was standing fine, next to Avery and his mother.

"Hey," Charlene said. "How's it going?"

"I'm alive, thanks to you, Charlene, and Darren," Seth said.

Dani studied Darren but didn't comment on the man's odd appearance. His hair or shredded clothes, or the soot.

"Thank you," Dani said to them both.

"I'm going to take Darren home and then go to the bed-and-breakfast," Charlene said.

"We'll meet you there," Avery said. "I promised Seth a tub of Rocky Road ice cream that I know we have in the freezer."

Dani said, "If it's okay with the medics?"

"He's good to go," the EMT said, handing Seth a release form from the back of the ambulance.

"We can walk to my house," Seth said. "Then we'll be there, Charlene."

"Very slowly," Dani said. "The mile Avery and I ran didn't seem that big of a deal on the way here. I have never been so scared." She reached for Charlene. "You didn't have to go in, but I very much appreciate it. You will always have a friend in me."

"Thank you," Charlene said. Good friends were treasures.

"I can feel the evil in this place," Dani said with a shudder. "I hope you aren't planning on reopening the theater? I will fight you on it," she said.

"No need for that." Darren hooked a thumb toward the smoldering brick building. "I'm going to tear it down, have it blessed, and then build a fountain here."

Dani blinked in relief. "That sounds great."

Seth and Avery both nodded. "Perfect," Avery said.

Charlene said her good-byes, and she and Darren walked through the curious throng of people, heads low, until she reached the Pilot.

She unlocked the vehicle and got in, surprised that she was trembling. "What a day."

Darren showed her his hand, too, also shaking. "I think I need a stiff drink. Too bad I drank all the tequila."

"Maybe the ice cream would be a better idea," Charlene said. "You need to be listening for Officer Bernard's call."

"That's true." Darren scratched his jaw.

They buckled up, and Charlene drove to the white historic home without another word. All she wanted was her love seat, her cat, and Jack.

Klara ran outside when she heard Charlene in the driveway. A pretty blonde followed her.

"DiDi," Darren said in a murmur to Charlene.

She sighed and got out of the car with Darren. Her two years of being a hostess made it impossible just to drop him off to face the music alone.

"What happened?" Klara asked, DiDi at her side.

"Matthew jumped from the building, on fire," Darren said. "My sister is alive." He turned to DiDi. "She tried to kill me."

At that, both women took his arms on either side and led him toward the house.

"I'm here," Klara said. "*We* are here for you."

Relieved, Charlene returned to the car. At least Darren wouldn't be alone. Abandoned. For that, she was grateful.

She arrived home, beat. Exhausted. It was three in the afternoon, and she had a happy hour to prepare for. She couldn't cancel—it was what she did. But oh, she needed a minute. And a shower.

Jack wasn't around when she arrived, so she snuck into the bathroom and put the shower on hot. She cried and cried over the injustice in the world. When she got out, she could hear Avery and Seth talking in the kitchen. The door to her suite was closed.

Jack was in her living room, concern on his features. "How are you? The fire at the bakery and the theater has been all over the news!" he said. "Are you hurt?"

"I'm just fine, honestly." She towel-dried her long brown hair, speaking in a low voice that would blend with the television in the background.

Jack studied her closely. "You have bruises on your arms. A cut on your hand!" He blew cool air over the marks.

"I must have gotten them while wrestling with the fire extinguisher," she said. "Glad that I learned how to operate a fire extinguisher as part of the new business safety training."

Avery knocked. "Charlene?" She spoke through the door. "Come have ice cream with us!"

Charlene nodded at Jack. "Coming!" Opening the door to the kitchen, she walked out of her suite and wrapped the towel around her damp hair like a turban.

Seth and Avery each had huge bowls of ice cream.

"Want one?" Avery asked.

She almost said no, but then nodded. "A small one."

They sat around the kitchen table, Silva blinking golden eyes from her spot by her dish. Seth had taken Jack's chair. Jack wasn't pleased about it but observed quietly from his place by the fridge.

"Thanks again, Charlene," Seth said. "You saved me. Mom wants to make you some of her lasagna as a thank-you. It's pretty good."

"She doesn't have to do anything!" Charlene nibbled a small bite of the ice cream and let the vanilla with chocolate melt over her tongue. "Oh, great idea." It soothed her raw throat. "My throat is sore from the smoke, I guess."

Seth swallowed a spoonful. "Or from confronting Matthew. He was spooky crazy."

"If you don't tell me what happened," Jack

warned, "I'll mess with the lights." He crossed his arms and emanated cool energy.

Charlene, feeling better now that she was home with her family, grinned at Avery. "I'm not sure what Seth told you, but Darren's sister, Mila, is alive after all this time. She was haunting the movie theater and had convinced Matthew to poison Elise as payback for wanting to fire him."

Avery's jaw dropped. "His sister was alive all this time, and he had no idea?"

"Yes." And nursing anger for him not rescuing her from their horrid life.

Avery took another bite, scraping her spoon across the bowl. "I feel so sorry for Darren."

"Me too," Charlene said. "Patty found the roasted garlic and dried flowers in the bakery kitchen and confronted Mila. Mila had made the poison, but Matthew put it on Elise's popcorn. He wasn't mentally stable." She rose from the kitchen chair and rinsed her bowl in the sink.

Jack hovered by her. "What happened to Matthew?"

Charlene turned toward Avery and Seth. "It's distressing that Matthew jumped from the roof to his death." A tragedy.

"My mom thinks the building is evil and is very glad that Darren isn't keeping the Spellbound open. Shortest job in history," Seth said.

"You're lucky you survived your employment there," Avery countered.

Jack shimmered by the sink with alarm. "You are all lucky to be alive."

Adrenaline fled and Charlene nodded, suddenly beat. "Yep. I'm ready for a nice glass of pinot grigio."

"I'll prepare things for happy hour so you can relax, all right?" Avery wiped a tear from her cheek. "I love you!"

"I love you too." Charlene smiled at Seth, adding, "Minnie probably has a lot already complete, so it shouldn't be much."

"Mom said you're a very cool woman. I agree," Seth declared, granting her a flash of his dimpled cheek.

Charlene's face heated and she opened the fridge to hide her embarrassment.

"Back off, boy," Jack rumbled, but he was chuckling. "You've got another admirer, Charlene."

She ignored Jack and said, "Minnie has an artichoke dip, with crackers. Hummus and celery sticks."

"I'll do it!" Avery rinsed her ice cream bowl. "Seth, did you want some more Rocky Road?"

"I'll wait and save my appetite for happy hour," Seth said.

"Wise!" Charlene closed the fridge, leaving the teens. Once at her custom bar in the living room, she poured a large glass of citrusy wine and sank on the sofa. Silva hopped up next to her, as confident as if she'd never been scared of the wolfman at all.

"It will be our secret," Charlene said to the cat.

Jack waited by the fireplace, watching her thoughtfully. "This was a strange one, Charlene. Very strange."

She heard Avery and Seth laughing in the kit-

chen and murmured to her ghost, "It was. Hypertrichosis."

"Seeing Darren like that made me want to practice as a doctor again. What do you think of that? I
can do it online these days."

Her stomach clenched. He was right. This was
the perfect time in history for him to work on the
internet and help patients. Jack very much wanted
to be part of his community.

Charlene sipped her wine and raised the glass
to him. "I bet we can figure it out. You'd need a
fake name."

"Now that this case is solved," Jack said, "I've got
the perfect plan in mind."

# CHAPTER 22

A knock sounded on the front door, and Charlene placed her wine on the side table. Avery
beat her to the entrance.

"We know who that is," Jack drawled.

The door opened. "Sam!" Avery said. "Please
don't be mad at me forever."

Charlene paused in the living room as Avery
widened the door and the handsome detective
strode into the foyer. Seth entered from the
kitchen, hands in his pockets, possibly the coolest
kid in the world.

"I'm not mad," Sam said. He looked for Charlene and studied her with his steady gaze.

"Hey!" She smiled at him. "I'm surprised to see
you so soon."

"Just wanted to give you a heads-up since you
left without saying good-bye." Sam's arms were relaxed at his sides, the very picture of a confident
man. Her stomach fluttered with attraction for
him.

"You were busy, and I didn't want to bother you," Charlene said. Or get detained.

"Klara arrived with her girlfriend, DiDi Larson, a lawyer," Sam said. "Mila is charged with several things, but she's been sent to a psych ward for evaluation. Darren went home."

Charlene didn't tell him she already knew that. "That's good news. They've had a tough life. Did Darren tell you about their condition, hypertrichosis?"

"What's that?" Avery asked.

"It's called wolfman disease, cruelly," Charlene said.

"Is that why Darren had that scruff all over his face? And Mila was covered with hair. Like a guy," Seth said.

"Yes," Charlene said.

"That's awful!" Avery's gaze filled with compassion.

"And extremely rare," Charlene said. "It's why he and his sister were taken to the orphanage after their mother died. The villagers were going to let them starve, can you imagine? The nuns fostered them, but then lied about Mila to Darren."

"Did Elise know?" Avery asked. "That Darren had the hypertrichosis?"

"No." Charlene shook her head. "He kept it a secret."

"I can't imagine Elise would be cool with it," Seth said, remarkably astute for a teenager.

"Avery, I appreciate that you wanted to stay away from the theater as I'd asked. That shows maturity," Sam said, giving Charlene the side-eye.

"Hey!" She crossed her arms.

Jack chuckled.

"It's my fault she was there," Seth said. "I'd called Matthew to see if he'd been in touch with Darren, and he said it was going to be work as usual, and so I told him I had a new job. He made me feel like I owed him for quitting, to bring back the uniform. I'm sorry, Detective Holden."

"Call me Sam." He narrowed his eyes at how close Avery and Seth stood, united. "Thanks for the apology. In the future, please understand that I ask things for a reason. I had Matthew under surveillance and was aware of his stay in the psych ward. Though he was the manager at the time of the jumps, there was no way to connect him to the suicides. The young girl he'd let in who was stabbed had been killed by her boyfriend."

"Not related, then," Jack said.

"I didn't know you had that information." Charlene raised her chin. "I texted you, Sam, so you knew where I was and why."

"I appreciate it. We were at Patty's when I got your text, and I sent the team over right away."

"I'm glad Patty's okay."

"Yep. Cursed your name, Charlene, but then confessed to tricking Elise out of her inheritance. Not a crime, and since everyone is dead now, except her, she wins."

"Didn't the bakery burn?" Charlene didn't think that was very positive.

"Yeah." Sam folded his hands before his waist. "I'm sure she's insured. She might rebuild."

"If I were her," Avery said, taking Seth's hand, "I'd take the loot and move to the Bahamas."

Sam chuckled. "Bahamas, huh?"

"Bahamas!" Charlene's breath caught.

"Just kidding," Avery said. "Salem is home. This is my home. I won't go too far."

Charlene's racing heart steadied. "Home is very important. It's what Darren wanted to give to Mila. Who knows if things would have been different for his sister if she'd been loved and nurtured?"

"Nature versus nurture," Jack said. "An age-old debate."

"Mila was living in the basement of the Spellbound Movie Theater. She'd tracked Darren from Munich and the Shultz Seasoned Salts campaign that Klara had begun in Germany. It was no problem for her to act like a ghost and play on Matthew's delusions," Sam concluded.

"How sad for her," Charlene said.

"She sounds pretty bright," Jack said.

Sam gestured over his shoulder to the open front door. "Charlene, might I have a word on the porch in private?"

"Sure." She followed him out. Jack was already there.

She furrowed her brow at her ghost, and Jack disappeared.

"When I dragged you out of the building today, my heart sank," Sam said.

"Why is that?" Charlene said, keeping things light as she liked to do.

He took her hands and brought her to the railing, and they both sat.

His gaze turned a deep, warm brown, and her stomach somersaulted. Her pulse skipped.

"I've been offered a promotion," Sam said.

A promotion? Why the long face if it was good news?

"You've wanted to be lead detective here for ages," she said. "Congratulations!" She'd open a bottle of bubbly and they could celebrate.

"Not here." Sam looked away.

Her hopes plummeted. "Where? Boston?"

"No. Portland."

"Maine?" That wasn't so far—an hour and a half, give or take.

"Oregon." Sam released her hands and scooted his back against the post.

"Sam, that's across the world." Charlene shook her head, her stomach rolling and jumping in protest.

"I don't think I can, in good conscience, accept it," Sam drawled. "Despite your promises, you can't stay out of trouble."

"Sam!"

Guilt and joy and regret collided within her.

"I've told them I need some time to consider it. I have until September to decide." With the gentlest of fingers, Sam smoothed her hair back from her cheek. "What do you think I should do?"

"I can't make that decision for you!" *Stay here, stay here, stay here.*

"Rover will be fine. My department will be fine. Jimenez and Bernard are both due for promotions of their own." Sam didn't break their heated gaze.

Charlene couldn't speak. Her tongue was literally glued to the top of her mouth it was so dry. Nerves. Tension. Panic.

"You aren't begging me to stay," Sam said, sounding disappointed.

"I want you to." She swished her tongue around her mouth and cleared her throat. "But I would never keep you from your dreams, Sam. I wouldn't do that to you." Her heart was on fire as she said, "We are too good of friends."

Sam flinched. "I really hate that particular *F* word."

# EPILOGUE

*August 1*

"You would never know this used to be the movie theater," Charlene said, adjusting her sunglasses as she straightened. She was dressed for a day of manual labor in the warm Salem sunshine. "Darren, you've done something amazing."

The brick building had been razed, the ground blessed by a Protestant minister, a Catholic priest, and a Wiccan priestess, just to make sure the soil was truly cleansed.

Avery, Seth, Sam, Franco, Kass, Kevin, Amy, and Dani were planting a perimeter of sage bushes around the fountain as suggested by Brandy Flint. "Thanks to you," Darren said. "I couldn't have done this without your help."

"I was happy to pitch in, but you made it happen." Charlene patted the flat of the shovel around the base of dirt. The sage had a wonderful scent, was low-maintenance, and warded off evil. Bonus.

The fountain had a peace sign as its base ₂ multiple water arcs crossing over in a half circle. was quirky and totally Salem.

"How is Mila?" Charlene asked as they moved on to the next sage bush. This time Darren dug the hole.

"DiDi is trying to get Mila expedited to a medical facility in Munich. Klara wants to know why I care. She thinks I should return to Saint Mary's and leave Mila to her fate."

"Why is that?"

"It's complicated. I tracked down what happened with Mila. It seems that an older abbess thought she'd save Mila from a life of uncertainty as Wolf Girl in the circus." Darren jammed his foot to the shovel with extra force. "To avoid being the object of scorn or ridicule."

"Oh, no." Charlene wiped her forearm over her damp forehead. "To protect her?"

"I understand that!" Darren blocked the sun with a large-brimmed hat and a long-sleeved sun shirt, and jeans. "But why the lie to Mila, that I had abandoned her?"

"That's cruel!"

"There are good things too. I mean, they taught Mila to bake. The fire had been a small one but had sparked the idea for the abbess's lie. To force Mila to accept her place in the church. Well, when the abbess died of old age, Mila went to the city with a more progressive nun and saw the advertisements for Shultz's Seasoned Salts. She's been plotting my downfall ever since. She wanted to kill Elise to make me suffer. Then, with Elise dead, it was my turn."

harlene paused for a drink from her water bot-
. "Can you speak to her? Explain?"

"Mila refuses to see me. She and Klara get
along, though. So, Klara lets me know how she is.
Sends my love to Mila."

Mila was very intelligent, Charlene thought, but
scarred by her childhood. "What is your hope for
your sister?"

Darren stepped back from the hole and Charlene put the sage bush in. He stomped it down.
The scent was heavenly.

"I want her to forgive me," Darren said softly.
"That will take a miracle."

"Miracles happen, Darren, don't give up." Charlene exhaled and looked around at the group of
chatting, happy people. "This place will bring such
joy."

Her miracle arrived in a blue SUV and exited
wearing jeans and a T-shirt that molded to a trim
physique. Chestnut hair, trimmed, and a mustache
that tickled when they kissed. "Sam's here!"

Darren chuckled. "You just lit up like a fire-
work."

"Can you blame me? This is our second date—
but we plan on taking things very, very slow."